I0634894

Dear Reader,

First things first: I hold all responsibility for any incon-sistencies, typos, or misuse of words that you may come across in this book. Despite having a great proof-reader, I still make mistakes. Please forgive me.

Secondly, I urge you to read through the glossary at the back of the book first. Even though the English lan-guage is fairly well known, there are cultural and time period differences that can add a "snag" to your reading enjoyment. That being said, the British version of the English language has use for some words that some Americans might not know of and vise versa. There are a few terms and idioms that might even surprise you. That brings me to the Scottish version of English. Many would argue that there is no difference and unless you hear the accent, you'd never know. I agree, but that also depends on the time period you're talking about because, at one point, the British and the Scottish did have a wee bit of a grudge.

That in mind, I urge you again to look over the glossary first. Unless, of course, you like being confused and figuring out the use of the terms on your own; then by all means, be my guest and skip it. Either way, I hope you'll enjoy the story and not dwell on the use of the English language too much.

Hearts and Stars,

J.T. Whitesell

CARRY
❧ ME ☙
OFF

CARRY

❧ ME ☙

OFF

J.T. Whitesell

ISBN-10: 0985643307

ISBN-13: 978-0-9856433-0-0

Cover Photo by: J.T. Whitesell
Cover design by: Richard Whitesell
Proofread by: Linda Bensinger

First Edition. Printed in the U.S.A.

10 9 8 7 6 5 4 3 2 1

For my grandmas:
Because one never held back from
discussing the possibilities.
And the other embraced life to the fullest.

Death cannot stop true love. All it can do is delay it for a while.

- From The Princess Bride

Death is an angel with two faces; to us he turns a face of terror,
blighting all things fair; the other burns with glory of the stars, and
love is there.

- T. C. Williams

Because I could not stop for death
He kindly stopped for me
The carriage held but just ourselves
And immortality

- Emily Dickinson

❧ TABLE OF CONTENTS ☙

ONE YEAR LATER

THE LAST TIME

Glossary
Acknowledgments

THE
᠍ EIGHTEEN ᠍
HUNDREDS

THE FOURTH TIME

From among the balcony the sounds of dining, discussion, enjoyment and love fill the house and swell the walls. The library is the only empty room at the moment and the dark shadows beyond the balcony doors whisper malicious intentions in my ear. I also hear my name being called. Someone is looking for me, hesitantly.

"Where is Miss Anna?" The question is breathless and apprehensive.

"Is she not with the ladies?" I hear the scorn and belittlement in my father's voice toward my caretaker. Coins and keys jingle in his pockets as he adjusts his breeches.

"No, sir." She sounds afraid of my father. Perhaps that is why she always succumbs to him. I suppose she feels obligated. Her brother works hard on our cotton plantation and yet my father still considers selling him to Mr. Jenkins down the road.

It will not be long before I am discovered. This evening is the celebration of my twenty-first birthday but it is too sophisticated for anyone to concern themselves with my whereabouts. My ostensible friends have not noticed I am gone, therefore none of my parents' friends will notice my absence either.

I have been feeling a bit despondent all day. Functions ought to be agreeable but nagging at the back of my mind is the knowledge that father will deny my paramour's request for my hand in holy matrimony. Mother's comments insinuate that he is fast with the ladies and a bad influence; getting into trouble and, apparently, rather rude. She claims it is his upbringing. Father agrees, saying that he comes from poor breeding. I know not with whom they confer.

In my flight from the celebration, at the top of the stairs, I collided with the one person whom I least desired to see me in such a state of distress. It was as if I had hit a wall. He wrapped his arms around me, despite any onlookers, to keep me from plummeting back down from which I came. Somehow I knew this was the last time he would hold me and I prayed that he would never let me go. No matter how many times we have met privately, I cannot get over how strapping he is. I stared longingly into his green eyes. By his distraught appearance I knew he had been given bad news.

I did my best to pardon myself and adjust my hair. For a man my parents so adamantly disapprove of; he brushed a stray curl off my forehead then raised my hand to his lips and kissed it softly. What seemed well rehearsed and practiced was his, "Happy birthday, Jo."

Looking down so he would not notice my rosy cheeks, I curtseyed, swiftly kissed his smooth shaven cheek and said "I will always love you." Then I ran into the library. Closing the door ever so slowly, he gave me a dismal grin. Just before I shut the door completely, I blew him a kiss and the most minuscule of waves.

Thinking back on that moment, part of me fancies that he had followed me into the library. The other part

2

of me yearns to check the door to be certain it is properly locked.

I sigh deeply. He would be better off with any other lady.

Hiking up my skirts, I drape my legs over the wooden railing that wraps around the balcony. Slowly, I finger the braid of rope in my hand. This will be quick. I have seen my father's slaves die by the noose half-a-dozen times or so. They always go with such pride. Is the *other side* that much better than my father's plantation?

I fix the loop around my neck very carefully. My mother will not be happy if a single hair is out of place when I am found. I can just hear her now, "Oh, my Anna! At least she passed looking as beautiful as ever!" Perhaps I will get to witness everyone's reaction as an apparition. I do not suppose they will mourn long—a fortnight, perhaps, if I am fortunate.

Will *he* ever love again?

I stand with my back to the house and allow my arms to suspend my body out, over the ground. If the rope gives I may end up with a broken leg, at worst, from this height. I gaze out at my father's cotton fields. If the horizon were visible in this darkness, I may feel better thinking that one step could take me miles away from here.

I close my eyes.

A familiar voice I have heard only in the dark recesses of my dreams sounds so close to my ear.

A dirty name
A dirty face
A curse to relive this place
Die for his shame
Die for the key
Die to become free

I shake my head to dispel the chant. Where have I heard it before? A hundred times before. I let out an exasperated breath and my hands slip slightly on the railing.

"Your means to extract sentience shan't null the misfortune you bear," a voice whispers in my ear. It is quite unlike the chant—unlike any voice I have ever heard before. My head swims with comfort and delight as I pull back against the railing—eyes searching the span of fields.

"You are only hearing things, Anna," I whisper to myself.

"Are you?" the deep voice whispers back.

I startle. Not because I am apprehensive, but due to the sudden pounding of my heart. The voice does not sound much older than myself. Perhaps this is only a ruse and that pesky stable boy is hiding in the bushes. Again, I scan the fields.

A dark figure stands on the lawn. It is hard to see him, but he certainly is not that obnoxious stable boy. This man is tall and lean. I find I am not feeling as miserable as I was, earlier.

The figure shifts his weight from one leg to the other. He reminds me of those tattered clothes Mr. Jenkins stuffs with straw and hangs from a cross in his fields to scare the crows away. This man does not hang though. A long L-shaped stick rests on his shoulders, parallel with the ground. His arms wrap over the protruding ends.

How can he be so far away and sound as if he is standing on the balcony directly behind me?

"Hello?" I exhale softly.

"Hello." His accent leaves me numb. Perhaps I should be telling Father the British are at his doorstep in addition to the Union.

"I beg your pardon, good sir, but are you an acquaintance of my father?"

4

"No, Ma'am." Even though his face is veiled, his voice smiles at me.

"If you would be so kind, could you please leave me be? I am terribly busy at the moment."

"I can see that, milady."

"Off you go, then. Back to the stables." I have yet to confirm who this man is, but that is of no concern.

He steps from the shadows. Light from the window below warms his pale face as he smiles, shifting his weight once again. That simple smile causes my heart to skip. He is definitely not the stable boy.

After a silence that seems to last an eternity I ask, "Are you so lax in your duties that you have the time to stand by and watch me all night?"

"I will see that my orders are fulfilled and then kindly move on. Although if you are so inclined to temper your impulse, I will take my leave now, no matter what the consequences."

This confuses me. "What is your name?"

"Doyle. Damien Doyle, Milady." He plunges the straight end of his scythe into the ground as he bows his upper body, "But my *friends* call me Doom. And you are?" His question sounds as if he already knows my name, but feels it is only polite to ask.

"Miss Anna Fairchild." I nod my head slightly since it is the closest I can come to a curtsey on the ledge of the balcony.

"Anna." He gazes off into the darkness. "Well, Miss Anna, have you come to a decision?"

"Concerning what, Mr. Doyle?" I have already forgotten why I am standing on this side of the balcony, clutching the railing for dear life.

"Does your heart still long to cease this evening?" His question sounds pained.

Before I can answer, Ms. Cune, my caretaker, bursts through the library doors behind me. Whatever my decision is does not matter. I am so surprised that my feet lose hold of the balcony's edge. Searing hot finger nails tear at my flesh. My name is screamed on the lips of a foreign tongue. And then the railing is no longer sustaining me.

Everything goes black as cold fingers release the rope from around my neck. A strong hand cups my face to wipe away the last remaining tear of my life.

THE
❧ NINETEEN ☙
HUNDREDS

THE FIFTH TIME

The mirror above the sink is cold against my palm. When I remove it, the print slowly fades, leaving only a residue that is the summary of my life. I don't even recognize my own eyes staring back at me. I pull on my lower lid, stained red with tears. Someone's been going ape on the bathroom door making me feel like they're trying to burst through the confines of my skull.

"Anna! Please, open the door!" The voice is familiar, but I'm totally bummed out so I ignore it.

Looking down at the counter, I slide my hand across my make-up mirror and watch the distortion of my face disagree with the act of destroying the neatly plowed, white powder rows. My hand doesn't stop as the mirror, and my only reason for living, crashes to the floor. I grab my hair, wanting to pull it out. Too many reflections of my face are strewn all over the milky beige tile—staring back at me with hatred.

My knees let loose and I fall like a rock. The broken shards of mirror cut into my hands as I break my fall. The banging on the door is totally killing this trip. I stare at my hands and watch the blood slowly drip off my fingertips.

"She won't answer. She got angry when I told her we'd take her to dinner for her birthday. I don't know what's wrong," says a meek, familiar voice.

"Give her some time." This voice is deep and needs to cut loose, like now. It haunts my dreams. It pretends to care for me by day. But at night, it turns my bones cold and I gasp for air—waking up to my own choking screams. "She'll come out on her own."

The crying I hear is my old lady's. She's the weak voice that also pretends to care about me. Her cries are unmistakable. I hear them a lot more than her voice. I don't think she knows how often I've caught her trying to hide her anxiety about the old man. He's never home and spends too much time at work—scheming his secretary. No one knows I know this.

Water mixes with blood on the mirror shard resting against my knee. I draw my finger over the glass and a red line appears across the reflection of my throat. "Whoa, it's like a sign," I whisper.

The pounding on the door dulls and a chant starts whispering in my head.

A dirty name
A dirty face
A curse to relive this place
Die for his shame
Die for the key
Die to become free

I think I've heard this chant before. No matter how hard I resist; my hand holds the blade to my wrist.

"You sure about this, Miss Anna?"

I look up and across the room is the coolest cat I've ever seen sitting on the edge of the tub. He's young, attractive, and darkly mysterious. Quite the hunk. He smirks as if to show his disapproval in a reassuring way.

"You're outta sight. Do I know you?" Because if I don't, I totally want to.

He shrugs.

"How'd you get in here?" I look away from his dark, alluring eyes and I see that I'm still holding the razor blade against my wrist. I can't move my arms. If I didn't know any better I'd think someone is wrapped around me; holding every muscle in place. I feel possessed.

"I have my ways." He looks up at the small window as if he came in through it. This hunk's broad shoulders would never fit through that small window.

"Who are you?"

"We've been over this many times, Anna. I'm not bloody enjoying all the ways that you make me watch you die." His face hardens and he looks angry, but not with me. Who could he be mad at, if not me?

"It's copasetic, man," I say, feeling a little guilty for not remembering him.

He exhales through his nose and leans toward me, supporting his elbows on his knees. "I'm at a loss with you, Anna. Every time I come for you, you look as if you'll fight back. I'm beginning to believe there is some hope."

Fight back? Hope? I look at the razor against my wrist. It's penetrating deeper than before. It occurs to me that he said "every time" and I wonder what he's getting at. "Lay it on me. How many times are we talking about?" I wish I didn't sound so enthralled.

"This is the fifth time," he says with such tenderness and fidelity that I feel relaxed and willing to go all the way with him.

"Far out. You some kind of angel?" I'm such a ditz, but what else do people ask their hallucinations before they die?

He sighs so deep that I drop my head in embarrassment and notice that the razor blade is on the floor, mixed with my blood and the broken mirror. My reflection resembles a chaotic, cubism still-life that looks as if it should be on the wall of Picasso's home instead of my bathroom floor.

"Look at me." He doesn't demand it, but I feel I would do anything he asks. When I meet his gaze he says, "Do I look like an angel, my sweet Anna?"

I hadn't noticed he's wearing all black. His shirt is snug across his shoulders, but loose around the waist and his dark jeans are slightly faded. He has no wings or a halo, which I've come to believe all angels have. Taking note of the scythe, all I can whisper is, "No," and swallow hard, "are you Death?"

"Not quite. I'm one of his... helpers. We're called Deathdrifters." He stops and draws in his breath. "I've said too much."

"Don't sweat it. If I die, I can't tell anyone. And if I live, no one would believe me anyway; suicide is a direct ticket to the nut house."

"I think this is the most brilliant you, yet. Unfortunately, it won't matter. I gave up a lot to be here. Next time, I don't know what I'll have to do." Slowly, he scratches his cheek as if it helps him to think.

"Next time?"

"You have to remember, Anna."

"Remember what?"

"We're running out of time." He looks up at the little window again and then stands.

"Little help?" I smile weakly and hold my hand out to him. I haven't had much practice at flirting and I don't know why I think if he takes my hand to help me up off the floor it will be considered as such.

"I..." He stuffs his hands in his pockets as if to restrain himself and shakes his head. His face is pale and it occurs to me that, perhaps, the blood on my hands causes his discoloration.

But that's not the case, because a thick, bulky hand with too many gold bracelets, chunky rings, and long, brightly painted finger nails slices the razor blade across my neck.

As I lie on the floor and look up at my two guests, that totally far-out face turns to sheer anger and though the voices in the room sound like they're in a cave somewhere, I can still hear them.

"Nastusia, I'm not letting this happen again!"

"Five to Zero, Doom. Time flies, doesn't it? I sure hope Grim gives us a sixth time." This woman's voice is familiar also. It's Ms. Cune, my old man's secretary. She's the one who slit my throat. Now my family will think that I've committed suicide. "See you in a hundred years, handsome," she says and I hear her bracelets jingle.

Once everything goes black, I feel weightless and comfortable. Death is surprisingly gentle. At least *this* Death is.

"My sweet Anna," I hear in the distance, "I'm so sorry. I couldn't stop her. I'll do anything to stop this curse. I'll find a way, I promise."

Even though I can't see anything, I feel his hand come closer to my face. It's as if a cloud is blocking out the sun. "Wait," I plead and his hand stops short. "All I ask is that my parents don't know about the cocaine when they find my body. Please, Damien?"

"You remember!" I hear the joy in his voice and wish I could see his face before I feel the kiss of death upon my lips.

THE
✇ PRESENT ✇
DAY

EIGHT DAYS
BEFORE

I have a nervous tick of tapping my ball-point pen on my desk when I'm thinking intently. My father hates it, so I do it more often if he's around. I enjoy this class, but it has too many pop quizzes for my liking. Since I'm finished before the rest of the class it's become a little monotonous listening to the ticking clock and the injudicious scribbling of my peers.

Looking out the window proves to be even less time consuming. If this class ended, instead of began, with a pop quiz, I could just walk out the door. The amazing thing about college is that the professors don't care if you don't care. I'm not sure how I feel about that.

After the half hour is up, Stan collects our papers. It's interesting how different life in college is from high school. Ms. Falucchi, my senior math teacher in high school, would never have let her students call her Mary. Stanley Donahue, Ph.D., on the other hand, just wants to be called Stan. You got it, Stan!

The class continues its usual routine for the next hour. Drab conversations on how we interpret the works of Margaret Atwood, Joyce Carol Oats, John

Updike, and John Cheever occupy today's arsenal. I did the readings and I enjoyed them immensely, but I don't care much about listening to the interpretations of others today.

It's Friday and my parents are expecting me to drive home for the upcoming break. Mostly, because my birthday is next Saturday. I'm reluctant to go, but they have a way of making me feel obligated. I was glad to finally get away from home by heading off to school. And over the past two years, I have found numerous reasons not to go home.

I suppose if the only reason I stay away from home is due to my mother's excessive drinking, which she does in order to escape reality, I might be able to stomach the up-coming week. Mostly my anxiety rests with my father. He's not the loving type. I can't recall any memorable moments with him. He wasn't around all that often while I was growing up. He always smells like some kind of cheap perfume that isn't meant for a man. My mother wouldn't wear it either.

Every night that I tried to sleep as a kid, I would hear my parents fight. The arguments always escalated to the point when my mother would ask my father to leave his lover. Why my parents are still together, I have no idea, but I attribute my nightmares to my father's infidelity.

I'm not sure what's been going on in my dreams the past few weeks. Most of the time, these nightmares consist of dozens of vague, shadowy figures coming after me. I'm in a torn, dirty dress trying to get away. A deep calming voice always wakes me. I'm covered in sweat and shivering. If it wasn't for that voice and sexy accent, though, I think I'd have lost my mind after the first couple of nightmares. Unless, of course, the voice indicates that I've already lost my mind.

Last night's dream, which was not filled with creepy shadows, has been running through my head all day. I keep hearing that calming voice ask if I remember his promise. For some reason I'm always dumb in my dreams. It's like yelling at a wall. I can hear myself in my head say, "Anna, you know better. Think! Ask him something beneficial." I don't, of course. That would be too easy and life just isn't like that.

Stan interrupts my thoughts and hands out a small paperback to each of us. He expects this to be read when we get back from break, but I know better. Only half the class is here because some students have started their week early. I would have too, if I had a better place to go. When we all return Monday after break, Stan will lecture about commitment and say we have an additional three days. That's more than enough time. This book isn't over two hundred and fifty pages.

At the end of class, I throw my books in my bag and toss it over my shoulder. I think this is the slowest I've ever walked back to my dorm room. Once I'm in my room, I see my roommate has already left. She wrote a note on the mirror with a dry erase marker. I smile before I see myself and then quickly turn to throw a few things in another bag—necessities mostly.

I tie my short, dark hair into pig-tails behind my ears. The front strands don't make it in the ties because my hair is too straight and conforms to the shape of my head. I change into pajama bottoms and an old t-shirt because when making long drives I like to be comfortable. I stop to stare at the phone. I consider calling home and saying that I'm not planning to make the trip until tomorrow. It seems like forever before I give in and lift my bag up on my shoulder. Grabbing my keys off the dresser I turn to the door and catch a view of myself in the mirror. I cringe. Why do I hate myself so much?

Well, first of all, my eyes are too small. They have an odd, greenish-brown mixture that's encompassed in a gray-blue outer ring. Everyone thinks I'm frail looking. They call me dainty. Whatever. I don't even wear a lot of make-up. Just a faint, light pink eyeshadow, mascara, and on my lips, I apply only a clear gloss.

19

Involuntarily, I walk up to my dresser and open the top drawer. I know they're in here because I haven't relied on them since mid-terms last semester. I also haven't been home since then.

"Leave them, Anna."

Shit.

That beautiful, deep voice is back again. This time, I know I'm not sleeping. I consider talking back to it, but I don't know who might be lagging behind in the dorms and walk by. I ignore the voice, glance out into the hallway and then quickly rummage through the drawer. In the back, behind a pair of socks I thought I lost a while ago, is a pair of half-inch, double-thick, black rubber bands. I slide them both on my left wrist and because they're a little big they don't get tight until they meet my forearm just under my elbow. I lock my elbow and stare at the black bands.

"Anna, sweet Anna, please don't."

I turn around.

I swear that voice was breathing on the back of my neck. No one is here. No one is in the room with me. I snap the band and relish in the pain. I understand this feeling, and oddly, it's the only thing that keeps me feeling safe as I walk out of the building.

PROVE IT

It's a two hour drive home and I hate the way on-coming cars blind me in the darkness. I roll down my window, not because I'm hot, but because driving is so boring.

Hardly anyone is on the highway this late at night. The Georgia humidity is intense this year. The crisp, evening air is causing increased visual impairment of the road. It could be boredom, but the fog forming off the hot concrete looks to be materializing into a figure— a figure exactly like those from my nightmares. It makes me consider what it would be like to get hit by a car that's doing almost seventy miles per hour. Would it be a quick death?

My mind has no effect over my body right now. The radio isn't on. I don't have a CD player or a tape deck in this old, beat up car, so who I'm speaking these words aloud to—I haven't a clue.

"Die to become free," I whisper.

Well of course, but free from what? Free from my hellish life? From my parents' craziness? Lack of a social life? Fear of the unknown? The list goes on.

I feel as if I'm forgetting what I've already said to myself. I'm sure I said more before that. I reach my left hand up on top of the wheel and my eyes lock on the black bands. The rubber is soft as I glide my finger along the smooth torture device. Can I count how many times I've snapped them since I left my dorm room?

Twice in the elevator. Once after tossing my bag in the trunk. Twice before I could bring myself to start the car. Once more because it wouldn't start. Three times in line for coffee at the rest stop. And once more just now.

My fingers extend, stretching off the steering wheel for each snap on my arm. Ten times and the red ring of pain glows impatiently around my forearm. For some unknown reason this reminds me of the calming voice from my dreams. The same voice I heard that didn't want me to put these on.

"If only he was real," I whisper to myself.

How foolish.

I grab the coffee mug from the cup holder and place it to my lips. It's cold. I don't usually dawdle with my coffee so how could it lack that glorious burning sensation? The clock on the dash should be correct and if it's losing time, then that's just one more thing that's adding to the depleting value of this car.

Taking a deep breath, I realize it's not the coffee that's the only thing beginning to shiver. The air conditioning on this hunk of junk doesn't work, not that I need it. Turning the heat on proves useless because I'm cold to the bone. I roll up the window thinking it might fix this weird sensation. No luck.

"Are you sure?"

"Shit!" I swerve in my lane. Why does this keep happening? My pulse is racing and I'm thankful that I'm the only one willing to drive such a long distance this late at night.

"I didn't mean to frighten you, Miss Anna."

"What the—," I always try to correct my language before I see my parents. "Frighten me? You're a voice in my head! If I was crazy, I don't think you'd have startled me to the point of almost ejecting out of this piece of—"

"I was wrong," he interrupts me.

"*About*?" I can't believe I'm angry with a voice.

"This is definitely the most brilliant you."

"You have comparisons? So not only am I schizophrenic now, but I have multiple personalities too?"

He grunts. "I'm not a voice in your head, Anna. Mentally and physically there is nothing wrong with you."

"You're leaving something out," I say. I can hear in his voice that *something* is wrong with me.

"I can't tell you unless you're sure." He sounds hopeful and I'm intrigued by this.

"What does that mean?"

"I'm risking everything I am for you, my sweet." This shocks me. Who risks everything for someone they don't know? And what's with the pet name? Is he just being nice? Of course he is, Anna, he's whatever you want him to be. He's in your head.

"Who are you?"

"Are you sure?"

"Sure of what?"

"Reality. You requested that I be real to you. Do you want me to exist in this world?"

"Uh..." This seems like a huge leap. How does a voice in my head become anymore "real" than it already is? And if "real" is a visual perception then what happens to me next? Nut house?

As if he knows my thoughts, he says, "Think about it and in the morn, if you would like to know the truth, which I am more than willing to give you, call for me and I will come."

"How?"

"You know how."

"No, I don't!" Just as those three words smack into my windshield, warmth returns to my body and the driver of the car in the lane next to me looks over. I hope he doesn't think I'm crazy, because now I know I'm not. Though I doubt I can prove it. Can you prove a feeling running through your veins?

As I pull into the driveway of my parents' house, I realize that I haven't touched the black bands since he spoke to me in the car—in my mind.

HOME UN-SWEET HOME

I check my watch and it's past midnight. Last week, I told my mother that I'd be home earlier than this. The light in the living room is on so I'm sure she's still up. Slowly, I get out of the car and walk around to the trunk to get my laundry bag.

The lawn has recently been mowed. New flowers have been planted along the walkway to the front door. It's always reassuring to know my parents like to hide the turmoil inside the house by landscaping the place into a sanctuary as if the devil doesn't reside within.

The door is unlocked so I quietly peer inside. The house smells the same—stale bourbon and menthol lights. I didn't see my father's car in the driveway which means he's not here, as usual. I sigh and set my keys on the table by the door. He won't be home tonight, so I might as well lock up now.

As the deadbolt seals in the misery, my mother stirs on the couch. I drop my bag on the linoleum and casually kick the brass foot guard on the door. My mother picks her head up, looks around the room and smacks her lips to clear away the dryness. Apparently, doing that didn't help so she swigs the bottle of bourbon still in her grasp.

"Morning, Mother," I say, looking at the mess of interior design magazines on the floor.

She scrunches her face up as if she can't see me without her glasses. She doesn't even wear glasses. "Oh, you're home." She digs her hand into the couch cushion and doesn't make eye contact with me.

"Looking for these?" I pick up the menthol lights off the coffee table and throw them on her lap.

"Thanks." She lights up without another word.

I walk over to the bay window and open it. I'm not too keen on dying of second hand smoke, which is odd because I'm not afraid to die at all. "Where's my father?" I don't really care to hear the answer, but if I don't make small talk we'll sit in silence the rest of the week.

"Same place as usual," she mumbles, trying to balance the cigarette in her mouth. She's not particularly good at talking with a cigarette and being drunk. Add walking to the kitchen into the mix and all I can do is wonder how many times she fell before she "mastered" the obstacles of the living room.

I snap the rubber bands on my arm lightly, looking around the messy room. "How is he?" I call.

"Angry when he's home—which is why he never is," she yells from the kitchen, even though she doesn't need to because sounds in this cold, rigid house travel like the air conditioned breeze that constantly runs through it.

I give up and close the window. "I'm going to bed," I say, picking up my bag and keys before I head to the stairs.

"Night," she calls back.

I hear her cough a couple of times as I ascend the stairway. She's violently rummaging through the fridge and I wonder if she's going to be all right. I stop and regret what I'm about to say, but that doesn't seem to matter.

"Mom?"

"What?" She closes the fridge and sticks her head into the hallway, looking at me like I've already asked her too many questions. I suppose one was more than enough.

"Do you need anything?"

"At the moment?" she asks. "No, but tomorrow night I may ask you get me another one of these." She swings the bourbon bottle over her head. At this rate, she'll need it way before tomorrow night.

My bedroom smells of stale air. I like it much better than bourbon and menthols. I put my bag next to my door and shut it behind me. Collapsing on my big, cloud-like bed gives me one reason to choose this place over my dorm. Outside of this bed, home doesn't hold a candle to school.

I roll over onto my back and my head hangs off the side of the bed. Something is wrong and I snap the rubber bands harder than before. From this upside-down perspective, I can see that my black curtains are pulled aside to let the light in. That's not something I would do. My fingers glide over the black bands on my forearm.

I do a backward summersault off the bed and stand with my back to the windows. I see that my desk has been organized. My nail polishes have been arranged, surprisingly, in alphabetical order. My papers have been piled up and my small, pewter grim reaper is being used as a paper weight.

None of this is something that I would do.

And my mother doesn't clean, unless she's changed in the last two years of me being away at school.

I snap the bands on my arm once and open my door yelling, "Mom, who's been in my room?"

I hear her clomping up the stairs and swearing under her breath. Once she's at the top, she takes a swallow of bourbon for sustenance. "Your father hired some prissy maid. She giggles too much, wears revealing clothes, and has some strange accent. I think she's Korean *and* Bohemian. I don't know and I don't care."

I dig my toes into the lush hallway carpet. "Why don't you just leave him?"

"Who? Your father? Never!"

"Why not?"

"Because he's your father, Anna." She walks past me and goes into her room. Not my parents' room. *Her* room. They've had separate rooms since I was in middle school. They tried to tell me it was because of my father's snoring, but I'm not stupid. I didn't get into the University of Georgia on an academic scholarship for being a moron.

I decide to go downstairs and turn off all the lights. My mother has a habit of driving my father mad. She'll mess up the house on purpose so this so-called cleaning lady will be too busy to notice my father. Then she'll leave the lights on all day if it means the electric bill will be higher next month. Mom also uses the oven a lot, but she doesn't cook without a good reason.

I flip the last switch on the wall at the bottom of the stairs and the blackness envelops me. The street light casts a warm glow through the sheer, canary yellow curtains. They glisten as they sway with the air current through the house, but I don't feel a breeze on my face.

"I'm sure I closed that window," I whisper to myself. I step closer to the bay window and before my one foot leaves the bottom step each of the four curtains move individually as if someone is dragging their hand across them as they walk past.

Nothing is here. I check the register on the wall but there's no current from the central air to move the curtains. The window is closed too, just as I thought.

I shrug off whatever it was I thought I saw. I just made a long drive so I'm sure I'm tired. The only thing to do is head back up to my room. I've got a lot of re-arranging to do.

Once outside my bedroom door, I grip the cold brass knob and see the black bands on my arm. I glide my fingers over the soft rubber. How does he expect me to call him back? I can't just yell at the top of my lungs and expect him to hear. As a matter of fact, I shouldn't have to say a thing. He should hear my every thought, shouldn't he?

Maybe not.

I twist the knob and reach my hand in to flip the switch. I don't recall turning off the light. There's a crack and a quick flash. "Shit," I whisper. I'm not about to turn on the hall light, because I can hear the drunken snores of my mother from her open doorway.

After I left home for school, my mother had taken to leaving the door open when she slept. It was her way of knowing when my father came home and if he came home alone. If the light being turned on in the hall wasn't a good enough indicator for her then the sounds of four passionately clumsy feet passing the open doorway would be enough.

I shut my door behind me and shuffle my feet across the rug toward my bed. Rearranging can wait until daylight. I slip off my jeans and lay on top of my quilt. Georgia is warm enough in spring that I don't mind not finding pajamas tonight. My room is hotter than Hades and all I can think is: This is home, Anna. Home un-sweet home.

As my eyes adjust to the darkness, I can make out the abstract design of my wall-paper border. I picked this one specifically for the black lines on the white background, which if you stare at it just right, the negative space forms a skull—hollow white eyes surrounded by black bone.

"I wonder what you would look like if you were," I hesitate, "real."

CARRY ME OFF

It's only been three weeks since my mother asked me to come home for break. And ever since that conversation, the voice of my dreams has kept me company. I wonder if he'll be the one to wake me from my nightmares tonight.

TOUCH OF DEATH

When I finally open my eyes, I realize it is Saturday. It was Saturday when I got home in the middle of the night, but I believe a new day doesn't start until you've had a good night's sleep. I roll out of bed and stand at my desk. I know I promised to rearrange everything, but now I'm not in the mood. It's much easier to just push things around.

With one quick swipe of my arm everything is on the floor. Where it should be! I pick up my little grim reaper and kiss it's hood. "You've always been there for me," I say as if he can hear me. As I place him back down on my desk I see what he has been holding in place for me.

In a room with stale air, I'm surprised I would need a paper weight. He has been standing on top of all of the essays I've done since high school. A few short stories, poems and research papers are piled up at the edge of my desk. They bring a smile to my face as I stroke the ink with the tips of my fingers. But staring at them won't move the day along any faster.

I grab clothes from my dresser and head to the bathroom. I don't care for hot showers. I like lukewarm.

The best of both worlds. The water pulses down on my face. I must have taken longer than expected because when I turn the water off I hear my mother shouting at my father. Once I'm dry I throw my clothes on to get back to my room as quickly as possible. Pulling my arm though my sleeve I notice my black bands aren't around my forearm. I know I didn't take them off.

Searching my room, I can't find them. I'm not a deep sleeper, so I'd have noticed if my mother came in and took them off. She definitely would have woken me up to ask about the red rings on my skin, which is now beginning to show signs of bruising.

I give up looking and plop down on my bed, running my fingers through my short, wet hair. I sigh heavily and fall back on my pillows. "Where are they?" I ask myself, aloud. I feel as if I've lost a part of my soul— the one thing that keeps me calm and comfortable in this place of doom.

Doom.

Why does that sound familiar? I feel like I should know that word not as a verb, but as a noun, which it is. A person. I shake my head. "No one names their kid Doom," I tell myself. Although, it might be an interesting conversation piece. I can't help but play with that thought, "Hello, My name is Doom Fairchild." I chuckle and roll over to look at my mini reaper. "Hi there, Doom Fairchild."

Last night's dream suddenly comes back to me in full force. I sit up to look out the window. The road is wet and therefore it must have rained. I recall in my dream, sitting up in bed and seeing someone standing by the window; closest to the closet. He wore a black, hooded sweatshirt and was soaking wet. He kept his hands in his pockets and remained still. I'm not sure he was even breathing. I didn't feel afraid then and I don't now as I recall the dream. It all seemed so real.

I remember him saying with a slight British accent, "This is how I look." Then he removed the hood and his cropped, black hair spiked out slightly over his forehead. He was tall, a little over six feet, and had broad shoulders. He looked strong, but not bulky like those frat boys on steroids. He smiled weakly at me and I must have blushed at the sight of his beautiful, dark eyes glistening from the glow of the street lights. Emotions battled inside me. I didn't know whether to run from the room or into his arms.

I don't remember saying anything, but he took one step closer to me, appeared pained and stepped back again. "I can't. Not until you decide what you want," he said, staring at the floor.

I can only guess that I asked him to come closer. Right now, thinking back about the dream, I feel as if I was under a spell. I've never seen that face before and yet, I was so drawn to a complete stranger. I've never longed so much for someone I've never met. Well, movie stars don't count, right?

Recalling the dream makes my heart ache. "I don't know what I want," I tell the ceiling. "How do I choose something when I don't know what the choices are?" Perhaps it's more suitable to talk to the floor. I mean, if he's not really a voice in my head then I doubt he was sent by God.

Heavy feet ascending the stairs distract me from diving back into my dream. I lip a prayer that those feet aren't headed toward my room. My peripheral vision catches a shadow stopping outside my door.

"Anna? Can I come in?" my father asks the wooden divider.

"Sure." I'm less than enthused.

The door creaks open slowly and a patronizing smile enters my room. My father sits on the end of my bed as if he's tucking in the four-year-old girl he used to adore.

Looking toward the window, I see that the rain has begun again. My father is smoothing out a small circle in my quilt with his hand. The repetitious movement draws my eye back to him.

"Your mother wanted me to tell you about the new cleaning lady before she comes over today."

"You found one that works weekends? Peculiar." I look at my nails and consider painting them black or deep plum today.

"Anna, please." I meet his gaze and see that he is not happy with the way this day has started out for him.

"What is it you want to tell me about her? That she's cleaned my room without my permission? Perhaps, that she's your new mistress and—"

"Anna!" He cuts me off and I see that his hand has gripped my quilt, ruining the smooth circle he just created.

"You can stop pretending. I'm not four anymore and I've known since that night."

"Anna, why do you always do this?" He rubs the back of his neck to calm the building tension. "Ms. Cune is very good at her job. I was hoping you might pick up this mess before she gets here. You haven't even been here twelve hours and it's a disaster."

I look at the items from my desk on the floor and it doesn't seem to be a disaster, as he calls it. "Less time doing her job; more time doing the boss," I mumble, hoping he didn't hear a single word of it.

He heard me, all right.

My face stings and I can taste blood in my mouth. I must have bit my tongue out of surprise when he slapped me. Water wells in my eyes from the burning sensation. I raise my hand to my face and the room is surprisingly cool all of a sudden. I exhale and a small cloud escapes from between my lips.

"I'm glad you came home for your birthday this year," my father says as he places his sinful hand on the door knob. He doesn't look at me and I assume that's because of his shame.

34

Die for his shame.

A guiding phenomenon pushes me to my desk. I pick up a pen off the floor and place the ball-point on the edge of one of my old essays to write down the four words that just went through my mind. And just like that, I feel colder and accompanied.

Slowly, I draw myself up from the desk and turn around. Over at the window, by my closet, is the same depiction from my dream. A dark stranger stares out my window at the rain.

"Um…" I don't know what else to say. Most girls would scream for help, but if he is here to kidnap me, right now, I'd go willingly.

He turns around and looks angry, dangerous even. But protective. I always thought no one in the world was paler than me or had darker hair, but this guy has both. His complexion is clean, eyes glisten with rage, and the shadows on his pale face from the hood over his head emphasizes his square jaw and perfect nose.

"Are you all right?" he asks me.

I feel as if I should know him. He looks a lot like the man from my dream last night, but something is off. I step closer and I can see he's trying to repress a smile.

"I'm fine. Thank you for asking." Two more steps and perhaps I can make out his face a little better.

He steps back with my every approach.

"He shouldn't have hit you."

"I shouldn't have mouthed off."

A few more steps and he'll be against the wall.

"You shouldn't have to hold back how you feel." He swallows hard. I think he knows he only has one more step before the wall.

"I think I dreamed of you last night," I say.

"Is that what you think?" He pushes his hands deeper into his pockets.

"I can't make out your face well enough, but yeah, that's what I think." I raise my hand to push back his hood.

"Don't…"

I'm not convinced. I smile and he gets more serious as he says, "I don't want to hurt you."

I'm confused and back up a step. "I don't understand."

"I can't stay unless you want my help. I'm taking a huge risk. One that I don't know if you'll ever entirely understand."

"Let me get this straight. You enter my room, uninvited, seem genuinely concerned about a little slap on the face and then say *you* don't want to hurt *me*?" I cross my arms over my chest and stick out my right foot so my weight is all on my left. "I don't think you can hurt me."

He grunts then says, "I don't want to *kill* you. Is that better?"

"Why would you want to kill me? I have nothing to offer you. In fact, an end to this miserable life would be a welcome change."

"I'm breaking every rule to help you. I just don't want to kill you in the process, so please keep your distance."

"You think you know the Touch of Death, huh?"

He allows himself to smile a tiny bit and I see the face from my dream. He's the man that took a step toward me. The stranger I longed for when I awoke. And as if he is reading my mind, he leans ever-so-slightly towards me and whispers, "I do, my sweet. I do."

SEVEN DAYS
BEFORE

He was gone the moment a knock came at my door. His face was only inches from mine and I licked my lips when I glanced down at his full, blush mouth. I would have given my life at that moment to kiss him. A complete stranger who said he would help me. With death? I think I'm losing it.

My heart is still pounding as I open my bedroom door. A woman I've never seen before, and don't care to meet at the moment, stands perfectly erect, glaring at me as if I'm a stain she can't get out of the carpet. I roll my eyes at my father's choice in women. Where does he find these people?

"Hello, Miss Anna. I'm Nastusia Cune." The sound of her voice makes my bones ache. "I'm here to help your parents keep house."

"Uh-huh." I turn away and sit on my bed. The temperature is still significantly lower than the hallway. I can see my breath again and wonder why this woman hasn't entered to reprimand me for the mess on the floor by my desk.

"I've been told you like your things the way they are, so I'll leave your room be."

"Why? You've already been in here at least once. I still haven't fixed everything you've screwed up."

"Screwed up? Such as?" Her eyes move from mine as she stares at my little pewter grim reaper.

"Don't touch Doom. He's off limits to everyone but me!"

Her eyebrows rise in curiosity and all she can say is, "Doom?"

I grab my pewter reaper and dangle him in front of her. She almost gives a sigh of relief and starts to walk away, but not without adding, "As it shall be. I'm at the mercy of your... *reaper*."

I slam my door closed and drop down on all fours to scrounge for my black bands again. They have to be under the bed. That woman's presence has my body trembling with anxiety. They're not here. Where are those bands? I'm helpless without them.

I bring myself back up on two feet and stare into my mirror. I look as if I haven't slept in days. My hair is finally dry so I run my hands through it to smooth it out. The top drawer has my make-up in it and I grab my concealer to lighten the dark circles under my eyes. I don't usually wear a lot of make-up, but after an encounter with that... *bitch*, I feel like death warmed over.

I pick up Doom and smile. "You are my protector," I say and shove him into my pocket.

"It's funny that you call him Doom," the voice of my stranger whispers behind me.

"Why is it funny?" I ask without turning around.

"Doom is how some have come to address me."

I spin around to face him, but he isn't there. "Uh, why do they call you that?" I'm not sure if I'm talking to myself or not. My eyes scan the room and after I don't see him, I close my eyes and think I'm just going crazy.

"I'm the Deathdrifter of the Damned. I only get the worst cases possible."

"And you've come to collect me? Great. How do I die?" I'm afraid to open my eyes and be disappointed that he won't be visible. It's not like I believe him, anyway.

"This time?"

Shocked, my eyes fly open. He's sitting on the end of my bed with his back to me. "What do you mean, this time?"

"I've been assigned to you *almost* every time you've died."

"Fantastic! I really am crazy. Forget medical school, no one wants a crazy woman caring for them!" I drop myself onto my desk chair to look at myself in the mirror again. My face is too thin, hair too dull. I have muddy eyes, and to top it all off, I'm now headed for the mental ward. Maybe I'll donate myself to the University's psych department. Here comes the guinea pig, Anna Fairchild!

"You're not crazy. We're seen when we want to be. Which is why I've gotten myself into so much trouble in the past."

"Bad boy, huh? Doom seems fitting."

"Damien."

"Hi, I'm Anna." I shake hands with the vacancy between us. He never takes his hands out of his sweatshirt pocket.

"I know that, Anna."

Of course he does. He's only said my name numerous times already. "So, how do you know me?"

"Like I said, I've been the one sent to collect your soul at each of your deaths, with the exception of the last two and this one. I sort of... bartered to be here."

"You're here to carry me off? I really am going to die, and sooner than I thought," I'm whispering to myself, but he hears me anyway.

"No. Not this time. This time I'm not doing my job. I'm keeping you alive."

"Why?" I ask. He's hesitating and I don't like the silence. "Never mind, I don't want to know."

He stands and comes over to me, but moves his hands from his sweatshirt pocket to his jean pockets. "Because..."

I look into his eyes and they don't look as dark and sinister as before.

"Because?" I whisper.

"Because the first time I took your soul from your burning body, I felt betrayed and... angry. You shouldn't die for his mistakes. He was, no, *is* selfish. It's your burden to carry this curse on your shoulders. You die on every one of your twenty-first birthdays and are reincarnated back into the curse every one hundred years. Someone so innocent and beautiful should have a long, happy life."

My face flushes. He called me beautiful. I now have the biggest crush I think I've ever had. And that accent isn't helping either. "I've never lived past twenty-one? Never been married or in love?"

"I'm certain you've been loved, Anna. Though whether you knew or not is of no concern to me."

"And you bartered to be with me, huh?"

"We all make mistakes," he says, sadly.

"Mistakes? You did your job, didn't you?"

"We're not allowed to feel *anything* for the souls we take."

"You said you've..." my voice catches, "*taken* me before. What number is this time supposed to be?"

He swallows hard once before answering. "Six."

"I've died five times?" I blurt out, appalled. I don't want to believe this. My eyes fill with tears and I try to push them back to the depths where they belong.

"We're not allowed to interact. That was my second mistake. When you were about to let go the second time in the depths of that lake, I let you see me. I thought I could restrain myself. I wanted to say something, anything to console you. You looked so sad and alone. I reached for you and you passed the moment my skin touched yours."

"That could have been poor timing. I don't think you should blame yourself." I clench my eyes tighter, keeping back the indication of my sorrow.

"No. I'm sorry, Anna, but that's not how it works. I know how to do my job. I just thought that I had enough power to change it. I don't."

"Tell me about the third time," I push the words past dry lips.

"My third mistake was when I gave up part of my List to watch you for a whole twenty-four hours before. You can imagine what trouble I'll be in when it gets out that I gave my whole List to Cameron this time."

A rumble of laughter comes out of me unexpectedly. "Cameron? Just Cameron? He doesn't have a nick name like The Bludgeoner, or something?"

He cocks his head to the side. "Trick. We call him Trick."

"That's lame!" I laugh harder and slouch down in my desk chair. He knows I'm hilarious—he just won't admit it.

His brow furrows before he says, "I watched you chop up meat for dinner and you decided to use a rusty old knife as your method. I tried to intervene by stopping Nastusia ahead of time. She's always been there—willing to help you follow through. She won't touch you directly until Saturday, your birthday, when it's time. But be careful around her in this house in the meantime. She will persuade you."

"What a downer. I die on my birthday?"

"It's part of the curse. And now it's become mine as well."

"You said the last two times you didn't get my name on your List. Why?"

"Grim took it off. I argued with him to let me try again by promising not to interfere."

"Grim? As in *The* Grim Reaper? Is that a nick name too?"

"Of course."

"Oh." I look at my hands and feel the need to keep them busy. I pull my little Doom out of my pocket.

"Can I see that?" He asks gently as if he doesn't really want to. I hold it out for him, but he tells me to toss it.

"I'm not afraid of dying," I say.

"Well, you should be. Now toss it." I watch it fly through the air and he grabs it with delicate ease. "I'm not supposed to do this, but do you want to see yourself die the last two times?"

"You can do that?" I lean forward. I've never been offered such an extravagant gift before. He nods once while inspecting every angle of the figure. "Yes, show me," I plead, though I'm not sure if I'm pleading for the vision or for him.

He holds the figure out to me and I touch the scythe with my fingertips. Instantly, my vision blurs into darkness and his face fades from view. I hear him whisper that it'll be all right. I must be panicking because he calms me with a simple, "My sweet Anna."

MY OWN DEAREST LOVE

That was the most exhilarating experience I've ever had—so far, anyway. I look up into his dark eyes of concern. I'm on the floor, my back propped up against my bed. His shoulders are inclined toward me. He has his hood back up and the sleeves of his sweatshirt are pulled over his fists which bear down on the plush carpet on either side of my legs.

"What happened?" I exhale slowly, glad to be breathing.

"I'm sorry, Anna. I didn't mean to..." He trails off and leans away from me. I think that is as close as I'm ever going to get to touching him.

In the visions, I watched as I hung myself from the balcony of a huge, beautiful white house. I saw Damien catch me just as my neck snapped and then take my soul as he wiped away my tears. Behind him looked to be a very angry, very jealous boy. I don't know if Damien knew he was there or not. And I don't know what connection I had to him either.

In the next vision, I saw myself standing at a sink in a bathroom which looked as if a sunflower threw up in it. I was gazing into a small mirror, dividing cocaine into thin lines with a razor blade. Then I changed my mind and pushed the mirror off the counter, onto the floor. Damien was there the whole time, but he didn't speak until I tried to slit my wrists. I can feel inside me how he made me feel even then. Did I love this stranger? Do I love him now?

His kiss took my soul after I begged him by name to hide my shame.

"You... you kissed me," I mumble, holding back any sign of rapture.

"I shouldn't have done that, I'm sorry." He looks away and asks, "Do you think you can stand? I didn't expect you to faint."

I sit on my knees, leaning toward him. My little Doom is haphazardly lying off to the side. "Don't apologize. I'm sure it was... wonderful," I whisper.

"Anna, please don't." He breaks our gaze and rests his back against my bed, propping his elbows on the mattress behind him.

"Don't what?" I reach out to touch his cheek, but he pushes my hand away with his sleeved arm.

"Anna! I'm going to keep you alive, not kill you for one moment that you'll never remember and a memory that only torments me forever."

"I'm sorry I torment you," I grumble and fold my arms around myself. I'm my own dearest love—my own true comfort.

"Look at me," he breathes against my ear. I meet his dark, trance-like eyes. "It's not that I don't want to. Ah, bloody hell." He pauses to run his hand through his hair, pushing off his hood. "You're all I've thought about for almost six hundred years. If I'm lucky enough to keep you after all of this, I couldn't be happier, but until then I'm doing whatever it takes to keep you alive."

"I'm sorry. I... I've never felt like this before. No one has ever cared about me. Not my father, and sometimes I doubt my mother ever did."

"He's selfish. This is all his fault and I really wish I didn't restrain myself from taking his soul when he hit you." Damien's eyes are blazing with rage at the thought of my father shutting me up.

"He's screwing the maid," I say, drilling at my eye with a fist. "Before her it was the neighbor. When my mother acted like a crazy bitch, she moved away."

"All Nastusia."

"She's the same woman every time? The one who's been ensuring all my deaths?"

"Yes. She doesn't know I'm here, but she's expecting me."

"I didn't see her in the visions."

"No, you wouldn't. She's a sorceress of great power. I'm not sure I can stop her alone."

"No one will help us?"

"I could ask Grim for help, but I doubt he'd give it to me."

"Is Grim stronger than Ms. Cune, er, Nah-stu-zah?" I sound out each syllable to make sure it's committed to memory.

He takes a deep breath and lets it out slowly. "In my opinion, yes. Grim can do anything, but convincing him to do so is next to impossible."

"Anything?"

"He can't or won't break the curse, I'm not sure which. He goes on and on about Fate."

"I was thinking more like remove The Touch of Death."

"Oh," he bites his lip, "well, it's his to give and to take away."

This excites me and Damien can see the hope in my eyes. He frowns and turns away, "What's wrong?" I ask.

"Don't expect too much. He's very stubborn."

"So am I." I smirk.

A quick knock raps on my door and when my mother's face peaks in at me, my eyes flash to where Damien was just sitting.

I can feel his presence in the coldness surrounding me, but I can't see him. "Yes, Mother?"

"Are you planning on spending the whole day up here?" She's over done herself today. Fried her hair with the flat iron this morning, re-dyed it in brilliant blonde and caked her face like a courtesan—complete with the bourbon and menthol smell.

My mother can be pretty when she wants to be. It doesn't help her to drink and smoke like a fiend. "Nice. You trying to upstage the help?"

She frowns. "I think you should get out today. I sent your father to the store to get something for dinner. You want to go shopping with me?"

"Spending all his money doesn't help the situation, you know."

"He can afford it," she beams. I think I just initiated the idea. "Why is it so cold in here?"

"I don't know, but I'm comfortable." I smile and pick up my reaper figure off the carpet. "I'm not in the mood to go out, you go."

My mother shrugs. She couldn't care less.

A current of cold wind brushes past my face. I close my eyes and let the cold linger, imagining him close. He's pacing back and forth in front of me and I think he's anxious. "What's wrong?" I whisper so my mother can't hear me.

"I don't want you alone in this house with Nastusia. Go with your mum." His voice is quiet at my ear, but stern and I want to yell at him for telling me what to do.

"I'm going to the library to get some school work done anyway and I might stop by and see an old friend." I lie with the best of them.

"Fine," she says, feigning disappointment. I've got a whole week of this yet. "Dinner is at six."

"Okay." I smile to reassure her I'll be home in time.

She shuts the door and I turn my head to whisper in the direction of the last cold gust across my face, "Meet me in the car." I grab my UGA hooded sweatshirt and leave my room.

PERFECTLY SIMPLE

I open my car door and plop into the driver's seat. I sigh heavily because if I had said yes to my mother's offer to go shopping, she wouldn't be sitting in the living room at two in the afternoon with a new bottle of bourbon.

"You can still go back in and tell her you'd like to go with her."

"You don't tell my mother no and then change your mind," I say. Turning the key in the ignition, the engine purrs, surprisingly.

"Where are we going?" Damien asks as I back out of the driveway and head down the street toward the main road.

"No where I can take us," I prompt.

I can't see him, but from his quiet grunt, I know he's not thrilled to do what I have in mind.

"Please?" I beg.

"I don't know. I can't figure out why he would allow this. It seems so pointless."

"Pointless?" He sighs at the tone in my voice. "Can I ask you something?"

"Of course, my sweet. You can ask me anything."

I smile. "Have you ever... looked in on me? I mean, have you been watching me... grow up?"

"No, but I collected the soul of a baby that was neglected by an orderly at the hospital where you were born."

"Neglected? You mean murdered, don't you? Who would murder a baby?"

"That's not the point, Anna. I collect the souls of the Damned. Grim let me keep that baby on my List because he knew the timing was right and you would have already left with your parents. I even checked for your name on the discharge sheet."

"Wait, you're given times at which people die?"

"Name, time, and cause of death," he states, sounding at ease about his work. What kind of person is relaxed talking about how often people die?

"So how can..." I try to remember the name of the Reaper he gave his List to, "Trick do your List and his own?"

"Why do you think we call him Trick?" There's a smile behind his rhetorical question. "He does his job well. The way it's supposed to be done. Plus, he's only been around for a short time and his List is... specific. He can handle it."

I pull into a parking space in the back end of the library's parking lot and turn to face the empty passenger seat. I wait, staring at where I think his face should be. I don't know what he's hiding from, but I hope he'll decide that he doesn't have to.

"Why are we at the library?" he asks with unease.

"Because no one comes to the library on Saturday. And no one will see us... er, me, talking to myself." I look up and down the length of the passenger seat. "You don't have to hide, you know?"

"I'm not hiding." I'm certain a frown is overwhelming his face.

"Take me to him. I want to discuss my... death."

"I already told you that I'm not letting you die this time." I blink and he's suddenly here, beside me.

"Does *he* know that?"

"Probably, which is why you're not on my List anymore."

"Who's List am I on?"

"Grim's."

"So if I live past my birthday, will I be taken off?"

"No. Fate decides on how and when, not a Reaper." He turns his head to the side, sheepishly, scratching his jaw. "If the curse is broken, you'll be reassigned."

Reassigned? Could anything else be so perfectly simple? "Well, I have other reasons to talk to him. Please?" I'm beginning to feel desperate. I can't think of any other way to find out more information. "You promised to help me, remember?"

He sighs. "I'm not promising that any good will come of it. Everything could get worse."

"I'll take my chances." I clap my hands together exuding excitement. "Let's go!"

IMMUNITY

The car went dark. Dark became light. Then light became white. Damien stands only a few feet in front of me and I can see him without the surrounding haze that is life.

"Am I dead?"

"No. It might take some time to find Grim, but he's around."

I can't take my eyes off Damien's back. Surrounded by the whiteness that is nothing makes him much more approachable. He's no longer wearing the dark, hooded sweatshirt that covered every inch of exposed skin. The black polo he has on now is tucked in, but bunched at his waist. Even though his shirt is black, he seems brighter—lighter somehow. It could be the light-wash jeans he's now wearing instead of the deep blue ones he wears in *my* world.

I reach out my hand to touch his back but stop short. I don't know what will happen if I touch him in this place.

I shake my head lightly to clear the accumulating fantasies. It does nothing to slow the beating of my heart. He turns around and my whole body quivers. His eyes are like stars on a clear night. That jaw line is hard and angular. He folds his arms across his chest and perfect teeth smile at me for the first time.

"What?" I ask.

"I'm considering an ultimatum," he says. I cock my head, wondering if he means with me or with Grim. "Come." He throws his head to the side, enticing me forward.

I follow him without the slightest hesitation. I don't know if it's him or the lack of distraction, but I'm captivated.

In this whiteout I feel as if our legs move but we make no progression. Suddenly, Damien stops and I stop next to him. "There," he points at nothing.

"I don't see anything." I squint in case this is an indication of needing a long overdue eye appointment.

"He doesn't want you to. Notice the temperature?"

"It's not cold here." I run my hands over my arms. "I thought—"

"Cold is an indication of death, but it's also evidence of a Deathdrifter's mood. This could be a good sign."

"Doom, this is not your signature," a rough voice, old with experience says, fatigued.

"No, it's Trick's," Damien says, indifferently.

A black blurry figure appears in front of me. There is no detail to this image. If he can make me see what he wants, he could be anything from a cockroach to a cupcake. But he smells like a garden.

"I see," he says with disapproval, "and this is all because of her. Again. Is there any guideline you won't break?"

"No."

The hairs on my neck prickle with the sudden change in temperature.

"I'm trying to decide what to do with you, so you better have a good reason for bringing the living here."

"I'm renouncing my status, Grim. I no longer want to be one of your Deathdrifters."

"No? Then you will lose your soul. Is that what you want?"

"Every hundred years, you take her soul to re-incarnate it into the curse. I know you have no choice in the matter, but I'm not losing this battle anymore."

"You're tying your fate to hers?"

"Yes, I am."

"Your name will not appear on my List until you're alive. I don't decide the time and place. You do this and you may die tomorrow—losing her forever."

"So give me life and then tell me when I'll see you again." Damien doesn't sound as if he wants to leave Grim.

"It is against policy to talk to the living, but that's never held you back before." The contempt drips from Grim's smoky lips and I shiver.

"Not even when you threatened me with life *after* her death, Grim." Damien sounds defensive, like a son standing up to his father's reprimand.

"Excuse me, Mr. Reaper? But what if *I* volunteer to be a Deathdrifter?" I ask.

Damien turns and makes to put his hand on my shoulder, but remembers himself and stops.

"Interesting," Grim says. "What kind of living soul do you think a Deathdrifter can be? Afraid to get close after all these centuries. Living a secluded life is not living, Doom. And unfortunately, you're already alone, my boy.

"And you," the blur adjusts to indicate that he's talking to me. "No females have ever been Death-drifters."

"First time for everything," Damien mumbles.

"Doom, you have so much potential. The time between her deaths and new lives, proves you have a weakness. I can't have a weakness in my apprentice."

"What do you mean by that, Grim? There's always something behind your words," Damien says.

I suddenly feel an even colder chill run through my body. I don't know whether it's Damien or Grim who is causing the rapid drop in temperature, but either way it can't be good.

"Give up on this decision and when I'm finished you will have my place. Change the rules to suit you as you see fit. Rid yourself of all weakness."

"Grim…" Damien sounds like he might give in. I can't bear the thought of him going through the pain of watching me die countless times until he can change all of this.

"Um, sir? I have a request," I say, trying to engage Grim in conversation. "You are familiar with my situation, yes? My family's curse?"

"What about it?" he chides.

"Damien has sworn to help me and—"

"He can't," I'm interrupted, "He has no power over the matter."

"No. I'm sure he does not." I see Damien's mouth open slightly as if to object. I don't actually believe that he can't help me, but the idea here is to agree with the one who has all the real power. "And I agree that it isn't wise for him to live. Nastusia is in my house as we speak. She knows he'll come for me and try to stop her. That has to give him some sort of leverage over her."

"What are you asking for?" Grim is intrigued, I can tell.

"I'm asking that he remain with me until my birthday, when whatever happens… happens." I pause to take a breath before the next choice of words leave my mouth.

"Anna?" Damien takes one step toward me.

"You're asking me to let him break another law." It's not a question.

Law. Guideline. Whatever. Grim knows what I'm asking for and he's not making it easy.

"I am." I pick my head up with pride and stare at the black fog which I believe to be Grim's eyes. "I have no memory of my past lives and if I die again, I won't remember any of this anyway."

"Eight hundred and nine years you've walked the land of the dead for me, Mr. Doyle. The last six hundred you've forgotten who you used to be, have you not?"

"I have not."

"You want this? You want to give up on the memory of them? Because if you live again; you'll make new memories. They'll be gone forever."

"No, not exactly, but I do want Anna, sir."

"A deal then. I'll relieve you of your List on the eleventh hour of each night lasting until dawn the following day. During the day, you will continue your work. If you succeed at stopping Nastusia, I'll keep my promise and return your life. If you lose this girl again, I will no longer be in need of your services and I will take your soul as a whole. Agreed?"

"A nod's as good as a wink, Charles," Damien says, without hesitating. I wish I had more time to think about what Grim just said.

"Good. Then we are finished here."

"Wait," I say, "about this Touch—"

"The deprived child may be granted immunity while here. That does not mean you are to return."

The smoky fog diminishes and I'm wrenched backward. My body slams against a solid form and it feels like a wall has stopped me from falling into a void. Arms wrap around me and a cold nose presses against the back of my neck.

"Thank you," he whispers. "I'd wait forever for you, Anna. Honest."

"Who said I did this for you?" I smile and turn to face him. I've only laid eyes on this man a couple of times. Talked to him spanning hundreds of years without recollection, but my heart doesn't seem to care about the logic.

I rest my head against his chest and close my eyes. He feels cold and firm. I pull away from him to look into his eyes and slide my hands from his shoulders to his waist. The taper of his body is exactly what I expected, but it never occurred to me that he would feel this good against my palms.

"Who was Grim talking about when he said you would forget them?" My brow furrows. I have always hated the look on my face when I do it, but this time I welcome it due to Damien's hands gently caressing the frown from my face.

He places his cool lips to my forehead and says, "I was born in twelve thirty-two and I died in twelve fifty-five."

"You died at twenty three? And you're... eight hundred and... thirty-two."

He shrugs and rests his chin on top of my head. "I left my wife and unborn son behind."

"I'm so sorry to hear that." I hug him tighter and push the jealousy I feel deep down. They're long dead and he hasn't been watching them relive a curse for six hundred years. No matter how many times I repeat that to myself, it doesn't make me feel any better. "You must miss them."

He shrugs and leans backward to examine my face. "I never met my son. I only saw him once and that was because I found his name on someone else's List. I found my wife had remarried and was with child, a third."

"Did it hurt to find out that she had moved on?"

He tips his head slightly, indicating a yes in my book of vague body language. "I threw myself into my work knowing that the child we had was going to be lost in battle. Our son died defending his home."

"That upsets you, I can tell."

"Yes." He hesitates. "I tried to stop feeling after that. I was doing rather well until I came for you. Watching you die, numerous times, has turned me into

58

a wreck which Grim hates to deal with every hundred years." He smiles slightly as if causing Grim difficulty is fun for him.

"Glad I could be of service," I joke.

He smiles his closed-lip smile and holds my face between his hands. I shut my eyes to savor in his touch. "If this is the one and only time I can touch you without killing you, I'll take it. No one has ever made me feel like this before, Anna."

With that simple comment I melt in his arms. His lips lightly graze mine as if he's afraid his kiss will still be the death of me.

It almost is.

TREPIDATION

We're sitting in my car in front of the library. The wind has picked up and I look at the clock on the dash which reads five. I now realize we took longer than expected. Damien is dressed head to toe in black again. It suits him. He pulls the sleeves of his hooded sweatshirt over his hands and I notice on his wrist are my black rubber bands.

"Um, where did you get those?" I'm afraid to ask for them back. I don't want to give him the wrong idea.

"Get what?" He's not paying attention to where I'm looking because he's preoccupied making sure none of his skin is showing or will inadvertently touch anything living—me, especially.

"The black bands on your wrist," I whisper and turn my head enough to shield my eyes from his view.

"I hate these. I took them from you because I don't want you hurting yourself anymore." He scowls while pulling on the rubber as if to break them from his wrist.

"Yeah, well, I've been looking everywhere for them. They calm me. I need them. Especially if you're not around."

"Why aren't you looking at me?" he asks. "I've memorized every one of your facial expressions over the past six hundred years. Hiding your face won't fool me."

I turn to look at him and his eyes already embrace a look of sorrow. He sees the unease I have for being without the bands and leans toward me. "Show me your arm," he whispers.

I pull my sleeve up and the red and purple rings glow with malice. "I want them back."

"No," he grumbles, and leans back against the door crossing his arms.

"How'd you get them off me, Doom?" I hiss so he can't misinterpret my discontent.

"You are a petite girl, Anna. They slipped down to your wrist while you were sleeping and I took them off. I *hate* that you do this to yourself. That *they* bring this upon you." I know his 'they' implies my parents and not the bands.

"Fine. Keep them." I can get more. I wish he had told me he had them, but I don't think my current mood would have been different anyway.

"I have to get my List back." He relaxes his arms. "See you anon, my sweet."

"Okay." I know I still sound upset, but now it's because he's leaving. "Hey, D!" I yell, but he's no longer in the car. "Don't be late," I tell myself.

Pulling back into my driveway, my father's car is parked next to my mother's and I consider parking behind his to keep him home tonight. That won't make a difference though, because he would just take my mother's car to spite us both. Besides, I'll pay for it eventually.

I've got four and a half hours to kill before Damien comes back. I try to think of every possible thing I can do to pass the time but all I've got is reading that book Stan gave out for homework.

I'm already half an hour late and expect to have missed dinner. Instead, I find my mother sitting at the table, alone, pushing cold mashed potatoes around with her fork.

"Sorry I'm late, I always lose track of time around books," I lie. The fact is, I can't say that I always lose track of time while making-out with Damien in some weird place that has no clock. There's too much to explain with that statement.

"It's fine."

"Do you want to watch a movie after dinner? I'm sure we could spend some time together laughing at a stupid comedy like we used to." Forever ago.

My attempt falls flat as she picks up her plate to carry to the kitchen. It's an indication that I'm eating alone tonight too.

"Where's my father?" I ask.

"In the den. He's probably seductively feeding that *cleaning* lady."

I sigh and take my plate to the kitchen to reheat it in the microwave. I'm better off taking a movie to my room to pass the time. Reading for Stan's class can wait. Besides, what's the point if I die on Saturday? Stan won't know if I've read it or not.

I see my mother take a new bottle of bourbon from a grocery bag. Good ol' Dad comes through again. I lean against the white granite counter top and watch her fumble with the twist off cap. Depression and lack of exercise is taking its toll on her. Finally, after I've watched her face contort with effort, she's found the key to her false happiness.

The microwave beeps and she jumps. I take my plate out of the microwave and decide to eat standing up. I'm shoveling food in my mouth so fast that I don't notice my mother leave as my father walks in. I rinse my plate and leave it in the sink because the dish washer is currently running.

"Hello, Anna," my father says from the entryway.

I glance over and see that his shirt is wrinkled more than normal as he hastily tries to tuck it back into his pants. The vertical stripes of his shirt reveal his inability to dress himself properly without a mirror.

"Hi," I mumble.

"Why weren't you home for dinner on time?"

"Lost track of time, but does it really matter? You apparently had no intent to eat with us," I sneer.

In two long strides my father is in front of me and has my jaw in a vice grip. "You should learn to be more polite. I didn't raise you to be so audacious."

"You hardly raised me at all." I'm not sure if he understands me. I can't move my jaw well enough to speak coherently. His face is scrunched up in anger and his breath reeks of fine wine. The kind we don't open except for "special" occasions. This coming Saturday is apparently not one of those occasions.

My father's hand wraps around the back of my neck and holds the bottom of my skull just as tightly as he had my jaw. "Are you saying I'm a bad Father?"

Okay, so he did understand me.

I don't say anything right away. One thing this life has taught me is to be fearless. I copy the anger on his face, but inside me is the little girl who always hid in the cupboard—shaking with trepidation. I wish I could open the door right now and tell her everything will be fine, but I don't have the key to unlock it. "That would be an understatement, *Father*."

He forces my face down on the granite counter and I stare at the black swirls in the stone. He places his lips so close to my ear that his nose is pressing against my cheek. "You can't help anyone until you help yourself." I shut my eyes and hold my breath. He claps his hand so hard against my back that I choke and cough. I should be glad he didn't use his fist, but the pain isn't allowing me to savor the satisfaction of that logic. As his hand loosens on my neck, I bring my head up off the counter with it. To my surprise, he quickly slams me back down on the counter. "Know your place in this house!" he shouts in my ear. I'm not moving as he lets go. My eyes are wet and my nose stings from trying to hold back tears.

Once he's out of the room, I let myself fall on the sparkling white tile. I hate this kitchen. I hate this house. I hate myself. Slowly, crawling out of the kitchen, I feel the ache of the slap on my back. My cheek is warm and stings to the touch. I hope it doesn't have a mark. Feet block my way to the stairs and I stop crawling. I look up and Ms. Cune is standing over me. An evil smile is plastered on her face and I realize that it's really her beating me through the use of my father. Not that he's ever been tender in the past, but he's never inflicted physical pain until she arrived as our neighbor years ago.

I hang my head and admit defeat. I'll never survive.

"No little Doom to protect you? How sad." She turns on her heel and walks out the front door.

I hardly make it up the stairs before my father opens the door of his den and leaves for the night. Once I get to the top of the stairs, I turn into the bathroom and strip off my clothes. Pulling my thin, long sleeved t-shirt slowly over my head, I notice a fragrance that isn't my own. It's a peculiar smell. Not one that you could give a name to, but if I had to, I'd say it smells like Death. Not what death smells like to the living, but what it smells like on an attractive, mysterious man. Death: The new fragrance for men—but impossible to market!

After I turn on the shower, I catch a view of my face in the mirror. Damien won't be happy. The redness is fading, but the purple is surfacing. The area is only the size of a quarter on my cheek bone. It won't be hard to cover with make-up, which may relieve some of Damien's anxiety. I twist at the waist to see the damage to my back and it hurts so much I give up and completely turn my back to the mirror to glance over my shoulder. Oddly, it looks as if my father, no, Ms. Cune, used a bat to hit me, instead of my father's arm. A bruise cuts diagonally from the top of my right shoulder blade to under my left one.

I sigh and step into the neutral water. I take long showers because they're nice escapes from reality. In here, it's just me and my mind and whatever I can think of to distract me from life. Unfortunately, my mind is blocked with pain—physical and emotional. I can't stop crying.

When I finish, I wrap the red towel around me and head to my room. Scanning what movies I own, I pick up the first comedy I see. I don't know if it will distract me the way I hope, but anything is better than nothing.

After changing into a deep purple tank and black shorts; it's not long after the movie starts that I begin to feel drowsy. I try to keep my eyes open to watch, but I know I won't make it through. I roll over so that my bruised cheek is against my pillow. I kick the quilt off the bed and use only my black and white striped sheets for comfort. I don't particularly care for this scene so I let my eyes rest.

STARRY NIGHT
EYES

I wake to a fuzzy black and white screen. I missed most of the movie and I can hear someone wearing a hole in my carpet. It's cold and the sheet isn't helping to warm me in the slightest. I look at the clock and see that it's five minutes to eleven. I pull myself up in bed and moan from the pain in my back. Wait. If I could adjust my gaze to read the clock when I woke up then I'm on the opposite side that I went to sleep on. Which means...

"Damien?" I whisper.

"What happened to your face?" He sounds furious. Just as I knew he would be.

"You're back early." I bring my hand to my cheek—even smiling hurts.

"I've been here for an hour watching you sleep. It wasn't until you turned over that I saw *that*."

"Oh." I'm not sure how to address him in this state of anger. "Do you watch me sleep often?"

"Anna, don't change the subject. What happened?"

"Nothing," I say, and look away.

"Nothing is black and blue and swelling on your face," he growls.

I jump out of bed and regret hurrying over to my mirror above my desk. Pain surges through my body, but it's tolerable. My hair is pillow teased and unkempt from falling asleep when it was wet. I push my hair back behind my ears and switch on the desk lamp. Damien draws in a quick breath. He must have just caught a glimpse of the mark arching over my bare shoulder blade. I look at the bruise on my face and it's swollen and darker than when I fell asleep.

"I can hide this," I say, glancing at his refection in the mirror. He's turned his head to the side.

"I know it looks bad, D, but it looks worse than it is." I turn to take a step and pain shoots down my back.

He sees me freeze out of his peripheral vision. Jerking his head slightly to look at me, he closes his eyes as he says, "Your face shouldn't be causing your whole body pain. What did he do to you? Tell me."

Didn't he see my back?

"It's not his fault." I'm still not moving. The pain will ease soon enough so I can go back to bed— hopefully. "Why are you way over there?" I try to sound seductive, but I have no idea how to do that.

"You come here," he says and swallows with too much effort. I frown and slide my foot along the carpet toward him. This isn't going to work. I'm going to have to tell him about my back. Why hasn't he looked at me?

"Why do you have your eyes closed? The bruise isn't that noticeable in the dark, is it?"

He exhales slowly and takes one hand out of his pocket to scratch his cheek. "You *will* tell me, Anna."

"That's not a reason to keep your eyes closed."

"I'm trying to be polite."

"Polite? What for?"

"You're hardly wearing anything," he whispers more out of embarrassment than for concern of being heard.

"Oh, I..." I slide my other foot forward so as to make it back to the seclusion of my bed. Pain renders me motionless. "I need help," I mutter.

He's in front of me before I realize he's moved. "What's wrong?" he asks, searching my face. Without trying, his voice makes me feel accepted, cared for, and desired.

"I can't move. It's my back. I feel like my spine is a metal rod." The pain is causing me to panic. I'm gasping for air. I've never felt this immobile. This helpless. He's still staring at me and I'm beginning to lose that emotional rush he instilled in me moments ago. "Help me." Tears burn down my face and I see his hand move toward me, but he still won't touch me.

"Do you have anything alive in this house that no one cares about?"

"Other than me? No," I retort.

"No cat, or perhaps a neighbor's annoying dog?" His voice quickens, eyes searching. Now he's panicking.

"I'm not letting you hurt someone's pet, Doom."

He scowls and disappears from view; purple smoke in his wake. I can't believe he just left me. Letting my knees collapse beneath me, I grunt from the pain climbing up my spine. My head falls forward and I curl my body into a fetal position. All of a sudden the world feels like its shifting and I'm cradled in Damien's arms. Still in the same fetal position, he has my head resting on his shoulder and my forehead touches the cold fabric of his hood.

Millimeters from my skin, his icy hand glides over my back. I grunt when it stops the second time, hovering over the bruise. "Stay still. I have to lift the back of your shirt." He shifts me forward slightly so my head rests against his other shoulder, his chin over the back of my head so skin can't touch skin. My tank slowly creeps up my back and when it reaches my neck I hear him swear under his breath. It's not a word I recognize and it makes me wonder what kind of words people used in the thirteenth century.

"Where did you go?" I ask. His cold hand continues to hover over my bare skin. I whimper from the sensation. "I thought you left me."

"I had to be sure I wouldn't kill you. I've never tried a glove as a barrier before."

"Whose poor kitten did you scare?"

"Anna, don't joke."

"But it feels a little better now." I want to add that the relief can't be as wonderful as his touch, but I think that goes without saying. The thought even makes me shiver.

"Mm." He nods and removes his hand. "I'm making you cold."

"I don't mind. The room isn't cold anymore, why is it just your hands?"

"I'm dead, Anna." He pulls my tank back down. "I'm always cold, but the room doesn't have to be."

His tone tells me he intends on breaking his deal with Grim to protect me, but I'm not about to let that happen. I pull myself up from him and stare into his starry night eyes. "Gloves, huh?" I take his leather covered hand in mine. "Talk about protection."

"It's not skin contact." He tucks a loose strand of my hair behind my ear and I break our eye contact.

"I'm a mess," I say and hide my face, yanking my fingers through the knots in my hair at the back of my neck.

He curls a finger under my chin so that I face him. "You're beautiful." He needn't say more. I move to wrap my arms around his neck—desperately wanting to kiss him. He's faster than me and I suddenly feel like a drunken sorority girl throwing herself at the first guy in sight. He holds my arms, keeping me a safe distance away. "I think you should lie down for a while. Don't put a lot of stress on your back right now."

I pull myself to my feet. I can be just as cold and unfeeling as Death. As I turn toward my bed, Damien grabs my wrist and looks up at me. He's still kneeling on the floor and he lifts himself so he is sitting on his heels, putting his nose even with my waist.

"Tell me what happened," he begs.

"You'll just get mad and it's not his fault anyway."

"I have ways of finding out the truth, you know." I don't know, but I can imagine.

"I think he was used as a vessel by Ms. Cune... Nastusia. I mean, it was like a slap on the back, but with a little more force. Only his palm touched me, and yet it looks like I was hit with a two-by-four."

He nods and is content with my answer, but that doesn't change the anger on his face. "I checked into the origin of this curse." He places his cheek, covered by his hood, against the soft cotton of my tank top. "I know why she's punishing you."

"Why?" I watch his hand play with the drawstring of my shorts. My eyes trace his jaw line to meet his eyes filled with despair and silhouetted in the moonlight. This information can't be good.

"Centuries ago, the first time your father was with Nastusia, he promised he'd leave his wife for her. When he found out his wife was having a child, he couldn't bring himself to leave your mother. Nastusia got angry. She watched you grow up while learning the Black Arts. When you turned twenty she cursed you to die on every one of your twenty-first birthdays until he willingly left his wife. The curse for him is to lose the child he chose over her. The child he watched grow up into a beautiful woman. After which, your mother is to go insane and your father is free to be with Nastusia—unless you survive."

All my past lives in a nut shell. All that time, all those lives—repeating like clockwork.

"How did you find out about this?"

"Trick."

71

I have to assume he means the Reaper and not that he's playing a joke on me.

"Okay, how does he know?"

"Every Reaper has a gift. A talent, you might say. Trick knows things. I don't know how, but he does. He is as successful as I thought he would be with both my List and his own."

"What's yours?"

"I have a calming presence."

Yeah, should have known. "And what did you find out from Trick?" I ask since he hasn't offered the information on his own.

"My scythe has seen a lot. Grim's has seen even more. If a Deathdrifter touches an inanimate object, he can see every event it has experienced. Trick has now seen all of your deaths that I've reaped. Unfortunately, he has some strange connection to one of them that I don't understand. It seemed to anger him but he says it's between him and Grim. He insisted I use Grim's scythe to go back farther." He turns his head so that I can no longer see his face. "He says he knows why Grim lets me break the rules."

"Why is Grim so lenient with you?"

Damien doesn't answer me. Instead, he brings himself to his feet and picks me up to lay me on my bed. "Rest now."

"You don't know or won't tell me, D?" I blink in quick succession and dampen my lips.

"Trick saw a hint of something but won't say what. Grim is good at hiding the truth so I can't give you details." He lies down with me, leaving his clothed arm under me so the coldness of his gloved hand and arm align perfectly with the battered mark on my back. "I don't want to leave you come dawn. I'm afraid he'll hurt you again."

"I'll try to keep my mouth shut." I smile and curl up to his cold body—our clothes and the sheet my guarantee of survival.

"If you think that will help." He runs a leather finger over my lips. I shudder, but not due to the cold. "You want the quilt? I don't want you to freeze."

I'm not answering him because I don't want him to break our proximity. He exhales on my cheek and then on my neck just under my ear. My heart races and I melt against him. It doesn't matter how cold he is because I think I have enough heat to fuel the both of us.

Pulling him closer, I try not to think about how I've been waking up to his voice for weeks but have only seen his face for the first time today.

He breaks my thoughts with a cool word whispered in my ear, "Sleep."

Shivering, I wonder if he can feel my warmth. I exhale slowly and he answers my question with a deep plea in his throat and chest.

SIX DAYS
BEFORE

I'm not sure if what I'm hearing is a bad thing or just a figment of my imagination. It's probably something insignificant and that's why Damien isn't bothering to pull himself away from me. Not that I want him to. I can only wish that he'd let himself lose control. He's doing an awfully good job at keeping me on edge.

"Damien?"

"Anna," he breathes against my collar bone, closer than he should be.

"Do you hear that?"

"Hear what, my sweet?" He's making me wish I never brought it up.

"It sounds like... like tapping..." I've lost myself in the caress of his chilly, gloved hand as it creeps up my thigh. I shiver when it sneaks over the sheet to rest on my ribs. "...tapping on the window," I exhale in a rush. My mind swims in a haze of delight. He picks his head up off the pillow to listen carefully.

His brow furrows and I think I hear him damn someone. He gently pulls his arm out from under my back and with the hope of making him forget the window; I arch my back, seductively. I'm hoping that he'll take notice of my false allowance of letting him up. Perhaps he'll forget the sound and draw his eyes back to me.

"Stay right there," he says with force. I tell myself that the harshness is more for his benefit than my own.

He looks out the window and exhales with relief. Pulling on the pane he says, "Carrying coals to Newcastle, are we?"

A tall, sturdy-looking young man crawls through my window. He has the stereotypical bad boy look. His straight black hair is parted slightly to the side and hangs just above his eyes. A black, unbuttoned trench coat hangs to the floor, and his pants hang low, looking a little too big. A ribbed, thermal shirt with a few holes and tears along the hem is stretched tight across his chest. He has the largest combat boots I think I've ever seen.

"Aye, well, I donnae like to interrupt," he says, red ash falling to my carpet. I don't smell smoke so I'm sure his cigarette is purely for show. Can I get second hand smoke from a dead man's cigarette?

"Bollocks, Trick," Damien says, annoyed; accent thicker than I've ever heard.

"Watch yer mouth in front of the wee lass, Doom."

Damien runs his tongue over his teeth as if to clean his mouth of the foul language. "Trick, this is Anna. Anna, Trick."

"Hello," I mumble.

The look in Trick's eyes makes me uncomfortable. He squints at me and the corner of his mouth turns up slightly. I'm aware of the fact that I only have on a thin tank top and shorts. It doesn't help that the sheet only covers my left leg. In a flustered mess, I pull the sheet up to my chin.

Trick nods his hello. "Yer only supposed to die once, ya know." He takes a step toward me and Damien places a hand on his shoulder. I gasp, forgetting that they're both dead. "She's scared," Trick says, sounding angry. He flicks his cigarette out the window.

"No. Anna has no fear of dying." Damien looks out the window, quickly. "For herself, anyway."

Damien's eyes meet mine. "It's okay. I'm already dead, remember?"

I exhale, blink hard with relief and nod. Trick chews on his lip as he looks me over. Slowly, he turns back to Damien. His fists are clenched at his sides and he's starting to worry me the way he glares at Damien. "Where's yer List?"

"I'm relieved until dawn," Damien clarifies.

"Ya lucky, Bastirt." Trick glances at me. "She cannae be that special."

"Believe me, she is." Damien smiles.

"Aye, feeling alive?" Trick asks, with resentment.

Damien's eyes narrow.

"Tis all over yer face. I felt it too, or did ya forget already?"

"Not now, Cameron," Damien chides.

It's starting to bother me that they're talking as if I'm not in the room. "Why are you here?" I interrupt.

"Came to deliver a message. I be gone soon," Trick whispers as if his feelings are hurt. I watch him take Damien by the arm to the farthest corner of my room and then flinch away as if he just touched a hot stove. "Yer burnin'."

"I'm fine," Damien says.

I can't hear the rest of their muffled conversation. The tone of Trick's voice is disturbed, but Damien sounds reassuring. Once Damien signs a paper and hands it to Trick he whispers something and Trick shrugs. Damien claps Trick on the back and sends him on his way. He closes the window quietly and does his purple vapor Flash back over to me; leaving purple smoke fading in his wake. I'm beginning to think this disappearing-reappearing act is his idea of impressing me. I mean it's only five steps from the window; it's just as easy to walk over.

He looks pensive and I can't help but wonder what's going on in that head. "What was all that about?" I ask.

"Nothing to make a song and dance about. Grim just wanted me to know about a change in the policy concerning us Deathdrifters." He smiles and leans down. The closer he gets, the colder I am. He seems to absorb my warmth. "How's your back?"

"Great! I don't feel any pain." I'm so surprised I have to ask, "How'd you do that?"

"Ice packs were a great invention," he says, smiling slightly.

Playfully, I grip the collar on his shirt and pull him closer. "You're not funny, Mr. Doyle," I say.

"I'm not?" He sounds hurt, but I know he isn't. Smiling, he leans down as if he's about to kiss me. I move the sheet to reveal my leg as before. Guiding his free hand to my knee, he's not as cold as he was and I begin to think that Trick was right about me making him feel alive and that I'm just not used to his cold.

As he positions himself on the bed beside me, I nudge my nose into the cave of his hood, under his chin. "Is Trick always that creepy?"

Damien furrows his brow, trying to understand why I'm asking such a question.

"I don't like the way he looked at me," I explain, feeling embarrassed to say this about his friend, but I don't want to hold anything back.

"Shite," is all he can say and I hear him release a deep, frustrated sigh in his chest.

"What's wrong?"

"He..." Damien stops and I'm not sure why. It doesn't feel like he's breathing anymore and I wonder if Death needs to or if it's just a force of habit.

"D?" I sit up to stare into his eyes. "You're not breathing."

"I'm dead, Anna. I don't need to." The pain in his eyes says something is more serious than his lack of vital signs.

"Then why can I feel your breath against my skin? How can you hold me and make me feel a heart that's pulsing inside you? I don't understand. Are you faking all this? How do I know who you really are?" Tears spring to my eyes for a man I hardly know. I hate that I've cried more in the last day than I have in the past six months. I knew I shouldn't have come home this week. I should have faked sick or gone to Miami with my roommate.

Damien sits up and holds my face gently in his gloved hands, resting his hooded forehead against mine. "This is no cupboard love, Anna. To be honest with you, my casual breathing is a habit. You don't just end the things you did in life once you become a Deathdrifter. Your mind still works the way it did when you were alive. I breathe because my brain tells me to." He pulls back to look into my eyes. "As for my heart—it only beats for you. It's your warmth that my heart needs. Feeling like this after all these centuries has made me entirely yours."

He wipes away my tears with his leathered thumb as I say, "So why did you stop the *habit* just now?"

"You made me realize something I did which I now regret."

"Which is?" I kiss his shoulder lightly, wishing we could go back to that world of white. "Maybe I can fix it." I keep brushing my mouth over the shoulder of his sweatshirt, breathing lightly onto his exposed neck. I wonder if he can even feel it. He has to. Otherwise, why would we even be in this position?

"No one can fix it," he finally answers. "I made a man feel after he decidedly chose not to once becoming a Deathdrifter."

"You mean because Trick felt what you felt when I died all those times?"

"In a manner of speaking, yes."

"So he's got a little crush. He'll get over it."

"I'm afraid it's not that simple, Anna. Trick... He..."

I feel that we have now made a complete circle in our conversation. "He what?" I ask and sit up straight, hands folded in my lap.

"He loves you, Anna." Damien looks down at my hands and begins to play with my fingers as if he's begging me for forgiveness.

"I don't know about that," I say to reassure him that there is no competition.

"Anna." He's dead serious. "He *feels* the way *I* do."

Lord, I am stupid. Damien is implying something so important and it's going right over my head. I feel like such an idiot. A man, a dead one no less, is confessing his love to me and I'm down playing it to a childish infatuation. "You love me?" I ask with idiocy.

He meets my eyes and says, "Yes, Anna. I love you more than anything—more than life or death. I don't expect you to know how you feel. I don't expect you to say you love me. I've known you much longer than you have me. But I'm hoping, someday, you will."

My hands hold his hood, though my entire body wants to risk touching his skin. I lean against his chest, considering kissing him so hard that I think I could break him. More likely though, his weight would break me first. He holds me back. I can't overpower him, but I feel his chest rise and fall under mine with another release of his *habit*. It's when I feel his heart flutter intermittently that I truly believe every word he's said.

"You're so... addicting," I say, staring at his gorgeous mouth.

He slides his hands down my thighs to catch behind my knees. With one quick pull, my knees are around his waist and his hands glide up my back.

I'm six days away from a man being in love with me for six hundred years. Saturday should be the upcoming sixth death for me, but I'd gladly die now if this man that I've known for roughly twenty-eight hours could love me in a way I may never know.

A CONNIVING
S.O.B.

I woke to his faint whisper in my ear. "My sweet Anna." I start to open my eyes, but he draws a cool hand over my hair and tells me to sleep. I mutter something incoherent and hear him sigh before I'm asleep again.

The morning light brings me out of my peaceful sleep and I decide to start this day off right. Grabbing my towel, I head to the bathroom. With every step I can still feel the residual tingle of Damien on my skin. The tepid water beats on my face and all I can think about is how badly I wanted more. I smile because Death doesn't have it easy either, apparently.

I wash quickly and hop out of the shower to wipe away the fog of my reflection. My eyes are a little puffy from the lack of sleep, but it's well worth it. I only hope that he's thinking of me like I am of him right now.

I run the towel over my body to dry off. I'm in the mood to go shopping. If tonight is anything like last night, then it's my turn to drive him crazy. They sell gloves at the mall, right?

Springing through the hall and into my room, I jump, landing on my bed; bouncing like a six-year-old kid on a sugar high. I grab my jeans from the bag I put by the door when I got home. I almost never wear these jeans because my roommate tells me they're hot and plans on stealing them. They're light denim, almost white, and have some scandalous rips and tears strategically placed. Normally, I'd never buy clothes that look overused and resold, but my roommate can be very convincing. Over my head, I pull on my black spaghetti-strap tank and a sheer blue, long-sleeved v-neck.

In my closet is my old, black and white tote. Sliding the accordion door out of the way, it's just where I left it; in a heap on the floor. It has an old book I never finished reading—the bookmark still in place—and some receipts on which the ink is blurred. Dumping the contents of my purse onto the closet floor, I gather the things I'll need at the mall: The one credit card I own, my wallet with sparse cash and check book, as well as my ID, cell, tiny make-up arsenal, and car keys. It's all thrown in the tote.

Hopping down the stairs, I reach my father's den door. It's not usually left open. A sudden movement draws my eye inside. My father is sitting on the lip of his desk with *his* maid standing between his legs. They're laughing like giddy teenagers.

I shut my eyes and hang my head, trying to block the four-year-old's fear of the first time she saw her father with another woman. I bite my lip trying not to say a word. It backfires.

"Does Mom know?" I ask what I should have that night so long ago.

"Anna, what are you doing here? I thought you went out with your mother?" Gently, like I've never seen him before and unlike the words that just left his mouth, he takes Ms. Cune's shoulders in his hands and backs her up. Standing, he adjusts his belt.

"Nope." I look at the grandfather clock in the hallway. My mother must have gone out early—it's only half past noon. "I'm going to the mall. I'll be back later." I head for the front door.

"You're going out like that?" he yells. If I didn't know any better, I'd think that my father worked in a nursing home. He yells when it's perfectly obvious that he'll be heard.

"I'm not eighty. I can hear you." I turn and my eye catches Ms. Cune staring at me. Her vibrant orange blouse is unbuttoned, lower than it should be for professionalism. At first sight, it seems her skirt could dust the floor better than the broom propped against the den's door frame.

This is the first time I really take notice of her. She is quite beautiful—for a sorceress who wants to tear apart my family and kill me in the process. Her hair is black, but it's dyed with a fiery red highlight. She has a very curvy body, but I don't know if my mother was right to call her Korean. She has small, squinty eyes and a heart shaped face; which I guess if you're narrow minded you could refer to her as Oriental. The design and color of her style I can see as Bohemian, but coming from a drunken woman, anything can be referred to by the first word that comes to mind.

I turn to the front door and when my hand turns the knob a cold rush takes over the room. "D?" I whisper through closed teeth.

"Out. Now." The words are so short and clipped I don't recognize the voice.

I continue walking and hear my father shouting for me to return. I think I hear him call me a slut and normally, I wouldn't take offense, but due to roughly the last twelve or so hours of being with someone I hardly know, I don't know what I am.

Fumbling with my keys, I drop them on the driveway when I hear the front door of the house slam. I won't be coming home now until after dark, that's for sure.

It's Sunday, though. What will I do when everything closes early?

Sitting in the driver's seat, I lock the doors and take three huge breaths. I could really use the black rubber bands right now. Searching my purse, I find my lip gloss, eyeshadow, and mascara. Using the rearview mirror, I wipe the shadow ball over each eyelid and then apply a quick swipe of mascara. Thanks to D, the bruise under my eye is almost gone.

With the key in the ignition and the engine finally running, I pull out of the driveway. At the first stop sign to pull out of my street and head toward the mall, I pop the cap off my lip gloss and run it over my lips. "Today is going to be fun," I tell myself.

"Aye," the same voice from the hall answers me. My car is cold and my stomach is fluttering.

"What are you doing here?" I ask, but get no reply.

I drive in silence with the cold enveloping me. Finally, pulling into the parking lot of the mall I try to find my usual spot. Parking a little farther out than normal, I cut the engine and throw my keys in my tote.

"Mind if I tag along?" the voice asks me.

"Yes!" I look around the outside of the car to make sure no one heard me yell at myself. "If you show yourself, I might be more inclined to *invite* you, but no guarantees," I say, much quieter.

"He was right."

"Who was right and right about what?" I'm losing my patience. This voice is not calming in the least. It makes me nervous and... and...

"Doom."

"What?" There I go again. Yelling.

"I'm 'ere to keep ya safe. Make sure ya donnae say something to cause yerself harm." There is a smile behind his words and I *do not* like it.

"We'll see about that."

He doesn't say anything. The car is colder than Damien had ever made it feel. I'm certain the car will frost over any minute. Suddenly, a black form blurs into existence in the passenger seat. I can't make out a face, but slowly it's becoming clearer. I get it. This isn't funny.

"Ya look... pissed?" he says, searching for the right word. "I like it."

"Very humorous," I pause, "is this how you got the name Trick?"

"Aren't ya curious why I'm 'ere, Anna?"

"You already told me. You're here to censor my words."

He laughs a little, but not in a kindly way. "Aye, ya got me there, but I've got an ulterior motive too."

"I already know that." Trick loves me by accident, but I don't want to be the first to bring it up. "Damien told me."

"Aye? Full of surprises, that one. Guess I donnae know him as well as I thought." He scratches his chin and then slides both his hands down his thighs to grab his knees.

"What are you talking about?" I know his name has to have a hidden meaning. Is he a conniving S.O.B.? Most likely. Would he stab Damien in the back? I'm not so sure.

"Grim has a new policy which he created just fer his favourite ass-kissing Carrier."

"Carrier?" I ask. "Sounds like a disease."

Trick snorts his amusement. "Deathdrifter. Tis what I call me kind; since we tend to 'carry' souls away."

"I see," smirking before I say, "and you're going to tell me what the new policy is?" I prompt him.

"Aye." I wait a moment in silence while he seems to try to figure out his wording. "A Carrier can return to life—"

"What?" I interrupt. "You've got to be kidding!" I'm so ecstatic I almost shake him, but I haven't forgotten for a second what happens if I do.

"If..." He calms me with an assertive look. His tall and terrifying build is clearly of Scottish descent. His wording and accent is a dead giveaway, but the features of his face, however, are someplace else entirely. The small, straight lips are close to his straight nose; perfectly placed on a square face. His small eyes and thick brows make him look contemplative. He certainly is more exotic than Damien.

Ah, Mr. Doyle—a true English gentleman with an accent to die for.

Not that a Scottish accent is any less... amusing.

"If?" I prompt, realizing that we've been staring at each other and reminding him that he was talking.

"If his Key still works."

"What Key? Works for what?"

"Once a Carrier is recruited, he accepts the responsibility by unlocking his Chest. Each Carrier must fill their Chest properly. And it ain't easy. The Chest has to be filled with souls—specific souls." He pulls a chain out from around his neck. It looks like an old skeleton key, but the head of it is a rose. I wonder where Damien keeps his. "Souls are small, tender entities, Anna. We're all assigned a certain type. The Chest won't relock if tis filled incorrectly."

"What happens to the ones that don't belong in the Chest?"

"The Chest expels them. They become lost and are called Haunters. Those souls cannae be reincarnated. Our job is to ensure the transition, Anna."

So this new policy means that if a Deathdrifter does their job correctly by taking souls only designated on their List, they'll be reincarnated like the souls in the Chest. Which means Grim will have to keep finding replacements.

"You tried to trick him into giving you his Key, Trick, didn't you?" I smile just because I have the opportunity to use his Reaper name for what it's worth.

"Why would I do that?" He stares at me as if I shouldn't be happy about a chance for Damien to live out his life with me.

"He's been a Reaper longer than you. Wouldn't you return to life if his Chest had more souls than yours?"

He shakes his head but doesn't stop staring at me. "I donnae care much fer the living." It feels as if he's trying to see something in me. "Ya should know one more thing. And I donnae think ya'll be happy after."

I don't want to ask. I don't want to know. If he's going to ruin this day—one that has been the best day of my life so far, then I don't want to hear it.

"I made a deal. If Doom loses ya a sixth time, ya spend yer afterlife with me. Either way, no more curse."

"You made a *deal*? How do you make a deal without either myself or Damien involved?"

I'm livid. The claustrophobia of the car is adding to my hysteria. I pop open the door and start stomping off toward the mall. This can't be. I'm promised to someone whether I live or die. I have no say in the matter. Well, that settles it. I'm not dying!

A SAFE
PLACE

I know he's following me. I can't see or hear him, but he's close as I stalk my way through the parking lot. A blue compact car almost backs out of its space into me. "Watch where you're driving!" I slam my palm on the trunk. The man in the driver's seat is angry. I hope I didn't hurt his precious metal baby. Humans can really damage a car if you hit them—assuming it works the same way as it does for deer.

"We ought to talk about this, Anna," Trick says. He can't follow me everywhere, right?

The mall is awfully crowded today. Sunday is the day for new sales, so why shouldn't it be bustling? My mind is swirling with so much information and turmoil that I can't remember why I wanted to go shopping. I stop in the middle of the mall. A man at a cell phone kiosk is yelling to passers-by, requesting that everyone use his employer. I'm not going *that* way.

"Why are ya ignoring me?" he asks.

I don't know what makes him think I'll answer in a public place. I'm not going to have people staring at me, wondering who I'm talking to. I shake my head, hoping that he'll see me answer so that I don't have to speak.

"I see, yer too old fer imaginary friends." I hear him release a low chuckle and my skin prickles. "Better?"

I turn around and Trick is walking out of a video game store. "What do you think you're doing?"

He shrugs. "Shopping?"

"We don't need to talk. You don't even need to be here." I'm becoming animated and Trick watches my hand fly around as I speak. "You're here to make sure my father doesn't hurt me, not strangers. The mall is a safe place, I assure you." I glare at him.

"Aye, but perhaps ya could use a friend." He looks at me with pity. I am not pathetic. Friends disappear without a word and if they do use words—they're negative ones.

"I don't need friends."

His eyebrows rise in disbelief before he sticks his hand in his side pocket to pull out a pack of cigarettes. I still don't understand his addiction. "Why do you do that? Is there really any benefit to it?"

"Aye, no cancer." He pounds the pack against his palm.

I roll my eyes. "I wish you wouldn't."

"Wish all ya want to, lass," he mumbles, placing the white stick to his lips.

"Please?" I look up at him through my lashes. If Damien is right and he really does care, maybe I can persuade him. "For me?"

He grunts, taking the cigarette out of his mouth and replacing it in the pack; back in his pocket.

"So this deal you made," I prompt.

"I told ya. If ya die a sixth time, ya... what do ya say, hang out? with me. Yer going to be a Carrier."

"I'll die a sixth time, eventually. I don't see how this matters," I say.

Trick gives me a wry smile, looking at me from head to toe. He knows this and seems to be looking forward to it sooner rather than later.

I find that even though he's walking next to me, he's following me. Wherever I go, he turns with me. I don't need to worry about how close I get to him because he's keeping account of the distance. I watch him avoid strangers very carefully and wonder if Damien would go out in public with me.

No one seems to find Trick out of place. Children stare at him, but that's what children do. They observe. Teenage girls turn to watch him walk by. He doesn't even seem to notice how they gawk. He's not exactly dressed for Georgia's early warm weather, but I'm not sure he even notices the temperature.

"Do you mind if we go to the food court? I'm hungry." I'm not sure if he eats or if he even needs to.

He shrugs in response. I'm glad he's so opinionated. I cut through a break in the brick median that's filled with flowers. I imagine that the architects thought this median would ensure that shoppers would walk through the mall in the same way that they drive, but that doesn't seem to be the case. People walk where they want to. I swerve through groups of people and make my way through the corridor toward the food court.

The only reason why I ever come to this mall is for the food. It has the best choices. Not that it matters—I usually buy junk food. To be good, I've decided to get a salad from Candice's. It's technically fast food, but it considers itself better. I mean with a name like Candice, your food has got to be better than Artie's, right? I choose a salad with almonds and cranberries. It comes with a sweet dressing I can't place, but I love it, nonetheless. The cashier takes my order then looks at Trick and turns red before she has a chance to say one word.

Okay. I get it. Mr. Bad gets the girls. Or at least he used to.

"Nothin' fer me," he says to the girl who's ready to tear off her uniform and run away with him.

I grunt and wait for my food. Trick looks down at me and smiles mischievously. "What?" I ask.

"Salad? Ya on some kind of diet or somethin'?" He eyes me from head to toe.

"Why do you care?" I'm not about to tell him that I think I'm fat. I know I'm not, but eating right leads to a healthier, *longer* life. That's the lie I keep telling myself, anyway. I can't really say that I'm maintaining my weight. He'd only ask why and I'd have to deny his allegation that it all comes back to keeping Damien happy. And, besides, he'd be right.

"I donnae care." He looks away before adding, "I just think ya could stand to gain a few pounds. Yer too frail." He makes to jab me in the side with his finger, but I move away, out of reach.

Is he blind? I'm certainly not frail. Petite, yes. Frail, no. "I don't want to gain or lose, Mister..." I don't know his last name. My eyes dart around to search my memory. Did Damien ever mention it?

"McKinney."

"Not surprising," I feign my indifference.

"What isn't?"

"That you're Scottish. Did you die at such a young age because your family was oppressed?" I quietly joke. I don't actually know how old he is, but he doesn't look over twenty.

"Aye, if ya count losing the only person who matters in yer life after yer maw dies."

"Huh?" Now I feel guilty. Maybe I should watch what I say more often. I feel a little nervous as the cashier places a plastic bowl on my tray and a cup to fill at the drink dispensers.

"Ya heard me."

"I'm sorry. I didn't mean to—"

"Forget it. Me father fell in love with the wrong Russian. We fled. End of story."

It didn't seem like the end, but I pick up my tray and avoid looking at Trick as I make my way to an open table, away from others. Putting my food down on the cleanest table I can find, I slide the wrought iron chair away from the table. It screeches and I clench my teeth as if it will help to dull the sound. It doesn't. I sit and Trick takes the seat across from me. Still keeping a good distance away, he's blocked himself in a corner where no one can walk around and accidentally touch him.

"Will Grim be mad that you're showing yourself like this?" I ask as I pry the plastic lid from my salad bowl.

"Aye." He reaches over and takes an almond from my salad before I have a chance to touch the packet of sweet dressing.

"I thought you said you weren't hungry."

"I never said that." He smirks while he chews the small almond with pleasure.

"But you told that girl—"

"I told her I dinnae want anything. I never said I wasn't hungry, even though I'm not. I donnae get hungry and I donnae need food, but I can taste it."

I roll my eyes as I exhale a sound of annoyance from my nose. "I really don't know anything about Death." I glance around behind me to see if anyone is close enough to hear me say such a thing.

The mall is crowded, but anyone near us is occupied with their own conversations. Anything I have to say is of the least bit of importance. I turn back to Trick and he looks away as if I caught him doing something he shouldn't have. "Where'd the name Trick come from?"

"Grim."

"Ah, the all powerful Grim Reaper."

"Just Grim. We're all Reapers."

"What? I thought you were Deathdrifters?" He's got me entirely confused. "Are the terms interchangeable?"

He shrugs. "No, not really. Reaper is like a clan name." He sees my expression and rewords himself. "Family name, like Fairchild."

"But you're not related, right?"

"Blood ties are less important once yer dead." He leans back in his chair, shaking his hair from his eyes, before he continues, "Our occupation is Deathdrifter. Depending on whom ya ask tis a kinder term than Reaper. Fer us, Reaper is divided by individual title, like how ya have a President, Vice President, Supervisor, and so on. I'm Trick Reaper. Ya already know Doom Reaper. There're about a handful of us."

"Okay, so if Grim is President, who is Vice President?"

"Doom."

I'm a little shocked. That explains why Grim is so concerned about losing Damien. He's next in line to run the... business? "Where do you come in?"

He displays his hand, showing me five fingers.

"So, you get a death name when you die?"

"No, ya get a death name, as ya call it, after ya open yer Chest. Another Carrier names ya." He steals another almond from my salad. I consider stabbing him with my fork, but it would be a wasted effort. I can't hurt him. Not physically. "Tis just a title. Tells other Deathdrifters what kind of souls ya gather."

"Oh." This is starting to make sense. Damien had said he took the souls of the worst cases possible. Trick must take those that have been... tricked? "What kind do you collect?"

"Suicides. The ones that donnae cheat Death."

"So shouldn't you be called Cheater?"

His lip turns up on the side, slightly crooked. "The survivors are the cheaters, Jo."

He's the trick. I get it. And what about Grim, why wouldn't he take those that were the worst cases?

Maybe this isn't making sense after all. "So... what happens when you fill the Chest?"

"Before? Ya filled another."

"What, no reward?"

"No."

"No day off?"

"Yer trying to find reason in this. Stop while ya still can."

"Oh, no, no, I think I understand everyone but Grim. Shouldn't he have the worst possible deaths to collect?"

"He does. When Doom refers to his souls as the worst cases, he means to him, they are. Compared to mine—" he squints as if he doesn't want to recollect those people, "Compared to Sleep, everyone's are."

"There's a Sleep Reaper? That's hilarious!" I can't help but laugh. I mean, of course, you'd need a Deathdrifter for those that die in their sleep, but still.

"He donnae find it funny."

"Sorry." I wipe my eyes. "So, um, Damien collects what kinds of souls?"

"Those fated to die young. Doomed."

"But that's just who's on the List. You can take anyone's soul, right?"

He nods. "But they're lost. Damaged. The Chest cannae reincarnate the wrong soul."

I look down at my salad. I'm not hungry anymore. I push the leaves around with my fork. There's a stray almond at the bottom and I scoop it up with the fork. "You want this?" I ask Trick, holding the fork out to him.

To my surprise, he puts his mouth around the fork. His hair, I notice has a slight cowlick and curves up, away from his eyes. He appears unkempt in a sort of soft, perfect way.

I shake my head clear of his allure. I had expected him to take the almond with his hand, but perhaps he didn't want the dressing on his fingers. I drop my fork back in the bowl and stand up.

"Where to?" he asks me.

"Well, I came out here for... something new."

I don't meet Trick's doubtful eyes. *Something new*? Why can't I tell him I want my own pair of gloves? I walk over to the big green trash can and push my tray through the mouth of this petri dish.

The cold exudes from Trick's body. I've noticed that these Deathdrifters only seem to lose control over temperature when something is bothering them.

"Why are you standing so close to me?" I turn, but he isn't here. I mean, I'm sure he's *here*, but I can't see him. "Oh, we're back to this, huh?"

"Blood is 'ere. We have to go. Now! Run!" I don't understand what he means, but the urgency in his voice clearly tells me what his face would, if I could see it.

SOMETHING
IRRESISTABLE

Trick is doing everything he can to get me to move without resorting to pushing me. I'm not sure why he's in such a hurry. I'm assuming Blood is a Death-drifter, but I can only imagine what kind.

"Move faster or Doom will have me bawbag in me throat," he grunts in my ear.

"I don't—" My inability to comprehend what's going on is interrupted by three loud pops coming from the food court. People are screaming and running all over the place. A stern voice on the P.A. system tells people to proceed in an orderly fashion and exit the mall. I don't know what's going on, but that announcement isn't doing anything the help people stay calm.

"What was that?" I yell above everyone's shouting, forgetting that Trick doesn't need me to yell.

"I'll tell ya later. Now move!"

I try to head back out the corridor I had entered. Too many people are stuffed in here like sheep being herded into a barn. It's going to take forever to get to my car.

"Did you see it? I was there. He shot her point blank in the chest," someone says. They're way too excited for such a dismal experience.

"Trick, is that true?" I whisper.

"Car, Anna, now! I'll be there soon."

"What? Where are you going?" I'm afraid. I don't know what this has to do with Trick, but I don't want to be alone.

"Anna, go," he pleads, sounding distraught.

If a Deathdrifter is worried then I suppose I shouldn't dawdle. I push past a man who's hardly moving. Security is trying to get everyone to calm down, but they all care more about finding out what happened than with leaving. I finally get through the doors and realize the people in the parking lot hoping to shop today are in for a surprise. Running to my car and throwing myself in the seat; all I can do is shake. Resting my forehead against the wheel, I stare at the needle on the speedometer. It reads zero miles per hour. It's as static as I feel. I can't move. I can't breathe. My vision is blurry from the well of water in my eyes.

"My sweet Anna," I hear a whisper in my ear.

"D?" I raise my head and wipe the tears from my eyes. "Where are you?" I'm choked up with fear and sadness.

"I'm here." His voice soothes me and all I want is for him to hold me.

"What happened in there? I heard a man say someone shot someone. Are they okay?"

"Why do you think I'm here?"

"Then they're... dead?"

"A jealous boy shot a girl because she got in the way. He shot his friend for showing interest in the girl. Out of remorse he shot himself."

I shake my head, not wanting to believe it.

"Love makes people do stupid shite, Anna."

I swallow hard. "Did you take their souls?"

"I took the girl. Trick took the boy who shot himself and Blood took the friend. I came to make sure you're all right."

"Those poor... it's so unfair." I can't stop my nose and eyes from running. I keep sniffling and I wish I had a tissue or something.

"You should go, Anna. I'll ask Trick to see you home."

"I don't want to go home. Stay with me, please? I need you."

"I can't. You know I can't." He sounds forlorn and I know he is when he adds, "Please, don't cry."

"I'm sorry. I'll be okay, I promise." I smile the best I can.

I hear him exhale heavily with regret. "I have to go. I won't be late, my sweet." I feel his restrained attempt to push my hair behind my ear from the cool breeze across my face. It's a promise even if he doesn't say so.

As I drive out of the parking lot, every entrance and exit is blocked by police cars, fire trucks, or ambulances. They stop every car that wants out and won't let in a single person with hopes of shopping on this beautiful and suddenly depressing day.

After about an hour, I'm the third car from the main road. I see a slender arm reach out the window from the two cars ahead of me. She must be handing her license to the sheriff. I scrounge through my bag and pull out my wallet for my ID. When I finally come to the front of the line, I roll down my window and the officer asks me where I was in the mall when the shots happened.

"I was leaving the food court," I say.

"And did you see it happen?"

"No."

"Is that your ID? I'll need to take down your information in case we have any further questions."

I draw my lips into a meek smile and hand over my ID. He jots down on his clipboard what I'm assuming is my name and address. He hands it back to me and lets me go. Another policeman is directing traffic and even though the light is red, I pull out at his direction and head home.

My mind wanders back to the events at the mall. How could someone be so jealous that they revert to violence to get what they want? This whole thing astounds me. Didn't any of his friends realize what was happening with him? Did he have any friends? Well, he did—before he shot them.

I find myself pulling into another parking lot. It's a small strip mall and has one women's clothing store in it. I've never been here, but it seems interesting and any place is better than home.

"Rose, Sara, and Fiona's Elegant Apparel," I say, reading the sign. "Well, let's see how elegant it is."

The bell chimes when I open the door announcing to the sales team that another customer has entered for them to prey on. But no one rushes to meet me at the door and force me to buy something no one in their right mind would. The first few racks have brightly colored shirts. I skip over them entirely because vibrant is not my style. I find that nothing in here quite suits me. Then a woman I don't expect to be working here asks if she can help me.

"I'm just looking," I say without enthusiasm.

"Is there something you're looking for specifically?" She's not backing down and it makes me wonder if she gets a commission off of each sale. Her long blue skirt is ruffled and looks like it hasn't seen an iron for ages. I suppose that's the style though. Her sunny yellow hair is pulled back into a bun and she wears no make-up. Her blouse isn't tucked in so it's hard to make out how heavy she might actually be.

"No. I don't know. I'm into darker clothes. I don't really need anything."

"Well, we have some nice camisoles that are dark and a few skirts."

"Thanks." I make my way through the store and notice that some shirts are hanging from racks up by the ceiling. A few mannequins flaunt the best ensembles that the store has to offer. I'm about to leave when my eye is drawn to one of the mannequins. "Excuse me." I project my voice because I'm not sure where the sales lady has run off to.

"Yes?" She appears out of nowhere.

"Where can I find that?" I point to the mannequin and realize she might think I mean the blouse it has on. "The plaid top, I mean."

"Oh, the camisole? It was made exclusively for our store. You can't find that anywhere else."

I swallow knowing that translates to expensive. But it's beautiful and I can't resist. "How much is it?"

"Sixty-five."

"Can I try it on?" I figure I can't lose any money in a dressing room.

The woman smiles and takes me back to the far corner of the store. "I'm guessing you're a 32B," she says with her eyebrows raised. I'm betting she thinks she's never wrong.

She isn't.

"Yes," I mumble. She pulls the curtain closed while she gets the camisole.

Once she returns she hands it to me and says, "Try this one. I hope you know it only comes in red."

"It's okay. I like plaid." I take the hanger from her and realize it's a set. The cami is solid from the empire waist down, but the fabric that covers the chest is plaid. The matching panties are cute considering the ruffled black edge around the waist which is the only solid-colored part on it.

I slip the top on and it fits perfectly. Turning side to side before the mirror, I can't believe I almost walked out without noticing it. Apparently you can lose money in a dressing room. And more than I expect because after I change I find myself asking the woman if she has a dress in the same design.

She scrunches up her face as if my taste in clothes is horrific. "What's the occasion?" the woman asks.

"My birthday is on Saturday. I'm hoping that my..." What is Damien to me, exactly? I can't say I'm dating a dead man and expect her to understand. She'd either pity me for my loss or kick me out of the store. I'm not sure how to say to her that I want a dress to make Damien's heart beat faster than it ever did when he was alive. Of course, dinner is supposed to be with my parents, which means Damien would never even see me in it. Now, all I want is to throw the whole dinner idea out the window and just be alone with him.

"I'm sure he's already planned a wonderful evening." She must think she understands my predicament as if it were just the excitement that is young love. "I don't think I have anything like that, but I do have something I think you'll like." She scurries out of the small closet this store is referring to as a dressing room. When she returns she hands me a beautiful deep purple dress.

Putting the dress on, it's cool and smooth against my skin. In front of the mirror, I like what I see. I like myself. The dress hangs perfectly from my hips and stops just above the floor. The material is a soft satin and it couldn't be more comfortable. It hugs my waist and gathers at the small of my back. The straps are wide and angle over the curve of my shoulders. It even makes my chest look bigger, but I believe that is due to the low neckline. I look at the tag and my heart drops. I can't afford a one hundred and fifty dollar dress right now.

I change back into my regular clothes and tell the sales lady that I love the dress, but I can't afford it right now. She smiles and says, "Do you still want the cami set?"

"Oh, yes. There's something irresistible about it."

I hand her my credit card and glance at the dress one more time and let out a long sigh.

"I'm sure he'll love whatever you wear," the sales lady says and hands me my receipt.

I smile, thank her, and leave the store. Wishing is not going to get me almost two hundred dollars for that dress. I look at my cell phone and see that it's nearly four o'clock. Where does the time go? I jump in the car and head home. I've got nowhere else to go and I'm feeling down about a dress that I wish I had a place to wear it to—and the money to pay for it.

INFINITE TIME

My bedroom is the only place where I can find solitude. The news is covering the incident at the mall today. I can't believe I was there. It seems like no matter where I go, someone gets hurt or dies. I've gotten used to the fact that it's me who gets hurt, but now that someone has died and I know what happens to their soul, I feel empty.

I haven't been home long and already my room is turning cold. "What does the soul do inside the Chest?"

Trick is leaning against the far wall. His hands are pushed deep in his pockets and his head hangs low.

He shrugs in response. "Wouldn't know."

"What's wrong with you?" I ask, in a tiff. I'd be happier if I wasn't reliving this afternoon on the TV. And no matter how many drawers I rummage through I can't find any rubber bands.

"Nothing." I know he's lying.

I don't say another word as I continue to listen to the TV babble on about the shooting. By now I've started searching the boxes under my bed. Damien couldn't have taken every single rubber band in the house.

A few more minutes go by and I hear Trick slide down the wall and sit on the floor. "If nothing is wrong then why are you being such a downer?"

"Donnae worry about it."

"If you don't want my help, that's fine with me. I don't really care what's wrong with you."

"Doom's going to have me ass on a plate," he mumbles. Why is it everyone wants to talk when you tell them you don't care?

And I'm gonna have D's ass if I can't find a single rubber band in this house!

I slap my hands on my thighs and stare around the room. "Everything will be fine," I say. "You had a job to do and I got home fine without you. I'll talk to him." I'm not sure what I just offered. I'm still not entirely comfortable with Trick, but talking to him is better than talking to myself.

He doesn't answer, but I catch him staring at the bag with the red cami in it. Suddenly, he turns his head and pulls out his pack of cigarettes, pounding them against his hand. I clear my throat. Remembering my request from earlier, he puts them back in his pocket.

"It's not your fault that some kid shot himself after shooting his best friend and the girl he had a crush on," I say.

"Never said it was."

I wait for him to continue. He shows no indication of carrying on this conversation, so I let it drop. "You want to watch TV with me?" I ask, sitting on the foot of the bed and giving up my search for any type of elastic.

He gets up from his spot on the floor and walks over to me. He looks as if he's debating between the floor and the bed before he finally sits down beside me. He's rigid and almost seems a little nervous. I change the channel until I find something more interesting than the news. I assume he wants to forget earlier just as much as I do.

Time slowly drags on and I'm getting more impatient. My leg bounces nervously and Trick stares at it but not in a way that says it bothers him. We hear the front door slam and my father start his car before driving away. I look at the clock and its quarter to ten.

"Yer fine fer the next hour if I go?" he asks while reaching into the inside pocket of his trench coat. An old piece of paper folded into fourths trembles in his hand. He unfolds it and gazes over it quickly with a frown.

"I'll be fine. Go," I say, feeling like a toddler who's been a nuisance to her babysitter. "It's ten o'clock, so my father will be out for the rest of the night." Trick knows this, so he must be *dying* to get back to work.

He looks at his watch after replacing the folded up paper in his pocket. "Doom will be 'ere shortly." He sighs. "He's never late."

I catch a glimpse of the watch he's wearing. I've never seen anything like it. In fact, I can't even read it. It's a dial with one large clock circling the outer edge. Four small circles lay under each of the quarter hours; one under the twelve, one above the six, and ones to the inside of the three and nine. Over lapping those small circles are ones slightly larger and display pictures of what I'm guessing are the phases of the moon. The four smallest circles are like smaller watches of other time zones. I can't read the dials, but they are set up in a familiar clock-like pattern.

The oddest thing is that the large hands move clockwise around the outer dial which I know to be the time of the living, but it's the four smallest that move counter-clockwise. I want to ask Trick how to read it, but he stands too quickly and heads toward the window.

All I can do is stare at him. I nod once to signify that I heard him, but I really don't have anything more to say. Trick opens the window and puts one foot out onto the roof which is the overhang of the front porch.

"Why do you do that?" I ask.

"Do what?" He stops before pulling his shoulders through the window.

"Go out the window? You didn't use it to come in. Why don't you just fade in and out like Damien?"

"I like to take me time." He stares at me as if I can relate. "Especially because tis infinite." He smiles his half-lipped, crooked smile and pulls his shoulders out the window. His black boot fades just before it passes over the window pane leaving a purple haze escaping behind him.

"Infinite time, my ass," I groan and return to flipping through the channels. It's ten thirty before I know it and the warmth of the room without a Reaper to cool it makes me feel dirty. I escape to the bathroom to shower and bring my new cami with me.

The water feels good, but I make it short because I know Damien will be early—like last night. I sit on my bed and paint my toe nails. I choose a dark wine to accent the red in the cami. I'm feeling more relaxed, but there's still a nagging desire to find a rubber band. When I put my nail polish back on the desk, I realize how dumb I am. This whole time I've had hair ties.

I decide to put my earphones in and listen to a new underground punk band that my roommate wanted me to check out forever ago. It's actually really good. I lay back and close my eyes; bobbing my head to the melody because I don't know the words. My finger plays with the hair tie around my wrist but I don't snap it.

"Who have you been talking to?" my father's voice pierces through a quiet moment in one of the songs.

"What?" I remove one earphone and let it hang. Did he come home while I was in the shower?

"I asked you who you've been talking to," he states with disapproval.

"TV," I mumble. Does he actually believe I would offer him the truth?

"I heard a man's voice. Who was in here?" He eyes me from head to toe and I realize I'm only wearing the cami set. This does not bode well for my side of the argument.

"Men can be on TV too," I say and begin to replace my earphone.

"It wasn't the TV, *Anna*." The way he says my name makes me hate it. The way Damien says it makes me think no other name could be as sweet. My father stalks over to the closet and slams the accordion door to the side.

"You've seen too many chick flicks," I say.

A breeze blows though the open window and my father's quick movement catches my attention. "Why is the window open?"

"For air…" I didn't know I should be living locked up and alone.

"Don't look at me like that, young lady," he roars.

"Like what?" I try to pay attention to the muscles in my face. I don't notice anything abnormal from my usual indifference.

"Like that!" He stomps over to me and rips my earphones from my head. "What filth are you listening to?"

I cross my arms and stare at him. I don't think my expression will convince him to give me my MP3 player back. He's invading the privacy of a twenty-year-old girl. No. Woman.

My father throws my Mp3 player on the floor and as I reach for it, he grabs my wrist and hoists me to my feet. "Who is he, Anna?"

"Who's who?" I feign stupidity.

"The boy who's been sneaking into your room!"

"You're crazy. No one is sneaking in here!" It wasn't a lie. He didn't have to sneak. He's either in here or he isn't. It's that simple.

I shouldn't have called him crazy. My skin burns from the slap across my face. This burning causes another type of burning in my chest. A burn of anger. I stare straight into his eyes. "Who I date is none of your business!"

"My daughter *is* my business!" He's squeezing my face in his hand. My jaw hurts from the pressure. I push away from him by banging my fists against his chest. His other hand holds me in place with his fingers digging into my bicep.

"Ssstop," I slur out because I only have use of my tongue to form words.

"I want a name." His eyes are glowing with anger. My hand goes numb because of the tourniquet he's created around my arm. I wince with pain as I flex my bicep. Bad idea. My legs go weak from the throbbing and my knees buckle. I wrap my hands around his wrist.

"Please. Let. Go," I beg.

He only lets go of my arm. Both his hands encircle my throat and he holds me against the wall, a foot off the ground. My feet, panic stricken, search for the floor. It's difficult to breathe and I can't beg anymore. He looks so angry—so determined to have me dead.

Everything starts to blur and flashes of darkness are all I can see.

Then I hear him.

"Put her down, Mr. Fairchild."

My body meets the floor in an excruciating way, but I welcome it compared to the turmoil of my father. I cough and wheeze as I try to catch my breath.

"Who are you?" my father demands. "How did you get in here?"

"I came in the front door. It was open."

"Da... Damien," I choke out.

He gathers me in his arms and I see him glare at my father. "I'm not letting her stay here any longer. She's coming with me."

He helps me stand and grabs the jeans I had on earlier off my bed. Before I know it, I'm in his carefully covered arms and he's carrying me out to my car. I don't know where he's taking me, but anywhere is better than home.

EVERYTHING I
NEED

In a flurry I am swooped out of my room, down the stairs, out of the house, and put into the car. I'm not sure if it's the pain in my arm and the throbbing of my neck that keeps me unaware, but before I realize it, Damien is backing out of the driveway and my car is purring like a kitten. It never runs this well for me.

"Put these on." My jeans are thrown in my lap. The car is cold, but the cloud of my every exhale is dissipating.

"You drive?"

He ignores me, glancing at my legs while I pull on my jeans. "Maybe I should take you to the hospital."

"No! I'm fine."

Damien's more irate than anyone I've ever seen before. He wrings the steering wheel and it almost bends from the stress. Unable to withstand the look in his eyes, I take in the condition of my arm. There's a red outline of my father's hand. I can feel a bruise rising to the surface from deep below.

Damien must be watching me as I poke at my bruise because he whispers, "Wait until you see your neck."

I flip the visor down and stare at myself in the little mirror.

"Oh," I gasp. Black and blue fingers wrap around my neck. If I didn't know any better I'd say Death himself had come for me and failed at taking my soul.

I flip the visor back up and slouch in the passenger seat. Pulling my legs up, I rest my chin on the seam of my knees. Damien's anger makes me shiver.

"Here." He sheds his hooded sweatshirt and hands it to me. "I should have remembered to get you a shirt."

I catch him glancing my way again, but this time it's at my new cami and immediately my thoughts go back to that dress. "It's okay. I'll be home tomorrow anyway." I slip the black hooded sweatshirt over my head instead of unzipping it. Due to the restrictions of the seat belt, it just seems easier this way.

"No, you won't." He glares at the road as if he can see my father standing there, ready to be run over.

"I have to. Where am I going to stay? I can't sleep on the streets, D." I stare at him and he looks pensive. I wonder what's going through his mind. I exhale a heavy sigh, "I know you mean well, but I'm going to have to return home, eventually."

"If I keep you out of that house, you won't be beaten everyday and that may lead to you staying alive past Saturday." He considers his words for half a second. "Yeah, we're not going back."

"You should know better than I do that she'll find me no matter where we go." I know he only wants to keep me alive and I'm grateful for that. And if what Trick said earlier about how a Deathdrifter can return to life is true, then that makes me only want to live if Damien's here to live with me. Otherwise, I'm stuck in the afterlife with Trick.

I turn to ask Damien how much he knows about the new policy that Grim instated, but as my mouth opens I notice a sign that says we've left La Grange.

"Where are we going?" I scan the road for another sign that signifies a direction.

Newnan? This is how I get back to Athens. Is he taking me back to school?

"I'm sorry, Anna. I don't have a plan. I just acted." A stern, tired voice comes from a Deathdrifter that never needs to sleep.

"Well, we could go to Atlanta. It'll seem less conspicuous for us to be roaming around there than in Athens."

"Mm." I think he's agreeing with me, but he continues to watch the road.

I turn my head and look out the window. It's a little over an hour to Atlanta and all I seem to have is my thoughts for company. "Um, Damien?"

"Yes, Anna?"

"Trick told me about the Keys."

"Did he?"

"He says if a Carrier fills his Chest, he can live again. Is that true?"

"Carrier," his brow furrows before he continues, "I've never met a Deathdrifter who's filled one."

"Do you know how full yours is?"

"No."

"Aren't you the least bit interested?"

"No."

I sit up from leaning against my door and stare at him. I refuse to believe that he doesn't want to live again. He told Grim he wanted to renounce his position as a Deathdrifter, so why wouldn't he be interested in whether or not his Key works? Unless... "Do you think it's unnecessary? I mean, since Grim says you can return to the living if you—"

"Anna," he interrupts, taking my hand from my lap to hold in his gloved one. "I'll do whatever I can to ensure you live long past Saturday."

"I know you will, but I'm talking about you. What will happen on Sunday? Will you just disappear? Will I ever see you again? I'm supposed to go back to school, and—"

"You heard Grim. He'll keep his promise."

"Then why aren't you as concerned as I am? I don't understand."

"Life has too many variables, Anna. I'll no longer know when life ceases for an individual—especially you. I'm... I'm afraid of the uncertainty of it."

I smile reassuringly at him. Even with the most morbid of conversations, he can be so sincere and heartwarming. "You know what's strange?" I ask.

"The living dating the dead?" He's straight-faced, but I smack his shoulder anyway.

"No! Well, yes, but only if you don't know the circumstances."

A smile prickles into the corners of his mouth. "What's so strange, Anna?"

I look at the purplish-blue marks on my arm. "Marriage."

His eyebrows meet in the middle before he says, "Hmm, please elaborate. What's so *strange* about marriage?"

"Well, what's the point? Eventually, it all comes to an end, even if the couple can't admit it's over. Why do people even bother?"

"If you love someone, you want to be with them. Always. Why is that so hard to believe?" He looks happy. The car is getting warmer so he must be thinking about his wife from centuries ago. I feel a pang of jealousy. I glance up and he's staring directly at me. "You're never planning to marry?"

"Not after living this life."

He looks disappointed and I think I see a hint of guilt. "Your father has hurt you in ways no one can imagine." I watch his expression change to tenderness as he glides his leather covered hand through my hair to push it behind my ear. His eyes glance back and forth between the road and me. "I wish I could give you more. Help you see the good in life."

"You're everything I need."

He exhales heavily and says, "I hope that's true."

INSTRUMENTS OF DEATH

I must have fallen asleep because I don't remember how I got in this bed. The room is dark. There is a low mechanical noise that I assume is an air conditioner. The fragrance is odd in a sort of sterile, living-in-a-bubble kind of way. A rough, thin blanket is weighing down an even thinner sheet and the pillows are softer than I like.

As my eyes adjust to the low light, I notice a glow is coming from under the door just a few feet away. "D?" I get no reply, but the light under the door goes out and a subtle creek comes from the hinges. "What are you doing?"

"Nothing." I find that I get that answer a lot.

"Where are we?"

He looks around the room as if it's obvious. "A hotel in Atlanta."

"Oh." That explains the poor bed quality and the sound of the air conditioner. I think hotels always keep them running. Even Georgia's coldest days are warm to a New York native. "What time is it?"

"Two."

Something is wrong. He's keeping his distance and isn't saying very much. It can't still be because of my father, can it?

"Did you get bad news or something? You seem so... reserved." I slip my legs over the edge of the bed and he comes to sit next to me, leaving what seems like an eternal amount of space between us.

"Where did you get this?" He indicates the shoulder strap of my cami. Then he takes his hand away, letting it fall onto his lap to stare at them—those instruments of death.

"A small store not far from the mall. I didn't feel like going home after you left me in the car. Why? Don't you like it?" I feign a pout.

He must not see this as flirting because he says, "Don't look that way. I hate leaving you." He looks me over again and I still see disgust in his eyes. "I like it, but..."

"But what?" I'm alarmed. I never thought he'd be so distant.

"Why red?"

"I like it." I pout, wondering why he finds it so off-putting.

He stands up and takes a few steps away from me. That's all it takes for him to reach the door and turn around again, pacing the small room.

"I'm at a loss right now," he says. I wait for him to continue, unsure of what he means. "I can't let—" He scratches his head as if to punish himself for some wrong doing. "You're not going home." He scratches his cheek. "I had to send Trick to get your things."

"I wish you didn't," I interrupt. "I see no reason for all the fuss."

"You see no reason?" His voice is stern.

I display my contempt by looking away from him and crossing my arms. I'm not sure why I think that avoiding eye contact and forming a barricade with my arms will make a difference.

"You've been home two days and already he's hurt you twice." He sighs. "Your mother does nothing but wallow in self-pity. You've got me wanting to kill anyone who gets close to you and at the same time wanting—" He stops. Stops talking and stops pacing.

He's done a wonderful job of grabbing my interest. "Wanting what?" I don't turn my head to look at him. With my peripheral vision, I can see his back is to me and his head is down. I imagine he's staring at his feet, but for all I know his eyes could be closed.

He sighs and scratches his cheek. "You really ought to be more careful of what you do during the day."

"What's that supposed to mean?" Now he's just making me mad. "I don't understand. Are you angry about the shooting? How was I supposed to know about that? You should be mad at Trick, he's the one that—"

I'm interrupted again, "I *am* mad at Trick. I'm furious with him." Again, he looks me over from head to toe.

"Good." Why do I feel like I didn't just win this fight? "Wait, why are you mad at Trick?"

"He's supposed to watch *out* for you!"

"He did... sort of. I let him go a little early and if I remember correctly—you were a little late." I turn to angle my back to him by shifting one knee up on the bed and pulling my heel up to meet my inner thigh.

"I don't blame him for that."

I stand up and walk over to him. His head is still down but now I know that he's been keeping his eyes shut. "You need to start making some sense." I poke him twice in the chest, but really, I mean to emphasize my annoyance with this argument; not with him.

"When I asked Trick to get some things from your house and bring them over before dawn, I found it odd that he already knew... about this." His eyes indicate my lack of clothes.

"What?" I step back. His eyes are frightening when he's angry. I've never actually been this close to him in this mood.

"He was with you." He grabs my chin between his finger and thumb. "You didn't know that, did you?"

"Don't you dare!" I pull myself from his grasp. "How was I supposed to know? I thought he left." My eyes search his face and now I see that it's not only anger that causes this look in his eyes. It is pure disgust and loathing. "You mean..."

"Deathdrifters are tossers, Anna. And I'm at fault for this one." He's disgusted and loathing himself, not Trick.

"Well, it's not like anything came of it, right? So he watched me change clothes. It's not like it's the end of the world." I place my hands on his chest after stepping closer to him. Trying to calm him isn't as easy as I thought. "Besides, not all Deathdrifters are... tossers, as you call them. You seem to be one of the few that aren't—I guess I got lucky."

He lets out an amused grunt. "I'm the worst one." He takes my hands off his chest and brings them down to my sides. At least he doesn't let go. "Anna, my sweet Anna," he drops his head, breath on my ear; not meeting my gaze. "The night is dangerous. You can't let me..." He lets go of my arms. "It can't happen."

"But—"

"Anna, if I touch you—actually touch you... Bloody hell, you have no idea."

I inhale a quick breath and hold it. I don't want to hear this. Slowly, shaking my head and staring at his chest, I can't bear to see the truth in his eyes. He's not actually saying any of this. It's all just a dream, right?

"Look at me, my sweet." He holds my chin in his gloved hand so I'll stop my slow defiance. I shut my eyes as tight as I can, trying not to see my father as Damien holds me still. "I've had all day to think about

124

this. I shouldn't have taken advantage. I shouldn't have pushed things so far last night."

"It's not like anything happened," my voice is only a whisper. "I can't believe you're wishing... that you never... bothered." I'm choked up. Tears flood to my eyes and he pulls me into his arms.

"I'm not trying to hurt you and I'm not saying I wish it didn't happen. I'm saying it shouldn't have and won't happen again."

He's not helping. "Why?"

"Because if everything goes badly before midnight on Saturday, I can't bear to think that you'll regret being with me. I can't believe that I don't repulse you on some level."

"Repulse me? What on earth are you talking about?"

"Precisely that. For me, earth doesn't matter. It's not my home anymore. I hardly know anything about this place. I've traveled over its surface millions of times, and yet, I don't *know* this place as home."

"And you think it's all that different for me? People are horrible creatures, D. They're selfish, narrow-minded, and greedy bastards. I'm happy you don't think of this place as home. I think that's the best part about you. How could you think that I'd be repulsed by you?"

"I'm dead, Anna. You can't seem to remember that."

"And you can't seem to forget it!" I pull away from his embrace and crawl back into bed. It's cold beneath the sheets, but not as cold as the room. His foul mood mixed with the air conditioner isn't helping.

"You're right." I hear his whisper not far from my ear and it sends a shiver through my body. "You're cold, Anna." He moves my hair away from my face and tucks it behind my ear. Without another word, he lies down next to me, but keeps the covers between our bodies. His arm rests over me and his gloved fingers interlace with mine.

125

I should push him away, but I can't. He's so comfortable and makes me feel safe. My body relaxes against his and he nudges his nose into my hair; away from my skin.

"Are you tired?" I whisper. I know I should know this answer but for someone who makes such a brash promise, he's not doing very well at convincing me of his dedication.

FIVE DAYS
BEFORE

As I open my eyes to the light seeping in from between the gaps in the curtains, I'm surprised to see two suit cases on the floor. If it's light, that means Damien has left for the day. The only question is whether or not he let Trick stay to watch over me. Though I'm not sure why I need a babysitter in Atlanta. Wait, make that a deathsitter.

"Yer awake."

I turn to see Trick sitting in the one chair this small hotel room has. He's watching TV, but it seems more like he's just staring at it and not really taking anything in. "He let you stay, huh?"

"Aye. Sorry about that. It was wrong."

I grin, flattered the slightest bit. "You're not sorry."

"Yer right." The TV screen goes black and Trick throws the remote on the wooden table. "Plans?"

"No." I look around for my pants. I don't recall taking them off, but I know I had them on when Damien and I had our little argument last night. I open my mouth to ask him if he's seen my jeans, but then I notice he's sitting on them. The one leg is dangling off the seat. He must know I need them and is testing me to see how far I'll go without pants. Jerk should know better. You can't fool with Anna!

A light knock raps on the door. It must be room service. "Can you get that?" I ask Trick.

"No."

"Why not?"

"Not supposed to be 'ere."

I pull my lips into a thin line and furrow my brow at him. He laughs and throws me my jeans. When I pull them on, Trick's already gone. As I walk over to the door, I button my pants. "Who is it?"

"Anna?" I hear my mother's forlorn voice.

How did she find me? "Mom?" I pull the door open very slowly, but I'm thrown backwards and hit the floor. I hear the door slam shut and a dark figure looms over me. "What do you want?" I push my hair out of my face and look up to find Nastusia towering over me.

She looks furious and ready to kill. "What are you doing here, my little pet?" There is no sweetness to her endearing nickname. Fire burns in her eyes. She doesn't touch me, doesn't come a step closer, but I feel my throat tightening and my body sliding across the floor toward the sliding glass doors.

I'm helpless. How can this be happening? It's not Saturday yet and Damien isn't here to help me. I try to yell for help, but nothing comes out. I squeak and kick my legs to no avail.

The sliding glass doors open and a rush of cold air enters the room. Colder than the air conditioner can ever make it. "Nastusia!" I hear Trick yell from the tiny patio. "Let her go!" I can feel his presence beside me, almost as if his arms are around me.

"And what can you do, Reaper?" she hisses. Her hand extends and from the dark corner of the room behind her, shadows extend toward us. My eyes get wide as the shadows form into figures. I'm hyperventilating and realize that I am, indeed, breathing. I try to get to my feet but find that I can't regain my footing.

"Stay 'ere, Anna." Trick whispers in my ear. He stands and has a large black and gold scythe. It reminds me of a fencing sword the way the metal intricately weaves around the L-shaped blade and extends down the rod to form another handle. It makes him look stronger and more powerful than his usual bad-ass appearance.

He makes a few swipes with his scythe at the black forms that surround Nastusia. They diminish and then reform. His attempt at ridding the room of them is a complete failure. Speed though is definitely on Trick's side. He moves effortlessly through the room and weaves between the shadows to reach a hand out toward Nastusia. She moves just before he can touch her.

"Nice try, young one. You should know better. Didn't that old man teach you anything?" Her hand creates a ball of dark, swirling smoke in her palm.

A dirty name.

I hear a familiar chant in the back of my mind as the dark shadows extend their reach for me. Their large forms are growing toward the ceiling and I can't help but curl myself up in a ball on the floor. I don't know what will happen if they touch me. I hope I don't die and I pray that Trick gets rid of Nastusia before anything else happens.

A dirty face, they chant.

I feel the shadows pulling at my clothes, hair, and skin. Their touch is hot and it feels like they could cause serious burns if they linger too long on my skin. I scream for help and feel my body being pulled out of the tightly knit ball I've constructed of myself. The shadows carry me over to the bed. I float above them, kicking and screaming for anyone or anything to help me.

A curse to relive this place.

I open my eyes quickly, catching a glimpse of Trick being held against the wall by Nastusia; despite him being bigger than her. He doesn't fight back with his whole body the way I would. His legs are limp and mere inches off the floor. His arms flex with the effort to tear her hand away from his neck. The Touch of Death has no effect.

Die for his shame.

I'm dropped to the bed and I feel a hard, long object against by back. Held down like this, I feel like an unwilling sacrifice to the gods. Only these are evil shadow gods, instead of the ones that supposedly bring peace or good fortune. The harder they push on me the more the long object digs into my back. A dark hand reaches for my face and I turn my head to the side. I don't want the darkness to take me. Cold metal presses against my cheek and I open one eye to see black and gold glistening in the sunlight from the window. Trick's scythe.

Die for the key.

I reach above my head and pull the scythe out from under me, slashing at the dark figures. They scream and cry out in agony. I don't know why they're more afraid of me than when Trick was hacking away at them, but whatever works. Pulling myself up, I crouch on the bed and divide the shadows with black and gold. They dissipate and their high squeals of the chant fade from the room. "Die to become free!" I shout as I lunge myself off the bed and force the black and gold death-bringer down on Nastusia's head.

I feel myself hit the wall above the bed and land safely on the mattress. I feel dizzy and weak. Looking up, I see Trick on the floor. He's rubbing his neck with one hand while he reaches with the other for his scythe. He raises it and a small amount of blood drips from the blade. Nastusia is still standing over Trick, but she's holding her head as red drips from between her tanned fingers. Her long nails are buried in her thick, matted hair.

She turns to approach me, whispering something that sounds like an ancient spell. I feel weaker and my eyelids get heavy. Just as Trick stands with his scythe, looking like the real-life version of my pewter reaper, everything goes black.

JUST YOU AND ME

Iopen my eyes and it's dark. Too dark. I suddenly remember what happened and I can't seem to catch my breath. I feel like I've been running for miles. My lungs burn and muscles ache. I can even taste metal in my mouth. It's so cold in here and yet I'm sweating.

"My sweet Anna, I'm so sorry." I hear the anguish in Damien's voice and I begin to cry. The turmoil of the day has come back to me and I feel lost and scared.

His leathered thumbs wipe away my tears and he pulls me into his arms, my head resting against his shoulder. I cry harder in his strong embrace, soaking his sweatshirt with my fear. I pull back to look at him, but he has this look that indicates he could kill someone at the moment, if given the slightest chance.

"Is Trick okay?" I ask.

"He's fine." He looks down at our hands and then meets my gaze again. "I'm going to tell him not to come back."

"Why? He saved me. I think you're mad at the wrong person." I'm desperate to defend Trick from Damien's wrath. I've never actually seen him act on his anger, but his facial expressions are enough to give me insight.

"I'm not mad at him about this. I'm angry with myself. I'm not leaving you anymore during the day. The List just isn't that important." He pushes a strand of my hair behind my ear. I tilt my head so that my cheek rests in his open, gloved palm. "Anna, I just don't know what to do anymore. I can't bloody save you. She'll come for you no matter what."

"Why did she come? Today, I mean. Why didn't she wait until Saturday, like she's supposed to?"

He scratches his jaw. "She's scared."

"She didn't look scared—try scary."

He smiles a little, but becomes serious again just as quickly. "Perhaps she knows she might lose this time. She's willing to break the curse herself in order to ensure your death."

"That doesn't make any sense. Why would she break her own curse? That would take my father away from her for good."

"Mm." He makes the sound that signifies he's deep in thought. "I think it's personal now. I've tied my fate to yours—as long as you die, whenever that may be, she wins. She'll beat me."

"Then what's the point of fighting?"

"I know I haven't made it seem like this curse is about more than you, but..." He lets out a breath of frustration. "I need you to survive."

"Why?"

"Because it matters to me. It makes a difference to your parents. They're not the people you think you know. It's their curse. It's you who reaps the penalty."

"That's not fair."

I'm a living reaper. I don't collect the souls of the dead; I collect the pain for my parents.

"I don't think Nastusia thinks it's fair that I keep intervening."

"I like your interference." I smile at him and he pulls me closer, turning my small body around so that my back is against his chest. He slides up to the headboard and pulls me with him. I nestle myself into his strong build and angle my head so that my ear rests over the spot where his heart should be.

"I've been thinking about Saturday a lot lately," he says. "And not only how I'm keeping you alive."

"Oh, yeah, why is that?"

"It's a special day for you."

"Special day, special death," I chide.

"Don't do that. I'm trying to explain something here."

"Well, explain then."

"I've thought about what we could do together—just you and me. I thought we could make it a right royal night out."

I shift and sit up to look into his eyes. "What does that mean? You want to wait until Saturday for a first date?"

"You'll have to excuse my ignorance, Anna. It's been over eight hundred years since I've courted a woman."

He makes me blush. I've never heard it stated like that before. "I think you're doing things here a little out of order, aren't you? I'm pretty sure I've read that the hero has to save the damsel in distress first, court her, marry her, *and then*..." I avert my eyes as I finish in a whisper, "make love to her."

"Anna..."

"Never mind, let's change the subject."

"You said you didn't want to get married."

"I did? When?"

"During the drive here."

"Hmm, I don't recall saying that." I glance to see if he'll catch on to my act. I clearly remember saying I wouldn't get married after living this life, but he brought it up... sort of.

135

"I am incredibly sorry for my intentions. I've tried to apologize, but apparently I didn't do it correctly the first time."

"Stop. You have nothing to be sorry for," I say.

He doesn't agree. His face is stern and his lips are pressed into a tight line. I'm not sure if I want to know what he's thinking, but I can't hold back my curiosity. "What are you thinking about? Do you have regrets?"

"No! Never." He pulls me closer, keeping his hood between our faces, which makes me wish that we'd go find Grim again. "I want nothing more than to be with you. I'd never regret even one second. You want to know what I was thinking?" I nod. "I was thinking about you. How long I have wished to touch you and when I did get the opportunity, spoiled, I only crave more."

"Then why did you say we couldn't—?"

"For the very reason that you laid out the order of events on how a man courts the most beautiful creature anyone has ever seen."

"Not anyone—just you." I turn away due to the embarrassment of my love life, or lack there of.

"Don't forget Trick," he mumbles.

"I *can* forget Trick because I don't care about him. Besides, I only owe him for saving my life."

"*I* owe him for saving your life. You don't owe him anything." Damien puts his nose to my hair and inhales deeply. "I thank him whole-heartedly for what he did, but he'd bite his arm off for the opportunity to keep you from me."

"I thought he was protecting me for you."

"You don't know. You can't understand."

I try to think of something to say to that. It's very distracting to have his cold breath so close the way he is. "Okay, if you say so."

My stomach growls and I grab my waist in pain.

"What's wrong? Are you hurt? You had some bruises when I got here that I did my best to get rid of."

136

He sounds panicked and his eyes search my face for the source of my distress.

"I'm just hungry. Stop worrying."

"You should eat. I'll get you something." He slides out from between me and the headboard.

"I'll come with you."

We head down to the main floor of the hotel and walk across the wide foyer to the restaurant. Not many people are walking about and it finally dawns on me that I have no idea what time it is. I glance around for a clock but there isn't one that I can see. Suddenly, as if on cue a clock chimes three times.

"It's three in the morning?" I ask.

"Yeah, you hit your head pretty hard." He wraps his arm around my waist. "Do you know what you want to eat?"

"I could eat a horse."

He cocks his head to the side to look at me in disbelief. I can't believe he's never heard this expression before. I'm sure it dates back pretty far or perhaps he finds it amusing that it's still used nowadays.

"A horse it is then."

FOUR DAYS
BEFORE

Damien watched me eat in awe. It was a little embarrassing to eat so fast in front of him—very unladylike. He smiled and kept whatever he was thinking to himself and we didn't bother hanging around in the restaurant long after I finished my meal.

Now that we're in the elevator and heading back up to the room, my heart sinks to think that there is only an hour left before the sun will be up and he will be leaving me again.

"What's that for?" he asks me.

"What's what for?" I ask, sounding more depressed than I intend.

"The sigh. Something bothering you, my sweet?"

"No, it's just... I wish you didn't have to go."

He grimaces—which is actually a really good look for him—and rolls against the elevator wall onto his shoulder to face me. "Perhaps I can stay today. I'll see if I can convince Trick to do my List."

I smile and nuzzle my face into the shoulder that's propped against the wall. He doesn't mean *convince*, he means *tell*. "I'd like that."

"Of course, you'll have to show some restraint."

"What?" I look up at him, confused.

"Just because I'm not doing my job doesn't mean I can keep you on your back all day." He taps my nose as if this simple gesture will relieve the withdrawal that is yet to come.

"I can handle it." I turn away so that my back is against the elevator wall. He gives me a wry smile. "What? You don't think I can?"

"Oh, I'm sure you can." The sarcasm in his voice is not subtle.

"Then why are you looking at me like that?" He shrugs in response and pushes his hands deep into his pockets. "You look like you know something I don't."

He closes his eyes and leans his head back against the wall. The elevator stops and the doors rattle before they begin to slowly slide apart. The elevator must be old because it took a lot more time than normal for it to reach the twenty-third floor. I push off the wall and take one step toward the opening doors. A cold glove wraps around my arm and holds me back. Quickly, I'm turned around with my back pressed against the opposite wall and the elevator door is shutting. "What are you doing?"

"You said you could handle it, but I don't know if *I* can," he says before he presses himself against me.

I shiver, longing to run my hands over his soft, cool skin, to feel the feathery texture of his hair between my fingers, and his firm arms wrapping around me. I can't feel any of that. And I don't know if I will ever get a another chance since we met Grim. He holds me in place, his hands clutching my forearms at my sides and my head pinned to the wall, afraid to move because his lips are millimeters from mine.

I'm not complaining. He's just humoring himself by making me stick to my word. I implied I wouldn't touch him. That doesn't mean he wouldn't touch me—within the confines of leather gloves and clothes, of course.

My breathing is erratic and I test him by slowly sliding my leg up the side of his. "That's cheating," he says with a cool breath against my neck. He pushes out his knee and knocks my leg to the side, holding it firmly against the wall.

"I think you're the one who's cheating," I say, gasping for air.

"You said you could handle it," he repeats against my ear and a shudder runs down my spine.

My heart aches for him and even though his skin is so cold, hovering just over mine, I feel warm inside. His fingertips are like ice through the leather, lightly grazing over my skin. They search the angle of my jaw, the slope of my neck, the hollow of my collar bone and the expanse of my chest that my tank top reveals. I want him so badly that when he begins to pull away, I angle my shoulders toward him, but I can't reach due to his hold. "You are so mean," I say, dropping my head.

He lifts my chin, teasingly, as if he's about to kiss me before saying, "We should get back to the room." I keep my eyes closed and nod slowly. He leads me by the hand back down the hall.

In the room, the curtains are drawn and it's rather dark as he closes the door behind us. From behind me, he wraps his cool arms around my waist and inhales the scent of my hair. Since there isn't much time left, I assume I should make the most of what we have. I spin around in his arms to face him and extend my neck with a prayer that my lips meet his, without punishment. His hands cradle my face, while mine run up the length of his torso from his waist to his shoulders.

An urgent moan escapes me and I feel him tense. He slows his already gentle touch and begins to break us apart. "D, I..."

"Shh," he cuts me off. As he pulls his body from mine, I still feel cold. And not in a way I like. Did I upset him somehow?

"Why is it so cold?" I rub my arms. The air conditioner isn't on and he isn't angry, at least his face doesn't look angry—that much.

"Where are you?" he says, but not to me.

"Tis almost dawn," an unhappy, Scottish accent resounds in the room. It's Trick who's making the room cold.

Damien looks back at me as he says to Trick, "You're taking my List today."

I swear the room just dropped another few degrees. Trick suddenly appears right next to me. If I move a mere centimeter I'll touch him.

"No. Tis not part of the deal," Trick says. "Besides, ya only have three minutes until dawn. Do ya really think what yer doin' is right? You cannae wear gloves all the time. If ya screw up and kill her, tis yer own damn fault."

"That'll never happen." Damien runs his gloved knuckles lightly down my cheek, and then brushes his thumb across my lips. I close my eyes to savor this final moment. My ear is close enough to Trick's throat that I hear him swallow hard and a deep vibration comes from within his chest. Damien is teasing him.

"No!" Trick's not backing down. "Am no' taking yer List."

"Making a song and dance out of this, are we? We'll both be in serious trouble, instead of just one of us." Damien turns to squint at him and puts the youngest Deathdrifter in his place. "I do believe this is the first time you've defied me, Trick."

"I'll take me chances." Trick crosses his arms. The two of them are creating arctic tundra in this room.

"You t-two better b-behave. I don't w-want to l-listen to your bickering a-all day," I chatter, arms crossed. If I were claustrophobic, I'd be having a serious panic attack right now. And by the look on their faces; I'm not dealing with two grown men. Today, they're children.

CHILDREN

After a couple hours of witnessing the childish, silent standoff from under a blanket that is male chauvinism; it was decided that I return home. I didn't initiate this idea and neither did Doom or Trick. Yesterday, in all the craziness of evil shadows, a demon sorceress, and tossed around suitcases and clothes, my cell phone had ended up in a dark corner behind the dresser that also served as a TV cabinet. At some point my mother had called wondering where I was. Normally, she doesn't care, but my father had been giving her a hard time about always knowing my whereabouts and she pleaded to no end for me to come home. The *children* finally decided it would be fine as long as they *both* came with me.

When I called and told my mother I'd be bringing two friends home, I heard my father object in the background. Funny thing was my mother said what I was thinking, "You won't be here, so why do you care?"

It didn't take long to pack up and check out of the hotel, which has me currently shivering and blasting the heat in the car in the middle of the Georgia spring time.

"It's a g-good thing you kno-ow how t-to drive." I shake violently from the cold radiating off the two reapers.

"Someone feels he *has* to," Trick mumbles.

"You d-don't d-drive?" I turn sideways in the seat to see both of them better.

"He's too lazy to learn."

"I donnae see a reason to partake in the ways of the living," he quietly defends himself and I find I'm straining to hear him.

"You ha-have a b-better way?"

"Aye."

"No, he doesn't." Damien glares into the reflection of Trick's eyes in the rearview mirror. The return expression from Trick makes me think he does but Damien is against me knowing about it.

It only makes me curious and want to ask Trick to clarify, but my chattering teeth are giving me a headache.

"S-seriously, guys, d-do I h-have to s-suffer the wh-whole way?"

Damien's eyes glance from the road to look at me. I think I just saw guilt—or at least I want to.

"Tell this wee bawbag to do his job and ya wonnae have to worry about how cold it is," Trick mumbles rather clearly.

"I'm not the only one causing this, *Cameron*." Damien squints into the rearview mirror to meet Trick's eyes as he uses Trick's living name.

"Don't call me that!"

"You're the only Deathdrifter that won't let anyone tie you to your life. You should be happy you died before you had anything of importance to lose."

I see the mix of anger and hurt in Trick's eyes. "If Anna wasn't in this car right now, I'd give ya the skelpin of yer life," he sneers.

"G-guys," I chatter, turning to sit properly again. "C-can we j-just get h-home?"

"I'm sorry, Anna," Damien says. I hear a crack that sounds like a bone breaking. Trick's arm is between the front seats; his hand is clenched down hard on Damien's wrist. Damien recoils and mumbles what I think is another apology. Trick just stopped Damien from touching my bare shoulder where my shirt has fallen to the side. I don't recall when Damien took off his gloves, but now I see why Trick thought using them was a bad idea. Habits die hard. But why wouldn't Trick let D kill me? Trick said I'd be with him after my sixth death; the sooner the better, right?

The boys take their time to relax and after a few minutes my chattering stops. "Trick could you meet us at my house? We're only an hour away and I'd like to talk to Damien about something."

"Aye, and let him *actually* hurt you? I'm stayin' right here, Jo. Consider me protection from yer *protector*."

I let out an involuntary, annoyed grunt. "My name is Anna," I mumble. He smiles crookedly, but says nothing. Perhaps I should let him stay—just in case.

"Let him hear it. It won't hurt anything." Damien sounds reluctant, but I guess he knows better than I do.

"Well, it's just... I know who you guys are, but what do I tell my parents?"

"Damien Doyle and Cameron McKinney," Damien states, as if I asked an obvious question.

I squint and grimace at him. "Yes, of course, the infamous Deathdrifters that just happen to be hanging out with me the week before I die!" I scoff.

"Anna," they say in a very irritated unison.

"What? Your answer wasn't exactly enlightening. What do you want me to tell them?"

145

"We'll make it up as we go along," Damien says as he speeds around a little old lady in a blue station wagon.

"Oh, sure. Fantastic. So, when I'm asked a question in private—because my mother is a gossip junkie when I have friends over—I'm supposed to hope that you two won't screw it up five minutes later? I'd like to work out a plan here, if I may."

"You may," Damien says.

"Aye," Trick responds.

"You two will be the death of me." I drop my arms from hugging the blanket around me because it's finally warmer in the car and they both seem to be repressing smiles. It's better to ignore them.

"You're both exchange students at my school and we decided to meet up in Atlanta. Now, why did I decide to do this?"

"Because we're pure helfy like," Trick says, satisfied with his answer.

I push my temple against my window and consider just getting out now—out of this car, out of this conversation, out of this life. They have no idea how stressful it is bringing them home—for real.

"I thought that answer was blatant," Damien says.

"Gads," Trick's eyebrows rise in amusement, "I thought it was blatant that we're helfy, but she hasn't accepted that answer yet either."

"Anna, don't worry. I won't let you get into any awkward situations with your mother. And I have a feeling you and she are right about your father. He won't be there."

"And how are you going to stop her from shaking your hand when she meets you, or... or..."

"Anna," Damien exhales slowly, "look at me."

He always says that when I'm anxious and somehow it always calms me down. I meet his eyes and he smiles faintly. "All right, I believe you," I say. "Everything will be fine."

146

First of all, nothing is fine as we pull into the driveway. My father is still home, his car parked beside my mother's. My mother is running out the front door to greet my guests—not me. I honestly think she's going to hug them, but she stops and smiles from ear to ear.

"Good day, Mrs. Fairchild. I'm Damien Doyle." He bows to her like a true English gentleman—pouring on the accent and all.

The giddy, little school-girl in my mother erupts and her rose-colored face tells me all I need to know: She's drunk.

Trick steps out from around the car with one hand in his pants pocket, holding back his trench coat. The other picks a burning, smokeless cigarette from his mouth—nice way to keep your hands away from introductions, Trick. "Cameron McKinney," he mumbles.

I glare at him as he puts the cigarette to his lips. His eyes say "I'm sorry" but he doesn't put it out.

"Well, Mr. McKinney," my mother turns even redder as she looks at Damien, "Mr. Doyle, won't you come inside?"

As the words leave my mother's mouth the front door swings open. "You!" my father yells from the porch. "You're lucky I didn't call the cops on you. Kidnapping my daughter like that!"

"Dad, he didn't—"

"Didn't what?"

"Kidnap me," I say as I turn my face away. I need to bite my tongue from saying anything more.

"So you're saying you know these guys? They didn't hurt you?"

Not like you do, I want to say. But before I can open my mouth Damien says what I never expected. "*I'm* not the one she should fear."

As Damien takes a step toward my father I see Trick put a hand on his shoulder.

147

Shit, I have a feeling *I'll* be paying for Damien's taunt later.

My mother puts her hand to her mouth and lets out a tiny squeak of jealousy. Her eyes glaze over as she gawks at Damien who glares back at my father.

"Now's a pure dead time to be inside, Jo," Trick whispers in my ear.

"You want help with dinner, Mother?" I start walking toward the front door where my father stands, unsure of what to do.

"Huh? Oh, sure. Does everyone like spaghetti?" She follows me, but looks back to Damien in order to direct her question to him more than anyone else.

"I'm going out," my father mumbles as he heads straight to the car. He backs down the driveway faster than any of us can get into the house.

"I'm certain that whatever you make will be to perfection, Mrs. Fairchild," Damien says as he follows us into the house.

"Where are you from, Mr. Doyle? You have a very interesting accent."

My mother brushes off Trick's accent as if talking to him is a nuisance. As if she doesn't approve.

"Try thirteenth century England," I mutter.

"What, dear?" She turns to look at me.

"Atlanta," I say clearly.

"Really? You weren't born there though, right?"

"No, ma'am. Across the pond." He smiles and she gives him a vacant stare. "Originally, Kilkhampton."

"Hm, Kilkhampton? I can't say I'm familiar with it."

"Near Cornwall, Mom. England."

Damien smiles and seems pleased that I know my British geography. Although, he isn't about to say that in the thirteenth century there was no Kilkhampton, but that it is the closest anyone can place on a map nowadays.

My mother's eyes flicker between Damien and me quickly, taking in our posture, the look in his eyes while

148

he smiles at me, and my shy smile at his involuntary attempt to close the gap between us. My mother can see our attraction and I hope she only thinks that our lack of physical contact is due to parental supervision. I'd be committed for having to explain The Touch to her.

Our personal solitude is broken when Trick clears his throat and says, "Gads, when's supper?"

"Belt up." Damien smacks Trick in the stomach. Trick looks annoyed, as if a de-clawed kitten just popped him instead.

The guys aren't hungry. Death doesn't eat, but apparently they feel jealousy.

This is going to be a long evening with the children who just happen to be Deathdrifters.

GOSSIP JUNKIE

To my surprise, Trick is a relatively slow eater. I suppose not needing to eat means you don't have to rush. I, on the other hand, am starving and focusing on the process of getting food in my stomach more than the conversation that's taking place. Damien even took extra time to 'learn' the process of making spaghetti with my mother. She found it exhilarating, while I found it rather annoying.

"How long have you lived in Atlanta, Damien?"

Great. My mother is now on a first name basis and since they're getting along, that can only mean bad news for me—ensured death and the loss of Damien forever this time. Both of those weigh equally on my scale of misfortune.

"Well, Mrs. Fairchild, it was so long ago that I don't quite recall." He pushes the remains of his food around his plate.

"You two aren't eating much. I hope it's to your liking," my mother says with a forlorn smile.

"Eh, tis fine," Trick mumbles, and then grunts due to a swift kick under the table from Damien.

"We ate on the way here, Mom. Sorry we didn't say anything earlier."

"Her 'we' refers to Cameron and me, Mrs. Fairchild. Anna wouldn't eat a thing." Damien scowls at me as if the event had actually occurred and I refused his offer of food.

"Anna, you really should eat more. I'm glad you had someone responsible with you. And Damien, please, call me Gloria. You needn't be so polite." The pallor of her cheeks flushes once again.

Damien doesn't reply. He's older than my mother and knows he doesn't have to refer to her as his elder, but this is his defense from telling her the truth—and to ensure her approval.

Trick seems to have given up without even trying.

"Oh, it's awfully cold in here all of a sudden. Anna, are you cold? I wonder if the thermostat is broken." My mother stands and rubs her arms as she walks over to the thermostat. She taps her finger against the small screen as if the number will change with that insignificant action. After scowling at the box, she comes back to the table and picks up her plate. "Anna, clear the table and come help me in the kitchen."

"Here, let me," Damien says, keeping his promise to not leave me alone with the gossip junkie.

"No, no, that's not necessary." She moves toward him and stretches out her hand. I've never seen Damien recoil so quickly. My mother is frozen in place, staring at Damien as if he has just done something obscure.

Trick walks around the table and mumbles something into Damien's ear and then lightly tugs on his sleeve. "We'll be outside, Mrs. Fairchild," Damien says with a twinge of guilt. "Anna?"

"I'll come out when we're done," I tell Damien, hoping my tone is reassuring enough. Since my father isn't home, it's okay with me that he waits outside.

My mother and I start the dishes in silence. Water splashes between us with each handoff of another dish.

I know she has questions—a plethora of them are sorting and rearranging in order of importance in her head. The more I think about it, the more anxious I feel. "Just ask your silly questions already."

She smiles at her hands as they play with the bubbly water. "I was just wondering," she pauses, "how long have you been seeing each other?"

"That's not what you really want to know." I hate it when she plays with me. Although, we haven't played this game of Ask-A-Question-Maybe-Get-An-Answer since I was in high school. Back then, I never wanted to tell her anything, now I'm not sure if I can answer her even if I wanted to.

"A day? A week? A month? I'm curious because you've never mentioned him before."

"When have I ever mentioned *anyone* from school to you? Do you even know my roommate's name?"

"No, but—"

"Exactly! So what is the real question you want to know?"

"Is he really from Atlanta? I mean, yes, I'm sure he is now, but that accent is rather strange. Are you sure he's from England?"

I can't actually answer any of these questions. I could tell her that I have been *seeing* him for almost a week. I don't think hearing his voice in my dreams counts. I can't say he's *known* me for six hundred years. I certainly can't say that in the span of six hundred years he's sure to lose a little bit of his accent. I mean he's only talked to other Deathdrifters and me. In fact, he could probably copy anyone's accent, so do I know for sure that he came from England originally? No. But I trust him and he has no reason to lie to me. She hasn't bothered to ask me if Trick is really from Scotland. Then again, I don't think she's all that fond of him or as concerned as Damien is about his little crush. Even if Damien doesn't consider it as such.

My mother frowns at me as I rewash the dish in my hand several times. I don't know how to answer her. I should be as vague as possible, but how would Damien answer her?

"If you won't answer those questions, then how about this one?" She turns to face me and rests her hip against the counter's edge. "Do you love him?"

"Oh, come on."

"Trick question." She smiles.

"What?" I drop the dish back in the sink. The mention of Trick's name brings to mind his furious and protective eyes from the fight with Nastusia.

"He obviously cares a lot about you." I stare at her. How does she know how Trick feels? "So does that other one, though I'm not sure what to make of *that* boy," she says in a condescending way. I exhale, glad I misinterpreted her. Then she picks up the dish that I dropped back in the dirty dish water and starts to rinse it. "It's obvious they both care for you."

"How so?" I scowl at the filthy water.

"I see the look in your eyes when Damien talks. I see how the other one watches your every move with conflicted concern. They're both watching out for you. And when your father came out on the porch, I saw Damien place himself slightly between the two of you while Cameron moved closer. I know things are hard for you when you come home and that's why you stay away so much, but I think you've found a rock in your whirlpool of a life, Anna."

"You have no idea."

"Perhaps I don't, but don't let the way your father and I are stop you from loving the person that is meant for you."

"I don't think it's going to be solely your relationship that makes or breaks what I want."

"What do you mean?"

"It's complicated and I don't know if I can explain it."

She thinks hard before saying, "Is Cameron the reason you two have an invisible wall between you."

"Oh, no. Cameron is... just a friend. That's all."

She takes a very dry dish from me and smiles. "I hope you're not being polite for my sake."

"Mm," I nod and try to hold back my smile, but my mother has already caught on.

She elbows me in the ribs and I lean away from her prod. "You win," she says. I have just bested the gossip junkie—without even trying—at her own game. And I have no idea how.

NO PAIN

Walking through the foyer, the grand-father clock strikes ten and I'm surprised at how quickly time flies. Damien and Trick are sitting on the front step and they seem to be getting along. At least they're talking civilly, anyway. I lean against the screen door and wait to see if they sense my presence.

"Yer sure he's going to do that?"

"You don't concur?"

"I donnae know. Seems a wee bit trifle, it does." Trick takes a drag off his smokeless cigarette.

Damien looks down at his feet on the bottom step. His legs are bent at the knees, but he relaxes on the stoop, elbows propping him up. Trick is sitting beside him, legs long enough to plant his feet on the grass. They must know I'm here because neither one of them is continuing their conversation.

I open the screen door and step out to lean my shoulder against the column. "You two getting along without me?"

"Aye," Trick grunts cynically, before putting out the cigarette that looks freshly lit.

"Fan-bloody-tastic," Damien says as he scratches his cheek.

I roll my eyes at the indulgent charade of his combination of superlatives and look out at the road. The cool breeze sends a shiver down my spine. Damien gets to his feet and steps closer to me. Looking up into his dark eyes, I wish he could hold me and reassure me that everything will end happily—that we'll never have to part again. His slight smile stirs my curiosity. "What?" I ask.

"You handled her very well. I'm not sure what you were worried about earlier."

"I just don't like to be in those situations with her. I've avoided them at all costs over the past few years. I'd like to keep it that way, if I can."

"Uh-huh," he says, and his smile broadens as if he's not really listening to me. His hand slowly comes up to my face and I close my eyes. I can feel the cold radiating off him, inches from my cheek, and I exhale slowly. My heart thuds in my chest—wanting his hand to touch my face and yet, I'm fighting the thought of what happens if he does.

"Donnae," Trick's faint voice cuts the silence.

I open my eyes and Trick is standing on the porch step just a few inches below us with his hand resting gently on Damien's arm. I catch a glimpse of anguish in Damien's eyes and I know he hates this as much as I do.

I turn away from the temptation of him and walk back inside to sit on the couch with my knees pulled up to my chin and my hands gripping my ankles. For comfort, and because of a childish habit, I grab the nearest sofa cushion and hug it tightly to my chest.

"What's the matter with you?" my mother asks from the archway.

"Nothing," I reply into the cushion.

She sits down next to me and puts her hand on my shoulder. "You can tell me. If you can't rely on your mother, who can you rely on?"

"Are you serious?" I look up to meet her eyes. "Where have you been earlier this week? Do you have any idea how hard things have been for me?"

The front door slams and my mother is distracted from my questions. Damien is standing in the foyer, dread written all over his face.

"What is it?" I ask, my voice shaking.

"We should go. *Now*." He takes three steps toward me, but my mother stands up and bars his way.

"Why? You don't have to run off now. Besides, what's so urgent that Anna needs to leave as well?"

"He's home." His eyes tell me that my father doesn't return alone.

"Is she with him?" I ask, pulling myself off the couch.

"Who? Ms. Cune?" My mother looks between me and Damien for the answer.

"Where's Trick?" I can only think of the last fight and how I don't want to be anywhere near her.

"Distracting them. Come on, we'll go out the back." He holds out his hand covered with his sleeve just as he had the night he first held me after Nastusia used my father to club my back.

"Wait! I don't understand. What's happening?" My mother rushes up behind me and takes my arm before I can reach Damien.

"I can't explain it now," I tell her.

When I turn back to face Damien I see what I have been dreading since he walked in the door.

"Ms. Cune?" My mother's confusion is obvious. Why is her cleaning lady dangling a friend of mine, unconscious, from one hand while my father is standing guard at her back as if he were reinforcement? It makes sense to me, but for my mother, this wasn't on the woman's resume.

159

"Nastusia! Give him to me!" Damien demands as he extends his arm out to his side. In his hand a bright white light flashes from his palm causing me to flinch. When I refocus on him he has a long black scythe with a blinding silver blade.

"Anna, what's going on?" My mother's more afraid than I am. I can feel her trembling grip on my arm. Her eyes are wide and for a moment I think it might be helpful to knock her out and claim this was all a dream. But what if I'm not here when she wakes? Who will explain it all then?

"Run, Mom! Please, just run," I plea and push her away without taking my eyes off Damien.

He stands his ground and doesn't let Nastusia take one step toward me. I don't know if he has a plan for keeping the shadows away, or not, and I hope they don't reappear now.

"Let him go," Damien repeats his demand but Nastusia hasn't taken her eyes off me.

"Let us trade, Doom. The Deathdrifter for the girl." Nastusia's sinister smile makes me cower.

"I'll trade you nothing! Give him to me!"

"Come and take him then." She laughs as she drops Trick to the floor and kicks him in the side. He rolls over in Damien's direction. Trick's groan provides me with some relief to know that he's not dead—anymore than he already is.

Damien takes one step toward her and she raises her arm, spreading her fingers wide. She makes a quick forward gesture from her chest toward Damien. A cat-like screech and a bright light fills the room. I hear a thud and when I can see again, Damien is on the floor with Trick at his side. His head rolls from side to side as if to help himself regain consciousness. Trick is awake but moving slowly. He gets on all fours in order to stand.

My mother and I are cowering on the floor and I see my father advancing toward us. He picks up my mother and tosses her to the side. She lands hard on her head and I think this is the first time I've ever witnessed him harm her. But his real target is me and not her. Clumsily, I try to back away. From around his leg, I see Nastusia hasn't left the edge of the foyer where the living room rug meets the linoleum tile.

Air is cut off from my lungs as my father lifts me off the ground by my neck. I claw at his arms, but it doesn't help. Fury feeds his torture and he feels no pain. Even as I kick my feet out at his shins, his face reveals no indication of the impact.

"Let her go, Mr. Fairchild!"

In my peripheral vision I can see Damien starting to stand. He's on one knee and hoisting himself up very slowly. Gasping for air, all I want to do is scream for Damien to hurry and make my father release me—even if he has to touch him.

Blackness clouds my vision and I hear them again.

A dirty name.

The voices ring out inside my head. I want to scream and beg for them to leave me alone but the chant continues.

A dirty face.

I see my father's face. Not the face that is strangling me, but the face that I haven't seen since I was four.

A curse to relive this place.

The scene changes and I'm watching myself grow up in the horror that is my father's infidelity.

Die for his shame.

The events of every one of my deaths flash before my eyes. Every one of them shows Damien's heartache as he looses me to be reborn into this curse. But one face of devastation lingers longer than the others—and it's not Damien's.

Die for the key.

I see a black box placed before me, but I've never seen anything like it and I don't know what to make of it.

161

Die to become free.

The feel of a long ago kiss—a kiss of another life—fades to loneliness and I feel as if my body is floating. I don't feel anymore pain. I'm not worried about the lack of air in my lungs. I'm light and carefree. Happier than I've ever been and now I understand.

Now I know what it means to die.

But do I want to?

JUDGE, JURY, AND EXECUTIONERS

A tender stroke of ice slides along my cheek, down my neck, and over my collar bone until it dissipates at my chest; just above the fabric of my shirt. Reflexively, my arms wrap around something hard yet familiar. I dig myself deeper into the warmth of the blankets. When I roll closer to the edge my head hits something solid and cold. I rub my eyes and the haziness of sleep begins to diminish, verifying that I'm not in my bed, but instead, on the couch. I just hit my head against someone's knee.

"D?"

"No," he says, disappointment lacing his tone.

I sit up and push myself to the other end of the couch, pulling the afghan around me. He's making the room terribly cold. Thank goodness my head didn't touch his skin.

Wait, did he touch me? I'm alive, so he couldn't have, right?

"Where's Damien?"

"He took yer maw upstairs." Trick stares across the room. "Waking up in her own bed will make it easier to convince her that tonight was only a dream."

This is the first time I've noticed Trick with his hood up. I don't recall ever seeing a hood attached to his trench coat, but I suppose, underneath, he could be wearing an unzipped, hooded sweatshirt.

Damien comes down the stairs and walks up to the end of the couch, behind me. "You all right? Let me see." He gently tips my head to the side and brushes my hair away from my neck with a gloved hand. He grunts angrily under his breath.

"Is it that bad?" I ask, my eyes closed. His gentle touch is all I've craved this evening and I really don't care if he's more concerned with bruises than with me.

He kneels on the floor, putting his head level with mine. "You've had worse," he whispers against my neck and his cool breath tingles, sending goose-bumps down my arms. Slowly, his cold breath follows the curve of my neck—ear to shoulder—reducing the swelling.

"He's coming." Trick thrusts himself off the couch and walks over to the bay window.

Damien stands, pulls his hood up over his head and Flashes so I'm sitting on his lap. I wave the swirling purple smoke from my face.

"Anna," he says as he wraps the afghan around me, "it's going to get very, very cold in here."

"Why? What's wrong?"

"Things are getting out of control. I've made a request and Grim won't act on it without the consent of every Deathdrifter."

"I don't understand. What request did you make? When? And why are they all coming here?"

He doesn't answer my questions. "If everyone gets angry, I don't know if you'll be able to handle the cold from all of us."

"As long as I'm with you, I can handle it," I say, as reassuringly as possible.

"Tell her the rest," Trick says, staring out the window.

"Rest?" I look up at Damien, but his hood hides his face from me and I can't see what his eyes might be able to tell me.

"I don't want to scare you, Anna, but—"

"Doom!" A thunderous voice echoes through my house. Suddenly, in the wing-back chair, a monstrous form appears and starts boring its red scythe into the carpet. The blade swings around and around, catching glimpses of light from the moon and shining it in my eyes.

"Morgan," Damien nods his head in acknowledgment.

"I didn't know you were so soft, Doom. You surprise me." The red Deathdrifter chuckles and turns his hooded face toward Trick. "Hey."

Trick lifts his black and gold scythe a few inches off the floor and then stabs it back into the carpet as his form of a greeting.

"What is this? Deathdrifters United?"

Morgan, or who ever he is, chuckles, so apparently I am pretty hilarious to this Carrier.

"That's one way of looking at it, darlin'," Morgan's voice rings with a smile even though I can't see him through his dark hood.

Damien's chest rumbles with anger, but neither of us says anything. I rest my head against Damien's shoulder and nudge it up against his hood. I hope that my stare gives this Deathdrifter the understanding that I am not afraid of him.

Within the blink of an eye two more Deathdrifters arrive in my living room. Each one takes a seat where they please, but as they do so, it seems as if they take an extra long time to stare at Damien and me. It feels like they're glaring at us beneath the shadows of those hoods. I'm not sure if I'm shivering from their cold or their assumptions of us.

Grim arrives last and he is not just a black blur for once. His tattered and faded black robe sweeps across the floor as he stands in the center of the room.

"You," Grim points at Trick, "over here."

Trick saunters over from the window and takes the seat he was in when I woke up.

"I'm glad you're all here on time. I know this is a little unusual, but I think we can come to a decision quickly." He stands and lifts his scythe. It's bigger than any of the others'. "First things first, gentlemen."

"Sorry, Anna. You have to get up for a minute." Damien gently lifts me up and slides me onto the couch cushion beside him.

The six Deathdrifters stand in a circle and angle their scythes so that the blades meet in the middle. As one, they recite:

"In vita mors est vivos et excrucior.
In morte est vita, propitious et rudis.
Sunt vera in morte est.
Pro nos sunt mors viatores,
Hic pro vestri animus."

Individually they state their name, from what I imagine is in order of rank.

"Sleep Reaper," one says holding a royal blue scythe.

"Trick Reaper," Cameron says with more enthusiasm than I've ever heard from him.

"Life Reaper," says another with a forest green scythe.

"Blood Reaper," Morgan's deep voice rings true; again with a smile lingering in his voice.

"Doom Reaper," Damien says, proudly.

They all take one step back and let Grim hold the floor for his own name. "Grim Reaper!" His voice echoes even louder than Morgan's had when he Flashed into the house.

Every one of them still has their hoods up as they take their seats. I stare at Damien in his black hood that hides his face from view and all I can say is, "My goodness, D. This is a cult, isn't it?"

"We won't be committing suicide or anything. Not tonight, anyway." There's a smile in his voice and he seems happier than before this whole charade started. He sweeps me back up in his arms and I nestle myself into the same position I had before.

I catch Trick glance our way, envious.

"As you may have heard, Doom is making a request that I feel I can not grant him alone. He needs the support of all of us for this," Grim initiates.

"We get that he wants to give up his List, but he's been giving away one day every hundred years. He does what he wants. What's the point of this?" Morgan is back to boring his scythe into the rug as he speaks.

"Doom, it is your place to make a formal request," Grim says.

"Anna, stand up. You won't feel any pain, but I'm bringing the marks your father made back for a moment," Damien whispers.

I lean forward and he starts to move my hair away from my neck.

"Wait one minute," says the Deathdrifter with the blue scythe. "How she know about us? Why is she conscious?"

"I've granted Doom the loss of his List from the eleventh hour until dawn. Allowing him to be with her longer than one day."

The other Deathdrifter with the green scythe says something I don't understand from the corner of the room.

"Doom, please begin," Grim says.

"Everyone, I'd like for you to meet *my* Anna."

Trick's head falls back against the couch with annoyance at Damien's claim over me. I can imagine him rolling his eyes right now.

I wave a little, feeling like a guinea pig brought to a kindergartener's show and tell.

"Anna has a problem."

I cringe. Does he have to start out like this?

"She's cursed by the demon sorceress Nastusia. It's purely a jealousy curse. The sorceress lost Mr. Fairchild's love centuries ago due to the loyalty he felt to his family, especially his daughter. Anna has relived this curse over and over though I've tried to stop it. Nastusia uses her power to control Mr. Fairchild, and in turn, Anna suffers." Damien turns me around so that my back is displayed to everyone. "He's done this," he lifts the back of my shirt to reveal the first hit, "and this." He pulls my arms outward to show the hand prints around my biceps. "And just earlier tonight, he has done this." He pulls my hair aside to show the fresh bruises around my neck.

I catch Trick's subtle change in posture.

"Mrs. Fairchild does nothing but drink and feel sorry for herself. Tonight was a rare occasion—both with Mrs. Fairchild and Nastusia. I believe this is because of me."

"What?" I ask. Damien's cloaked face angles toward me slightly, but he doesn't stop making his request to the judge, jury, and executioners.

"She knows that I'm helping Anna." He turns back to everyone else, "And that you all know about it. My request is that you all take parts of my List, let me stay with Anna—day and night—to protect her. I also beg you to take The Touch away from me as well until the end of this."

"Let me get this straight." Morgan stands and paces the room slowly. "You talk to a soul numerous times, which is against policy. Then you haunt her dreams and let her see you. Which I believe is outlined in the manual as *against* policy. You give up your List any time you choose and then you take a living soul to see Grim, in The Whitelands, and then you're rewarded for breaking the rules by being relieved of your List anyway. And now you want to *indulge* like the living; without having to live?"

A loud crack comes from the couch. Trick's leaning forward, staring at the floor. No one pays him any attention. Was I the only one who heard the sound?

"The way he makes it sound, it's as if you should be in jail or something," I say to Damien.

"I made my request. Now vote." Damien sits down and pulls me by my hips until I'm nestled on the couch, between his thighs.

Everyone vanishes from the room, including Trick, leaving us blanketed in a purple fog. I'm not sure what to make of tonight.

"Why did they leave?"

"They're discussing. They'll return when they decide." His tone is heartbreaking and I twist slightly so my shoulder is against his chest, my hips still parallel with his. I reach up, over his hood and caress his jaw line but it's colder and harder than normal.

"You're so warm," he says as if he's in a trance. "You're like fire." He swings my legs up so they drape over his legs and down the length of the couch. I still can't see his face under the hood. Glancing down at his hand that's caressing my thigh, I realize that Damien isn't his normal self. He's so cold and the glove is too loose. It slides down and his wrist is nothing but bone.

"D, your hand!"

"I'm sorry." He Flashes out from under me to pace the room. "I don't mean to scare you. Morgan interrupted me. This is what we are. Reciting the pact makes us this way. Once Grim releases us everything will be back to normal. I promise." He drops his arms and the gloves fall to the floor.

I consider what happened tonight and how much he's giving up for me; friends, trust, loyalty, a job he's done... forever.

"Was that Latin? What does it mean?" I change the subject.

"In life there is death, the quick and the tortured. In death there is life, the gracious and the uncivil," he takes a deep breath, "But in death there are those with true life. For we are the Deathdrifters, here for your soul."

"It's beautiful." And a little creepy. I stare up at him and he nods slowly. "How long do you think it will take them?" I search the darkness beneath the hood for a skull, but all I can see is never ending black cloth.

"Depends."

"What do you think they'll decide?"

"They'll back me and let me protect you."

"I hope so." I run my hand down his arm despite the lack of mass the sleeve implies. Time is my only enemy at this moment.

THE SILENCE
OF DEATH

An hour has passed and I'm beginning to wonder if Damien is as worried about the outcome of the 'meeting' as I am. I'm not sure why they wouldn't let him try to save me. I can't see the logic in their possible denial, but that could be because I'm so tired.

"What if…" I hesitate because I'm not sure I want to hear meself say this out loud, "What if they don't let you stay?"

"Anna," he breathes, and my heart flutters to hear my name on his velvety voice. "Don't worry."

I close my eyes from weariness of the wait and no sooner do I feel prying eyes among us.

"They've reached a decision," Grim says.

My heart thumps so loudly it might as well echo through the house. Damien is too patient or perhaps he's not reacting in a way that I can sense. I'm about to beat the decision out of Grim, but he pulls out an old weathered parchment from his tattered robes.

Grim unrolls the scroll to make his announcement. "We, The Deathdrifters, under the decree of Grim Reaper, have come to a consensus on the matter of the Fairchild curse.

"First, we are not ones to take lightly the gift of life, but we also know and understand the glory of death. And though, we do not make a habit of helping the living, we will make an exception, this one time, pending the acceptance by the blighted.

"Second, the Deathdrifters will have a replacement, of their choosing, since Doom has chosen to tie his fate to the living over his position among us."

"Great!" I can hardly hold my excitement, but when I sit up, I notice Damien hasn't moved yet. Accidentally, I catch a glimpse of his hand, which is still only bone, as it forms into a fist over his knee.

"They're not done," he grumbles.

Facing Grim, I see that his boney fingers are curling around the parchment tighter than necessary.

"At dawn the stipulations are as follows: Doom's scythe will be withheld—rendering the Flash, veiling yourself from the living, and visiting The Whitelands useless. Your Key and Death watch will be stowed under the supervision of Life Reaper. And lastly..." Grim hesitates and I swear I saw his hood flinch in the direction of Trick. "...relief of The Touch will be split. You'll have from the eleventh hour until dawn as your only reprieve as it was with your List, which will be distributed appropriately to the Reapers not engaged in the Fairchild curse.

"This is the verdict the Reapers have bestowed. The signatures below reflect that these hold true until the end of time."

Grim walks over slowly and hands a quill and the parchment to Damien. He looks it over slowly and rests it on the empty cushion next to him.

"What's wrong? Sign it!" I say, and reach over to grab the paper that holds my life in ink.

Damien tries to grab my arm, but ends up gripping a black and gold scythe instead. I recoil because Trick is standing so close that his cold radiates through the afghan. "Anna, it's not worth signing."

"You're an odd one, Doom." Morgan steps forward and he's surprisingly taller than Grim. "I thought you loved her warmth enough to accept anything." He chuckles reminding me of an old horror movie. It's a lot more frightening being in the movie than watching it.

"You're a dim bastard, Blood!"

I jump. Not because of the volume of D's voice, but because of the power in it—and maybe the volume as well, but not as much.

I pull the afghan around me tighter. Damien gently lifts me so he can slide out from under me. I've never been more frightened as I watch Morgan advance on him. Both are the same height as they glare at each other with only inches between their chests. Without looking, Damien takes the fleece throw off the recliner, wraps me in it and then turns back to Morgan.

"I argue the toss," Damien addresses Grim at Morgan's side.

"They're trying to be fair," Grim states.

"You haven't exactly been the ideal Reaper lately, Doom." Morgan seems to be holding a vendetta. If he's next on the 'MVP list' below Damien, I can only imagine what coded message he slipped into the verdict.

"So I've taken some of my own liberties over the past six hundred years. Don't you wankers have anything else to concern yourselves with other than with what I'm doing?"

"Doom," Grim reprimands.

"Don't yell at me about it!" Morgan shouts.

I'm getting more confused as their argument escalates. Grim is doing a fairly decent job of not choosing sides, but now Damien has Mr. Green Scythe defending him and Mr. Blue Scythe is backing up Morgan. Trick is standing by the bay window. He has no intention of getting involved.

I don't see this argument ending any time soon so my only option is to read the parchment and see if I can decipher it.

All of the Deathdrifters have signed it. I wonder if that means Damien is fighting for nothing, although I don't know yet what it is he's fighting to change.

"Um, excuse me, everyone?" No one seems to be paying any attention. I glance at Trick and he's the only one looking at me. "Hey!" I yell as loud as I can.

They all stop their arguing to stare at me. I'm speechless all of a sudden. "Uh," I stutter, and look down at the parchment crinkling in my hands. "I see it says here that this contract is only binding if *I* sign it. Where does Damien sign?"

"He is just a vehicle," one of them mumbles.

"Mine isn't needed, Anna," Damien says softly. He must have seen the confusion on my face.

"Then instead of fighting over this, why don't you all tell me what this means in *living* terms and I'll decide if *I* want to sign it."

"By all means, darlin', ask away." Morgan's entertained at my expense again and he sits down to drill his scythe back into the carpet. Grim and Damien remain standing in the center of the room.

"Why is The Touch the only aspect of being a Deathdrifter that stays?"

Morgan begins to laugh and says, "That's your first concern, darlin'? Because if it's gone, then so is he. No more Doom Reaper."

I scowl and look back over the parchment. What else could anger Damien so much? "Anna, you have to understand," Damien starts, "what's written there is coded. One statement can mean three, maybe four different things. And once you sign it, *you* can't go back."

"What about this has you so angry?" I ask him.

"They're trying to make you my replacement, Anna. They think I'll fail. If you sign it the way it's written and you die..." He trails off, not wanting to commit the rest of his thought to words.

"But you won't let me die, right?"

"Everyone dies, Anna," he mumbles.

"And when I die, I'm..." I glance from the parchment to Trick, who's looking out the window, paying the rest of us no mind. "What do you want it to say?"

The silence of death rings louder in my ears than the siren of a fire truck.

"I don't want you to have to see the cruelty of death in all its ways. This job isn't all beer and skittles, Anna. It's one you shouldn't have to endure, if you have the choice."

"Aw, what sweet rubbish, Doom." Morgan turns his head to me. "Don't you want to know whose idea it was to add that in?"

Damien doesn't say anything, but I'm more than curious. "Who?"

"Hey, Tricky, tell us again why you wanted to make sure she'd *always* be around?"

Ah, yes, of course.

A sweep of icy air runs through the cold room and Damien squares his shoulders to Trick. "This is your doing?" Damien growls.

"Ya asked fer me help, Doom. I warned ya, but of all the living souls fer ya to choose, it had to be *her*. Ya made a choice and now I've made me own."

"You made sure this would all work out for your benefit, didn't you? You little prat!" Damien punches Trick in the face and I know Trick doesn't feel it as his head juts backwards, but my heart feels for him.

I may regret this action later.

Slowly, reaching for parchment and quill, I scribble my name on the dotted line.

THREE DAYS BEFORE

No one realizes what I've done. There's a drone of shouting between Deathdrifters. Damien and Trick are attempting to inflict pain on one another, which has no impact for either of them. It's not until their hoods fall back that Damien realizes his bones have skin again and all of them know the verdict is complete.

Damien's eyes avert from Trick to me as I hand the scroll and quill back to Grim.

"I think it's fair," I say, to no one in particular.

"Anna, no." Damien releases Trick's coat and walks over to kneel in front of me. "Please," he whispers.

"I'm okay with this. I trust that you and Trick will protect me."

His sigh tells me he doesn't agree.

Grim's hand grips Damien's shoulder as a sign of encouragement. "There's one more thing. Something that's not in the parchment."

"I don't want to hear it."

"I do," I whisper.

Grim doesn't tell me though. He floats backward and disappears from my living room. Morgan, or Blood Reaper, depending on who's addressing him, is still sitting in the wing-back chair. Trick is at the window, rubbing his face from the residual degradation of Damien's pounding.

"What are you laughing at?" Damien growls at Morgan.

Blood Reaper stands, shakes his head and says, "The three of you are going to have all sorts of fun. Wish I could watch." Then he disappears, purple swirling in his wake.

"You may go," Damien says to Trick without looking at him.

"Doom, I..."

"Piss off, you dim bastard!"

"I cannae!"

Damien grunts and throws himself down on the couch. I'm not sure what to say or who to say it to, and I'm not sure why Trick wants to stay.

"Who wants to clue me in here? Trick? You seem to have all the answers."

"Just bloody tell her already," Damien says, relaxing on the couch with his face to the ceiling, arm draped over his eyes. "You've been biting your arm off to snog her."

Trick squints at Damien. "We're both staying. Doom is free of The Touch at night and I have the day. But, Jo, I'd never..." He doesn't finish.

I think I understand. If Trick is staying his List must be relieved too. I wish I could hit him right now, but I don't have a death wish. Not tonight anyway.

"Never what, let me live? You want me to die so I'll be with you, right?" I see Damien pick his head up and glare at Trick. Did this not cross his mind already? "You want to keep us apart, don't you?"

He glances to the side, considering—I'm not sure what.

"You have no right to decide what or who I want! And I've got news for you, *Cameron*, even if I do die; I won't be spending my after life with you!"

Trick flinches.

I must have really sparked Damien's interest because he takes my hand and when I glance over, he's smiling slightly.

"What?" I shout, lost in anger.

"Don't wake your mum."

That's his advice? I thought he was mad too.

"I'll go, if that's what *she* wants, but I'm coming back at dawn." Trick stands and takes two steps toward the door and then he does what I thought I'd never see him do without reasonable cause. He disappeared—and not through a window or door.

"You're adorable when you're angry. At someone else, anyway."

"Why aren't you still mad at him? He's wants me to die!"

"No, he doesn't. He'll give you anything your heart desires. But I don't want to talk about him. Come."

I finally realize we're making contact. Real contact. And I'm still alive! I shuffle my feet across the carpet as he pulls me closer to sit with him on the couch. His arms wrap around me and the room's cool breeze diminishes. A chill runs down my spine while Damien nudges his nose against my neck. He's not cold. Well, not *as* cold, anyway.

"What did Grim mean when he said there was something else?" I feel his body shrug around mine. "Aren't you curious?"

"I've had enough bad news today." He lifts me in his arms and readjusts my posture so I'm cradled sideways on his lap instead of my back against his chest. "Tell me, Anna. What is your happiest memory?"

"Being with you," I say without hesitation. I know what he means, but I can't honestly answer him.

"I mean before me—from your childhood—a holiday, perhaps?"

I furrow my brow, trying to concentrate on what I remember best about all those horrible times. Evil memories swirl through my mind. The ones I've longed to forget stab my heart and I don't understand why he's asking me this.

"You don't want to talk about today, I don't want to talk about the past."

"I see."

"Well, what about the future?"

"What future?" he murmurs through a tight jaw. Has he lost all hope of saving me?

"Tomorrow or..." I hesitate unsure if I'll get the birthday that I want.

"Or?" His knuckles run down the side of my face until his fingers cup my chin to turn my head, his eyes lingering on my mouth.

"Saturday," I whisper.

"That conversation will lead us back to today, Anna. Are you still trying to piece together tonight's events?"

"Saturday's my birthday. All I want to know is if you'll... be here with me."

"I'm not going anywhere. Unless you tell me to."

"My parents always plan some stupid dinner which usually consists of a quick, quiet meal and then everyone heading off in their separate directions. Normally, I don't mind, but..."

"You want me to be there, don't you?"

"Yes," I exhale and finally meet his eyes. Those dark eyes are so warm that I feel like it's a humid fall night; the sky scattered with stars and a light breeze rustling golden leaves.

"Then I'll be there. Besides, I'm not leaving your side on Saturday."

"Now it's you stirring up my thoughts about tonight." I bite my lip to let him know I'm not implying that he *talk* about anything. Not now, anyway.

"I have my own ideas for making memories tonight," he says, in a hushed, velvety voice that stirs my blood and makes me blush.

"Care to share?" I unzip his hooded sweatshirt and run my hand over his chest to unbutton the collar of his black shirt.

"You have a pool, don't you?"

"Yeah, why?"

"We'll have to be quick, then."

He scoops me up off his lap and takes me out the back door to the pool deck. Setting me on the wood railing, he positions himself between my legs and says, "Look up."

BROKEN PROMISES

Gazing at the stars, they've never looked more beautiful—so bright and fragile. I feel as if I can reach out, collect them in my hands and protect them from the day—from when the light diminishes their beauty from everyone's eyes.

I can hear Damien mumbling, but I'm not able to make out what it is he's saying.

"Damien, what are we doing?"

He raises his head. "This."

Placing his hands on either side of my face, as if I'm a china doll, and just before his lips meet mine, I hear him breathe, "My sweet Anna."

My lips tingle against his. It feels like sparks erupt between the heat of mine and the cold of his. A drop of warm water runs down my cheek, but I'm not crying. Another drop follows and then another. It's so warm that I'm curious and pull away from his gentle, lingering kiss.

Water coats my face and hair. It feels so good, so warm. "It's raining?"

I look up and clouds blot out the stars. Damien's damp hair still holds its perfectly short, spiky shape. The angles of his jaw and cheeks are accentuated by the water glittering on his face. His dark lashes seem to glow and then I realize his black button down shirt is clinging to his shoulders, chest, and arms. I pull him closer and wrap myself around him. Legs clutching his waist and arms entwined around his neck, I kiss his cheek, his forehead, nose, chin, and ear.

"This is better than the pool," I whisper, parting his lips with mine.

I know he loves the warmth of me so I'm not about to deny him any of it. My fingers seem to take on a mind of their own and recklessly unbutton the rest of his shirt to slide it off his shoulders. The thin undershirt doesn't take long for me to grab and pull over his head. His body is cold under my hands and all I want to do is keep him as warm as possible.

His body is wet with the rain. My hands slide over him quickly and it appears as if he's smoking. I know he's gorgeous, but this takes on a whole new meaning. His body is cold enough that the warm rain is causing steam to rise off his body. It's foggy and hardly noticeable but it's there.

I'm so lost in him and trying to get his clothes off that I've hardly noticed how he's been holding me; as if he'll break me—as if he's reluctant. We talked about intimacy at the hotel. He told me he'd never do anything like this. A fearful pain strikes me in the chest. His hands have been perched on my hips to keep me from falling off the railing, but otherwise, he hasn't exactly touched me. My shirt is soaked and yet he doesn't seem to notice anything but my lips. What if he's only considering giving in because I no longer have a chance anymore on Saturday?

"D, wait." He pulls back to look at me. "What are we doing?"

"You wanted to know what I was thinking about, remember?"

"You were thinking about me losing control while you just stand there?"

He furrows his dark, gorgeous brow as if he doesn't understand my concern. "Damien, what you told me at the hotel and what's happening *right* now contradict each other. What's changed?"

"At dawn, I can't touch you anymore and Trick can. I can't handle that." When I drop my legs he steps back and picks up his shirt to slide back on, but doesn't bother to button it. I must look really confused right now, because I'm not sure if I can remember my argument while he looks so tempting, so breathtaking standing only a few steps away.

"I want you, Anna, I really do, but I made a promise and I'm fighting not to break it."

"Please, broken promises I can handle. But only because you think we'll have another chance after Saturday." I hop down off the railing. "I don't want your pity."

"You think I'm not going to do everything I can to keep you? As you said, you have two to protect you. Meaning I have to work harder so that Trick doesn't touch you."

"He won't kill me by touching me if he's truly relieved." I roll my eyes.

"I know that," he growls. "I have other reasons to keep him from doing it."

"Like what?" I hop down from the railing and take one step. Damien doesn't move, doesn't seem to notice me or have any plan to answer me. He stares at the water in the pool, watching the warm rain tickle the surface.

"Kiss me," I demand.

His head shifts slightly in my direction, but only to see me in his peripheral vision. He's probably trying to match my expression to my voice. The corner of his mouth rises in amusement. I put my hand out, but he doesn't come any closer.

Letting out an agitated sigh, I pull off my thin, soaked shirt and drop it to the floor of the deck. Damien turns his sight back to the water.

"Ready?" I ask.

"For?"

I close the gap between us with two quick steps and plunge us into the pool. For my own plan, I didn't prepare very well. I cough up more water than expected and my throat burns from the chlorine.

"Are you all right? Why'd you do that?"

"Trying... to," I cough in a fit while he rubs my back and starts laughing, "lighten the mood."

"I see." He lowers his shoulders below the water and slowly moves back to the wall of the pool.

I follow him and when he places his hands on my hips to guide me to him, I pull off my drenched tank. "Touch me, Doom, before I make you regret it."

He lets out one quick snicker and says, "Regret not touching you? You can't change the last six hundred years."

"Oh, yes I can," I say, and graze my lips over his. I exhale so he can feel my warmth and I know I've got him trapped.

His hands run the length of my back, down to my waist. I slide my hands up his chest, pushing his shirt off his shoulders then finally unbutton his pants. He pulls me closer once I'm able to toss them up on the deck. He pulls my legs around him to straddle his waist.

"Shall we get out?" he asks me, kissing my neck and shoulder.

"Not yet."

His hand glides over my back. "You're so warm," he whispers in my ear.

"Only for you," I say, and nip at his ear.

He stifles a moan, but does a horrible job of hiding it as his grip tightens on my back and his other hand slides along my thigh. The flutter in my stomach is exhilarating and my breath catches in my throat. Spinning around, he stands and sets me on the edge of the deck with my legs still wrapped around his waist.

"Budge up," he whispers.

I slide back as he pulls himself out of the pool and in a fluid motion he scoops me up to lay me on the recliner that's pushed off to the side of the deck. With more effort than it's worth, we manage to pull off my soaking, skin-tight jeans. He leans over me, running his hands up my legs and lingers at my thighs. I close my eyes so I can enjoy his touch. His hands move up my hips, tracing the curve of my waist, and stomach. I try not to laugh from this gentle sensation that tickles ever so slightly in the most pleasurable way.

I feel his weight press against me and he's not as heavy as I imagined. His lips trace every inch of me. When they reach my neck, his hand slides one bra strap off my shoulder, then traces back down my side.

"I like this." He fingers the elastic of my underwear and I glance down, even though I know what he's talking about.

"Good. Now hurry up and take 'em off."

"No rush, my sweet. I asked you what your most memorable moment was and you said me, so I'm making sure that this is it."

"So the other times don't count?"

He scowls. "No."

I can't help but laugh. "Why not?"

"Because," he says against my skin. "Now stop distracting me."

"You want *me* to stop distracting you from *me*?" I laugh harder at how absurd this is.

"Anna, I can always stop."

"No." I feign unhappiness. Trying the most seductive voice I can, I whisper, "Please, Damien, don't stop."

He groans against the curve of my hip and then gently grazes his teeth over my skin, playfully—as if he could eat me up.

Lying beside me on the recliner, he cradles me in his arms and holds me close, kissing me delicately. His lips are like ice cubes and I'm starting to shiver. I know I can't hide it from him but his lips are soft and he makes me forget the turmoil so I don't want him to stop. It feels too good to have my bare skin against his, and even though he's cold, I'm willing to keep him close forever.

"We should go inside. You're shaking."

"No. We're not done," I say and push him on to his back so I can explore his perfect chiseled abs, strong biceps, and masculine curves. I run my fingers over every angle and hard muscle in his body. He closes his eyes and lets me do as I please.

I kiss his chest and make my way to his waist. His breathing, which I recall as a habit, seems to quicken. Moving aside the elastic of his boxers, I find the soft curve of his hip and kiss it lightly, my tongue sliding over his cool skin. I can feel him stiffen. His weight shifts and I wonder if he feels any of this. It occurs to me that if he can't feel the impact of pain; is pleasure different?

"What does this feel like?" I ask him.

"Brilliant."

"I gather that," I kiss his hip again, "but you don't feel it when someone hits you. So, how do you feel this?"

"Anna, I thought we discussed this."

"Did we? We discussed your *habits*."

"Please," he begs.

"I'm just curious," I say, crawling back up to him, looking into his dark eyes.

"We feel pain—it just doesn't linger. But warmth does. The pulse running through your body..." His finger runs down my cheek, over my shoulder and then his palm slides down my arm. "That's what I can't get enough of."

"That wasn't so hard, was it?" I press my body against his chest and he kisses me so deeply that I moan and run my hands through his hair.

"Doom."

Damn it.

Before I can open my eyes, Damien Flashes out from underneath me and his black button down shirt is dry and draped over me—hiding any view of me in my underwear. He's already back in his jeans and standing in front of Trick as if he could kill him. The sun light peaks over the horizon. Our time is up.

"You bloody—"

"Tis dawn," Trick interrupts him, looking toward the pool.

"I know what time it is!"

I'm wrapping Damien's shirt around me and feeling lucky that Trick can't see me with Damien standing between us. The shirt hangs just long enough to hide the lace over my butt as I pick up my two tops and jeans from the side of the pool.

"Anna, go inside."

Where did he think I was going? I glance back and see Trick toss his smokeless cigarette over the railing into the grass. That single action makes me wonder how long he's been watching us. How much did he see?

I'm running into the house, trying to stop the tears from mixing with the warm rain on my cheeks when I hear Trick yell, "Ya fuckin' promised me!"

CHEATER

I'm still soaking wet as the sun peeks through the living room curtains. I can't stop pacing and I have no idea what's going on in the back yard. Are they trying to kill each other? Can they kill each other? Doesn't seem likely.

And what did Damien promise Trick anyway?

I hear the floor creak above me which means my mother is awake and will be down soon. That also means I have perhaps five minutes before she catches me walking around wearing Damien's shirt. The only thing I can hope for is clean clothes in the laundry room.

I find an old pair of track pants that I haven't worn since high school and one of my black tank tops. I change as quickly as I can, but still wear Damien's shirt, unbuttoned, over my tank. The sleeves are too long so I roll them up to my elbows. When I come out of the laundry room my mother is making breakfast and Damien and Trick are sitting at the table. Neither of them looks happy.

"There you are, Anna. The boys said they didn't know where you were."

I don't bother to respond. I stare at Damien, who's perfectly dressed and dry, and wait for him to look at me. He stares at his hands that hold a cup of coffee. I wonder if it warms him the way I do.

Trick is sitting sideways at the table with his shoulder toward Damien, the other over the back of the chair, facing my mother. The *boys* are ignoring each other.

"Good morning, Anna," Trick says, a small grin stretching across his face.

"Mm," I grunt and open the fridge to see what my choices are this morning. I'm too angry to talk to anyone right now. I decide on juice and lean against the counter across the kitchen from Damien and Trick. Damien has yet to look at me still.

"Eggs, boys?" my mother asks as she walks over to them with the pan and a spatula.

Trick shakes his head, stands and walks over to me. Every time he's near my parents it's as if he has some sort of grudge against them.

"No, thank you," Damien says. My mother scowls slightly before turning back to the stove.

Trick places a coffee cup in the sink. His hand runs down my shoulder to my elbow—a trail of ice—and he holds it there on my bare skin. "I'm sorry about... ya know," he whispers.

I suddenly recall a face in my mind. It's a young girl. One I've never seen before. She blushes as Trick leans in to whisper in her ear. She's beautiful. I can't help but wonder if he loved this girl.

My heart races, reassuring me I'm still alive. A cup shatters and my mother jumps. Peering around Trick, I see Damien sitting at the table with his eyes shut tight and purposely not breathing.

"She's fine," Trick grumbles so faintly I know only Damien and I can hear him. I can because he's standing way too close to me and Damien can because... well, he can hear everything. It's only my mother who doesn't hear while she cleans up the mess, mostly because she's worried about Damien's hand which he stuck under the table since nothing is wrong with it.

"Let me see your hand," my mother begs. "You might have burned it. That coffee was hot."

"It's cold," he says.

"It can't be." She touches her finger to the coffee spill on the table. "It is cold. How can that be?"

He's been cradling that cup in both hands—both of those ice cold, freezing hands. All I want to do is hold him. Reassure him that everything is fine. I know I can't touch him, no matter how badly I want to, but I have to say something.

I walk over to him and stand at the end of the table. "Damien," I whisper. He still won't look up at me. "Please, look at me."

"I can't."

I kneel down beside him. "Why not?"

"It hurts too much."

"I don't understand. What's going on?"

"I have to leave for a couple hours. I'll be back."

"Go? Go where?"

He doesn't answer. With every bit of swift caution he weaves around me and the table to distance himself from my mother without touching anything. Before I can think of anything to say he's out the door and half way down the block before I can't see him anymore.

"This is because of you!" I glare at Trick.

"Anna, he's your guest. Be polite," my mother says, but unconvincingly.

"Polite? Oh, mother if you only knew the half of it!" I storm out of the kitchen and up the stairs to my room. I haven't slept yet, but I figure being nocturnal is the way to go from now on.

When I slam my bedroom door closed, I see that Trick is already sitting on my bed.

"Get out." I walk past him and pull a clean shirt and pajama pants out of my dresser.

"Someone needs a hug."

"I don't need anything from you!"

"I meant me. I could use a hug." He's all teeth and sparkling eyes. It's gross... in a kind of cute, boyish way.

"You don't deserve it."

"Aye? And some British dobber who wants to bonk ya on a driech day does?"

"Excuse me?" I turn to face him and he looks way too comfortable on the bed I plan to sleep the rest of the day away in.

"Ya heard me."

"So a pompous, wanna-be-badass, half-Scottish, half-Russian, peeping-tom is better for me? Is that what you're saying?" I shake the clothes from the dresser at him. If he's not going to leave, what's the point of changing?

"Aye, in a manner of speaking."

"Well, I don't want to hear it." I walk past him, out of the room, and into the bathroom to change since my room doesn't seem to be emptying any time soon.

When I return, Trick hasn't moved, but now he's in a black t-shirt and very baggy gray sweat pants. "If you think you're *faking* a nap with me, I'll have you know, it's not happening."

"How'll ya know if yer asleep?"

"Great. You just ruined sleeping for me, too."

He pats the side of the bed. "Sit. Talk to me."

"Trick, I'm tired. I want to sleep." He puts out his arms as an invitation. "Alone," I add.

"Anna, let me tell ya something." He fidgets as if he's having trouble finding the right words. "I've never loved anyone more than the lass I wanted to marry when I was alive. I was robbed of that opportunity by Doom. Aye, I'm furious with him. He gets anything he wants." He sighs, scratches his knee and looks at the empty space on the bed beside him. "I only want to feel yer warmth, smell yer hair, hold ya in me arms, Jo.

Please, just this one time, let me have what I've been cheated of."

"Nice try, but I'm not doing anything to hurt Damien. I love him." Did I just say that?

Trick looks hurt as he gets to his feet and turns away, toward the door.

I just admitted to Trick that I love Damien and Damien doesn't even know it. He's told me countless times that he loves me and now that I have the guts to say it I've ruined it by telling Trick instead.

So why do I feel like a liar?

"I know ya think ya do. And I know he loves ya. He has fer a long time. Unfortunately, he has a way about him that makes others feel... comfortable. At ease. Safe. He owes me and agreed to let me have this time with ya, which is why he's mad. Perhaps he trusts ya enough or perhaps he thinks I'll get ya out of me head. But if ya make me feel the way he gets to—"

"You're crazy." I interrupt. "He'd have told me if he was okay with this. I'm not some piece of meat you two can toss around and share."

"Neither of us intends on sharing, Jo. Ya live, he wins. Ya die, I win. Tis that simple."

"How do *I* win?"

"Ya win either way." He comes back to tower over me, looking hurt and vulnerable.

"I don't believe this. D would never agree to any of this."

"Yer right, he's on his way to The Whitelands with me scythe to get his back. I convinced him he'll need it since yer home. And someone has to protect ya in the meantime."

A quick burst of annoyance rushes through my nose. I hate that Damien had to give up so much of himself last night and I'm glad he's trying to fix it, but I don't like this. I cross my arms and hope that the time without him will fly by. Although, it seems as if the clock has stopped.

Now who's the cheater?

I sink down to sit on the end of the bed. "What do you want?" I ask him.

He looks down at me as if he doesn't want to ask. I'm so exhausted and this isn't fair at all. How am I supposed to know what to do? If I fall asleep and he... I don't even want to think about what he'll do. But if I let him touch me, or worse, kiss me, then what? Will he leave or will he be harder to get rid of?

He sits beside me, placing his hands on either side of my face and I bite my lower lip. I can't believe I'm nervous about something I don't think I want.

"If I let you kiss me, will you leave me alone?" My eyes glance at his mouth.

"Aye. If that's what ya want *after* the nip."

"What does that mean?"

"Ya might change yer mind. Ya might choose me."

"That won't happen," I whisper.

The corner of his mouth lifts. "Come 'ere, Jo."

My heart skips.

I lean forward and then stop, unsure if I can really go through with this. Trick closes the rest of the distance between us. He must know I'm considering backing out because he lingers over my lips, his thumbs run over my cheeks, fingers slipping into my hair. I part my lips slowly, as I say, "I don't—"

In less than an instant, Trick pushes his lips against mine and I use what strength I have to push him away. It's not enough. His mouth is hard and he kneads my bottom lip between his in the most un-flattering way. His tongue slithers out of his mouth and parts my lips as I fight to close them—to keep him out. I might as well be licked by a drooling dog.

I give up, hoping that he'll lose interest quickly. Letting my body relax, his grip loosens, but not to the point of releasing me. His kiss slows and he withdraws that probing tongue from my mouth. He's tender now that I'm not fighting and I can't believe that I'm beginning to enjoy this.

One of his hands moves to cradles my chin as he kisses me softly. His mouth grazes slowly over my bottom lip and involuntarily, I moan for more. His urgency increases as if he's trying to gather all my warmth in case he'll never get a moment like this again. My heart contracts, secretly praying that this isn't the only time. I wrap my arms around his neck. His other hand falls to my leg as he guides us down on the bed.

Trick's way of kissing is nothing like Damien's. Damien knows my face, he knows... Whoa, Trick knows more than my face. He makes me melt with a single touch at the back of my neck. Tipping my head back, his cool lips graze the hollow at the base of my throat. I gasp, lacing my fingers into his hair. How does he know?

He whispers words I don't know in my ear, but they're sweet and intimate and... it's as if my body knows more about him than I realize too. I'm trembling in Trick's arms, craving for more of him. My hands memorize the curvature of his jaw, neck, and chin. My leg creeps up the side of his, his hand following the line of my thigh toward my hip. Before I know it, I'm matching Trick's desire with my own. My hand glides down the front of his shirt until I can slip my fingers under the hem. He's so soft, and yet so solid.

In the darkness of my closed eyes that girl I saw when Trick touched my elbow is back. She turns, curtseyes, and blows Cameron a kiss. Her dark hair is curly and lays thick down to her waist. Her corset is tight and cleavage pushes against the restraint of her dress. She giggles, waves, and then says, "Good bye, Cameron."

In my head I hear a faint, "Please, donnae go."

Poor Trick.

I taste salt and realize I'm crying. When I open my eyes surprise and then concern crosses his face before he lets me go. Then he instantly becomes indifferent. "I donnae see what the big deal is," he says. Rolling away and getting to his feet I'd swear he looks hurt—almost concerned for making me cry.

Feeling a little rejected, I shrug in response.

"Is it all right with you if I sleep now?" I avert my eyes, wondering about Trick's memories of the girl.

He pulls the covers down and lets me climb under. "Aye, but I cannae go." I snap my head in his direction. "Because of yer paw," he clarifies.

"Fine."

It's taking longer than I expect to fall asleep. I roll from side to side but I can't seem to get comfortable. I hope it's not because I'm subconsciously afraid of what Trick will do while Damien's gone.

After tossing and turning for what feels like forever, Trick gets up from sitting on the floor and lies in the bed beside me. I freeze, hoping he'll leave me alone, but he pulls me toward him. I'm reluctant until his voice placates my heart.

"Come 'ere," he whispers.

Soon enough I find that he's cradling me in his arms; my head resting comfortably on his shoulder and our legs intertwined. We fit together perfectly with his cheek resting on top of my head. I release a contented sigh and in seconds I'm lulled to sleep.

THE PRICE
TO PAY

At some point I woke up to the sun burning my face and a cold weight curving to the shape of my body. I rather enjoy the mix of hot and cold combining on either side of me. I try to roll over but a low grunt of displeasure keeps me from moving. I freeze, recalling that Trick crawled in bed with me.

"Are you awake?" I ask, though I should know he isn't.

He grunts again just as softly but sounds content as he nudges his face into the back of my shoulder.

To my surprise, I like this feeling. I feel at home in a way I never have before—as if something has been missing and I just found it. Taking a deep breath I slide my hand along the back of his and interlock our fingers over my chest. It's only this one time. This can't happen ever again I tell myself.

I must have fallen back into an even deeper sleep, because I'm being violently shaken and someone is urgently calling my name. I feel cold and sticky, and my heart feels like it will burst through my rib cage at any moment.

Opening my eyes, the room is lit up by the lamp on my side table and the hallway. Everything is blurry but there are three people standing around my bed.

"What's going on?" I yawn.

I feel cold radiating off something very close to my face. When ice brushes my cheek, I flinch backward.

"Anna, what's wrong?" Damien asks, his weight tilting the bed down.

"Nothing." Focusing on everyone in my room, I see that Trick is by my desk, back in his usual trench coat, with the remote in hand. The third form is difficult to make out but hasn't moved since I woke up.

"What happened while I was gone?" Damien asks.

No one answers. I wonder if he's addressing me or one of the other dead people in my room. Then Damien says something I can't understand and the third blurry form answers him in the same dialect.

This isn't Grim's voice like I had thought it would be. The form isn't revealing itself and I'm beginning to wonder why he's here.

Damien's fingers run down my arm and I find that I'm inadvertently pulling away from his cold again. His face appears concerned as he gets up from the edge of my bed and walks over to the blurred form.

They begin their secret, coded conversation and it sounds like it's elevating past the point of anger—whatever past anger is.

"Will someone tell me what's going on?" I interrupt.

It's as if I don't exist. Damien stops talking to the blurry figure which vanishes as soon as he says something that sounds like "Do." Then Damien turns to Trick and says, "You want to explain yourself?"

Trick shrugs. "I made sure she dinnae enjoy it fer *yer* sake?"

"No, not that."

I did enjoy it toward the end but D doesn't need to know that. "For what?" I ask and push the covers off to make my way to the end of my bed, closer to them.

"I cannae change her memories, only show her what she once knew. Ya did it, so donnae act like I'm the bad guy."

Damien grumbles under his breath but doesn't deny it. "I don't want you near her anymore. I can do this without you."

"Life is me replacement?"

"He's proving better than you so far. Now clear off."

Trick stands and I look away. Staring at the floor is the only way to avoid the hurt I know is in his eyes. I feel as if this whole thing is my fault. I know it's not, but I can't help but feel a little bit guilty.

"I donnae want her hurt. I donnae know how ya can do this. How ya expect—"

Before I can take another breath Damien's hand glows white, like it had in the living room to fight off Nastusia, and then Trick is gone. Damien pinches the bridge of his nose as if it will control his anger.

"I'm sorry, Damien. I was afraid and confused. I thought if I let him..."

"Please, Anna. I'm not worried about the kiss. I'm concerned about whether you remember your dream though." He scratches his cheek, hesitantly.

"Um, well, it was cold and rainy. I was crying, but I don't know why. My feet hurt and I think I was lost." I still feel cold and vigorously rubbing my arms isn't helping. "I feel like I've lost something very important to me, D."

Damien takes the blanket from the end of my bed and wraps it around me.

"If you remember anything I need you to tell me right away. I'm not going anywhere." He smiles down at me as he lifts my chin to gaze into my eyes. "I think you'll be happy to hear what Life Reaper had to offer."

I pull my head from his grasp. "That was Life Reaper who was here a few minutes ago?"

"Yes." He exhales heavily and runs his hand slowly along his jaw, chin to ear.

"What language were you speaking?"

"Sumerian." He sits down beside me on the bed. "Life is old and stuck in his ways. He prefers that things never change and he can be quite stubborn, but everyone wants something, Anna, even the dead."

"Wait. How many languages do you speak?"

"Uh..." He looks up as he counts silently. "Sixteen? I could be missing some."

"Wow. Does Trick know Sumerian?"

Damien looks perturbed. "No. He's lazy and spent long enough learning English. He's also the youngest of us and doesn't care about anything except making sure he's doing what he needs to in order to get by."

"I thought he was trying to kiss *your* ass all this time."

"He was. Now that I've given up my spot as Grim's successor, he wants it."

"If I die, you won't have to give that up, right?"

"Anna, I gave that up when you met Grim in The Whitelands. After Saturday, I'm no longer a Deathdrifter no matter what happens."

"So you might not live..."

"Life Reaper is offering me Friday and Saturday in exchange for my Key."

"You can't give up your Key! You need it. And you won't be able to protect me from Nastusia Saturday night if you're alive. She'll kill you. We'll both die. Then where will we be?"

"We'll see if she notices."

"You don't think she'll notice? Her power will tear you to shreds unlike last night."

"Life is smarter than that. He won't allow me to be completely defenseless."

I nod and hope that's true. He had so much faith in Trick and yet here we are sending Trick away because he's meddling in my life and trying to seduce me. I guess that's the price to pay.

"I talked to your mum about dinner on Saturday night." He's changing the subject. I hate that.

"What do you mean?" I glare.

"A birthday dinner that will be worth remembering for once."

"And what will that be? Fast food?"

"Anna."

"Sorry. I don't know what's gotten into me."

He scowls and squints at me. He's feigning insult. "Try Nikolai's Roof in Atlanta."

"Goodness no, you're joking!" I push him, but he doesn't move. "That place is beautiful! At least I hear it is. And it's incredibly expensive. Is it really black tie?"

"It is." He stares at my hand.

"And do you own a tux, good sir?" I lean into him and place my hand against his chest.

"I own anything I want," he says, hesitantly caressing my thigh.

"Good point." My hand flies to cover my mouth with sudden concern. "But I don't."

"We'll find you something in the morn, if you like."

"No. I know just what I want." The dress from that small shop I found this past Sunday dances in my mind. I only have to figure out where I'm getting the money to pay for it.

"Anna, you're still shaking. Are you cold?"

"A little. I don't know why I'm shaking." I hold out my hand and watch it tremble.

"Budge up." He tosses his head toward the pillows. "I need you to try and remember your dream."

Situating myself back into bed, I lay my head on Damien's lap. He strokes my hair and it feels so nice and comforting despite his hand being so cold against my scalp.

"When will you be alive? I mean, when will Life grant you... life?"

"At the eleventh hour on Friday."

"So, that's just daylight today and Friday of no touching, right?"

"Yes, my sweet. Unfortunately."

"Okay. That doesn't sound too," I yawn, "difficult."

"You slept all day. Are you still tired?"

"Probably over tired. If I move around I'll be okay." I pick my head up off his lap, but he pulls me closer to his chest.

"No. Sleep. I have a feeling you didn't really sleep at all."

I can't help but yawn again, "What do you mean?"

"You're still tired from the dream you can't remember. It's as if your dream has drained all your energy."

Makes sense.

"Stay with me while I sleep?"

"Of course, my sweet. I'm not going anywhere."

EXCITEMENT
AND FEAR

"Anna..."

I hear my name and open my eyes. I'm not sure where I am. I sit straight up out of fear, remembering something. It was red and plaid. A scarf? No... it was a sash blowing in the wind outside my window. Was it just a dream or was it real?

"Anna?" my mother asks from the doorway. How long has she been standing there?

"What?" I still feel cold and my mind is racing around all the events of my dream.

"Is he asleep?"

"Uh," I glance down at the form lying at the edge of the bed, "yeah," I lie. I'm not about to explain how sleeping isn't possible for a Deathdrifter.

"Are you feeling all right? You look pale," she says with concern.

She's been doing surprisingly well since Damien has been around. I haven't smelled a lot of smoke looming in the air, she hasn't been griping a liquor bottle, and her emotions are stable. He really is a healer even if he does collect souls.

I run my hand through his hair and he pretends to stir as if he's been asleep, reacting to my touch as any normal, living person would. I lean down and see he's restraining a smile.

"Mom…" I hesitate, unsure if I'm ready to ask her this.

"Yes?"

"I need something to wear to dinner with Damien." I look down at him again, reassuring myself he's here. "Would you be able to loan me a little money? Normally, I wouldn't ask, but this is… really important to me." It may be my last birthday. Ever.

I hear her make an exasperated sound through her nose before she says, "How much?"

"Fifty," I whisper.

"And where is this special item of clothing?" There's speculation in her voice. She must not trust my taste in clothes.

"A small store I stumbled upon the other day. It's pretty. You should come with me."

"Fine. We'll head out early." She starts to leave, but then turns back. "Is he coming too?"

"No, guys don't like shopping, right?"

"I wouldn't know." She turns away and the tone of her voice makes me wonder what mood she'll be in when we do go out today.

"You don't want me to come?" Damien asks quietly, his eyes still closed.

"I'd like to surprise you, but I doubt I'll have the opportunity." I run my hand along the corner of his jaw under his ear, and then trace his lips with my finger.

"It's almost dawn," he says, and pulls my knees so I slide down the bed next to him.

Leaning over me, I can feel his cool breath graze my lips. Running my hands through his feathery soft hair, he kisses me slowly and his cold hand runs down my cheek, along my neck, and over my shoulder. When he reaches my waist and slides his fingers under the hem of my shirt my heart skips a beat and I flinch.

"Anna, what's wrong? That's the fourth time."

"I know. I'm sorry." Something about this seems wrong. I've been waiting so long for The Touch to be relieved and now that it is, something's off. What's changed? "You're just so... so cold."

He pulls away from me and sits up, swinging his legs off the bed. He rests his head in his hands. Is he angry with me?

"It's not the cold. I need you to think. I can't fix what Trick did without knowing what it is."

"Who says it has anything to do with Trick?" I'm more defensive than I should be.

"Anna, I'm not stupid."

"I had a bad dream. I'm just a little on edge at the moment, all right? It's not Trick." I have no idea why I'm forcing this.

"Then tell me about the dream. Maybe I can help."

"Well, I remember being a mess. I mean, literally. My clothes are torn, I have one shoe on, and I think there are cob webs in my hair. It's also really dark. I'm scared and this figure looms over me trying to grab my throat. I turn to run but I think I fall down the stairs."

"Who's trying to strangle you?"

"The face is hazy at first. I expect it to be my father, but..."

He waits to for me to continue and when I don't, he says, "But?"

"It's you," I whisper.

He turns to look at me. A mixture of guilt and fear on his face. "Oh, Anna. My sweet Anna, I would never hurt you. I couldn't. I can't."

"I just wish I knew why I was running in the first place. I know you won't hurt me. I don't even really feel like it's you I should be afraid of."

"Why is that?"

"Because in the dream, you're not cold. It's as if you're not really *you*."

He turns away from me to stare at the floor. "And you've never seen Trick in this dream?"

I shake my head. "No."

He scratches his cheek, debating. "If you don't mind, I'm going to see if I can find Sleep Reaper. I have to ask him what this means."

I nod and glance over at the clock. The sun will rise in only a matter of minutes—give or take a second or two. I crawl up behind Damien and kneeling, press myself to his back and wrap my arms around his neck. I kiss his cold ear and say, "Even if you are colder than I can handle right now, I'd still love nothing more than to warm you, heart and soul."

"You always do." He turns to face me and pushes a strand of hair behind my ear. "Anna?"

"Yes?" I meet his gaze and he looks as if he doesn't know how to say what he's thinking. I'm suddenly feeling very nervous.

"I know I've put some pressure on you and I don't want to force you into saying something you don't mean."

"What are you talking about?" I can feel my fluttering heart quiver in my chest. My stomach somersaults with a mix of excitement and fear.

"It's not just the warmth of you that I crave. Not just the feeling of being alive. You're gorgeous, strong-willed, smart, and afraid of nothing. But you're also fragile and have dealt with issues that are not your fault and yet you're paying for them. The first time I collected your soul, I knew you were special. There was something in your eyes that I had never seen in anyone else's. You had hope, peace, and pride. You didn't want to die and it sparked my interest to know why someone would give in with all those emotions bottled inside.

"Every time I spoke to you before you committed suicide, although technically, it's always murder, you've always been so beautiful and reassuring. You were reluctant to end your life, but there was no way to tell you how I felt about you. You never knew who I was. You were never the kind of girl to believe what I had to say. I took a risk this time and I'm glad I did."

I interrupt because I can't stand where this conversation is going. "Stop sounding like you're saying goodbye."

"I'm not saying goodbye, Anna. I'm trying to tell you how important you are to me. How much," his eyes meet mine, "how much I love you."

He's staring at my lips and I know he's waiting to read the words out of mouth and not just hear them.

"Damien, I..." Why can't I say it? I told Trick, of all people. I sit up to push him down on his back. He smiles up at me as I lay my body on top of his. "I'd gladly die if it's the only way we can be together."

"I'd never let that happen, Anna. Never."

I close my eyes and part my lips ever so slightly. I've never wanted to feel his skin against mine as much as I do right now. Leaning in, I'm surprised that my lips never meet his. He's gone and the sun is peering over the horizon, through my windows.

TWO DAYS BEFORE

I can't decide if I should just get out of bed now and start the day or wait here in case Damien comes back. I know he said he was going to look for Sleep Reaper, but how long can that really take? And what happens if he does find him?

Sleeping is futile though and I might as well get up. Grabbing a t-shirt and jeans, I head to the shower. I'm incredibly happy about buying that purple dress and I hope to... Death? it's still there.

Once I'm clean and dressed, I bound down the stairs and find my father standing in the foyer with Ms. Cune. I'm afraid to move or draw any attention to myself. I don't see my mother and fear she isn't awake yet.

"Anna, your mother tells me your boyfriend is taking us out to dinner at Nikolai's Roof," my father says.

"Uh, yeah, I guess." I'm not really sure how right that is exactly, but everyone else always seems to have more information than I do.

"I'll be sure to order the most expensive thing on the menu, if that's the case." He gives me a wry grin which makes me want to punch him.

He turns to walk out the door and it dawns on me that it's only Thursday and he's on his way to work, which leaves me alone with Ms. Cune.

Without making eye contact, I slip past her and down the hall into the kitchen. From the fridge, I grab the orange juice and milk and set them on the counter. Then I pull out a bowl and glass from the cupboard and head to the pantry for cereal. Ms. Cune is blocking the pantry door and I know I'm screwed.

"So Doom is calling himself your boyfriend now?"

"I don't know. He hasn't exactly said that in front of me, so whatever my parents perceive is up to them, now isn't it?"

She doesn't respond except with a sinister smile and I wonder if she's ever going to move so I can eat breakfast. Although I'm not sure how badly I'll need breakfast after she kills me.

"You're quite an interesting girl."

"Thanks," I say, without a care in the world. "Mind if I get some cereal now, or are you going to attack me with your shadow men so that breakfast will be the least of my worries?"

"Don't be so melodramatic, dear. I like to keep things interesting, is all. Watch you squirm like a worm on a hook."

"Oh, I didn't know you cared for fishing. Tell me, why would a demon sorceress, such as yourself, care to use such childish antics? I would think you'd be much more creative with your torture."

"You have no idea, my pet." She takes a step towards me. "A kiss is a dangerous weapon."

"What's that supposed to mean?"

Again she doesn't answer me. She leaves the kitchen and heads to the closet to pull out the vacuum cleaner. As if she really needs that. She should just

212

wave some stupid wand or recite some incantation and make the whole house clean. Well, maybe we don't pay enough for that. What's the going rate for demon house cleaners, anyway?

I open the pantry door, pull out a box of cereal and head over to the counter where my bowl, juice, and milk sit.

I jump with surprise at the sound of rhythmic pounding. This morning is giving my heart quite the workout. Trick is sitting on the counter, banging his boot against the cupboard door. He's rolling something hard and angular between his palms.

"How long have you been there?" I chide.

"Long enough. Hungry?"

"Yes." I move the bowl further down the counter— away from him. "There is no need for you to be here."

"Perhaps."

"So leave!"

"Aye, I will... eventually."

I let out a long deep sigh. Stubbornness must be a prerequisite to becoming a Deathdrifter. I pour my cereal and milk into the bowl, and then pour a glass of orange juice.

"Tell me, how long have ya lived in Georgia?"

"Why, Trick? What's it to you?"

He narrows his brow, trying to find the right words. "Small talk." It sounds like a question in his accent.

I sigh, shove the milk and orange juice back into the fridge and then take everything over to the table.

Staring at him while I eat isn't bothering him the way I'd like it to. "Eleven years," I say.

"Do ya have family 'ere?"

"No."

"What brought yer family to La Grange?"

"Business."

He hops down from the counter and takes the seat across from me at the table. "Anna, please, I'm trying."

"And you're asking questions to all the things you should already know."

"Aye? Says who?"

I drop my jaw to say... something, anything, but nothing is all that comes out. I search his face for any kind of lie or falsity, but he seems sincere and honest. Maybe he doesn't know anything about me. I've gotten used to Damien already knowing me, more than me— Old Me—Other Century Me that I don't care what he likes about me now.

"We moved here from New York," I say. "My dad's business got relocated and he runs this portion of the company. If we'd stayed in New York, he'd be doing a different job all together by now."

"What do ya want to do with yerself? After school, I mean."

"Funny you should ask. Aren't you advocating for my death?"

"Gads, yer cruel. But aye, I guess I am."

I scowl, hoping that he sees I don't condone his humor.

"Well, I *planned* to be a Pulmonologist. Which is why I *hate* smokers."

"Aye," he nods. "Good thing I quit," he says looking so far inside me that I know he's being honest.

"What?"

"Oh, good morning," my mother says as she enters the kitchen.

"Morning." Trick nods his head, without looking at her and lifts a cup of coffee I hadn't noticed to his lips.

"Where's our handsome Mr. Doyle?"

"Damien," I groan, rolling my eyes.

"I donnae know. Errands perhaps," Trick mumbles.

"Oh? Nothing too important, I hope."

"Aye, I'm sure tis important."

"I suppose that means he took Anna's car. I guess I'll be driving today." My mother puts the rim of her coffee mug to her lips and blows the steam away.

"Uh..." He better have. I glance at Trick.

"Aye." Trick answers for me and I hope he's right. "I'll be outside if ya need me, Jo." He leans over the table and whispers to me, "Where're yer keys?"

"In the bag by my bedroom door," I reply in a hush.

Trick looks at my mother. Her back is turned, fussing at the sink. He puts his hand on the table in front of me and says, "Donnae go anywhere without it."

When he walks over to the sink and sets his empty mug next to my mother's I see that he's put my pewter grim reaper on the table before me. I grab it and turn back to the entryway, but all I see is purple vapor in his wake.

"This better not take too long today," my mother grumbles.

Good ol' mom. I was wondering when her grumpy side would return.

I shove the tiny reaper into my pocket. "As long as the dress is still in the store it won't take long at all." I'm not too excited about doing this when she's cranky.

"Fine then. Ready?"

"Yup." I check the window, hoping my car is gone from the driveway. Otherwise I have some serious explaining to do.

THE COLOR OF DEATH

As soon as I step out of the house I see that my car is gone. It's reassuring that Trick followed through but it's also surprising because I don't have a clue where it is. I shrug off any apprehension of what Trick actually did with my car and climb into the passenger seat of my mother's SUV.

Our ride is silent until I start flipping through the stations of the satellite radio this huge excuse for a locomotive has. After enough satellite surfing and hearing my mother grumble about what passes for "good music" we pull into the small strip mall I had described to her.

"Oh, good, it's open." I jump out of the car—almost break my ankle due to how much higher I am in my mother's car than in mine and briskly walk into the store.

"May I help you?" a light, bubbly voice asks.

This is not the same woman from last time. This one is younger. Petite. Pretty.

The door chimes behind me and my mother gets right to the point, "You have some sort of purple dress?

My daughter said she saw something here earlier this week."

The clerk looks deep in thought. "Do you know where it was in the store when you saw it?" she asks me.

"It was on that manikin." I point to the only one the store has today. "Although, right next to it was a cami set I bought, but that manikin is gone."

"Oh, yes! I remember now. I'm changing the clothes on that one in back. I think the dress is still on the restock rack from earlier this week. My mother and I don't have much time to get merchandise back on the floor."

Nice to know, but I really don't care. I watch her walk into the small room where I tried on the cami and dress. Seconds later she returns with the dress in hand.

"Is this it?" the girl beams.

"Yes!" I'm so excited I want to grab it out of her hands.

The dark fabric shimmers in the light and the satin begs for me to run my hands over it. I imagine what it'll feel like to have Damien run his hands over my waist and hips with this cool, soft, and luscious material against my skin.

"Satin?" My mother interrupts my reprieve. "Let me see."

She walks up to the counter and handles the fabric rougher than I like. "This hem is loose." She points to the bottom of the dress where the stitching is frayed. "And there's a small hole along the seam at the waist. Right here on the left. I've never found a fabric to hold up well with poor stitching. Anna," she turns to me, "you'll be lucky to keep this on the whole night."

"I'm hoping not to," I mumble to myself. I think the clerk heard me because I catch a small smile cross her lips.

218

"What was that?" my mother raises her voice as if to demonstrate to me how I should enunciate each syllable out of my mouth.

I sigh but don't say anything in return. My mother always does this. She wants to talk this poor girl down to a cheaper price tag.

"Oh my!" Here it comes. "One fifty? Surely, you can't sell this rag at that price? I'll give you seventy-five for it."

"Ma'am, I can't give you fifty-percent off. I'll be fired."

"Oh, surely your mother won't fire you."

"No, but my grandmother will."

"What can you offer me then?"

"Um, one hundred?"

That sounds great to me. I'm willing to pay fifty if my mother still is.

"Ninety?"

The poor girl can't win. She crinkles up that face of pure, soft skin and pulls her pony tail over her shoulder to pick at the broom-tailed tip. "I suppose I could do ninety."

"You know I'll still be paying over one-fifty for this dress after taking it to a tailor today."

Way to pour on more guilt, Mother.

"I'm sorry, Ma'am," the girl rings up the dress at ninety dollars and to my surprise my mother hands over her credit card.

I feel inclined to slip the poor girl a twenty so that she can tell her grandmother, or mother, or whoever that she didn't go lower than expected, but my mother ruins this thought by saying to me, "You can pay for the tailoring."

Great.

The clerk and I meet eye to eye for a split second and I think I see pity, either that or understanding. I'm not sure which.

219

My mother hands me the garment bag and I see the name of the store for the second time: Rose, Sara, and Fiona's Elegant Apparel.

"Thank you, Fiona," I mumble and follow my mother out the door.

"We're going to my tailor. She'll make sure that dress is worth every penny."

"And then some," I add.

At the tailor's, Mrs. Durmot has me standing in her living room for over an hour.

"The hem and small hole are easy enough, but I'd like to alter the bodice and cut. It'll be magnificent!"

How anyone enjoys sewing this much is beyond me.

"Uh, what do you plan to do?" I ask.

"Don't worry. You'll be beautiful."

I mutter incoherently, feign a smile and try to look at ease.

"You kids and your fashions." She shakes her head and then turns me around to unzip the back of my dress. Apparently, she's done with me.

Mrs. Durmot always does wonderful work for my mother, but sometimes, she just creeps me out.

"I need this for Saturday night so I don't want you to overwhelm yourself," I add.

"Don't be silly, my dear. I have all the time in the world."

From what I've learned this past week, she's got one rude awakening coming.

"What time can I pick it up?"

"I'll call and let your mother know."

"Okay. I'm not sure what time I'm leaving for dinner in Atlanta."

"And reservations are for what time?"

"I don't know."

"Nikolai's Roof?" My mother must have filled her in. "Probably eight and how are you getting there?"

"Driving." It's not like I'm taking a helicopter or anything.

She pats my cheek as if I'm dimwitted. "Is this nice boy picking you up?" The way she says 'boy' makes me cringe. Damien is older than this woman and she's old enough to be my great-grandmother. Thank goodness he's stuck in an eternal age of twenty-three and understands how society has changed through the generations.

"He set this up with my parents, not me," I answer.

"He didn't tell you?" my mother asks.

"Tell me what?"

"You and Damien are going Saturday night. He's having dinner at the house with us tomorrow."

"But just this morning Dad said—"

"You know your father. He'll say anything to get you worked up."

I'm so confused I don't know where to begin with my outrage. Yes, it'll be heaven to have dinner just the two of us, but I was sure he said it would include my parents.

"You look fabulous in purple, dear," Mrs. Durmot says to break my inner turmoil.

"Thank you." I blush, staring into the deep rich purple and thinking of Damien's response when he sees me.

"Odd, though."

"What is?" I ask without looking up from the mesmerizing color.

"Purple is the color of death. What made you choose such a dark and dismal hue?"

"Funny. I thought this was the color of royalty and black was the color of death."

"How many dead people do you see turn black? They turn purple. Red and blue, my dear."

TOUCHLESS TORTURE

Mom and I spent more time with Mrs. Durmot than necessary. Now that we're home, it's dark but I can see two figures sitting on the front porch. One is reclined down the expanse of the steps—feet in the grass and elbows propped on the top step. The other figure, looking smaller and less relaxed, is sitting with his arms propped on his knees—hands clasped tightly.

I jump out of the car, slipping between mine and my mother's as she pulls into the garage. I skip up to the guys. "Hi."

Damien smiles up at me. "Hello," he says, laying on a thick English accent he doesn't need. "Good day?"

"Uh," I groan. "I've never been more embarrassed."

Trick looks up at me with slight amusement. His dark hair hangs in his eyes. "No? What about—?"

"Don't remind me, jerk!" The pool incident is not a memory I want to recall. But since I'm in a good mood because of my dress I attempt to kick him. Trick moves as if he knew what I was doing before I did and fortunately I miss his leg.

"Don't touch him," Damien says.

I furrow my brow. "I thought he had the day to be free and you the night?"

"Aye, but Sir Royal Bawbag over 'ere got his way. Again," Trick says, frustration leaking out between his tight lips.

Damien rolls his eyes but makes no comment.

"I thought you were looking for Sleep Reaper? Isn't Grim the only one who can—"

"The parchment is not under Grim's power—only his supervision. As long as every signed member agrees, it can be manipulated," Damien interrupts me.

"But I didn't agree," I mumble.

"Yer not a Carrier," Trick answers. "And I was... persuaded."

I look around to make sure my mother isn't in the vicinity of our conversation. "Then what's the point?"

"Usually a parchment isn't designed to limit another Carrier's abilities. It gives a Carrier power over other beings—such as ya," Trick says.

"But in this case, power is already divided," Damien continues for Trick, "and so we can ask for another's portion of the parchment to be altered."

"So Life gave you life for tonight through Saturday?" I ask.

"No. Life is under some... restraint and now it's only Saturday that I will be alive. I stay that way if my agreement with Grim is met Saturday night." He means *my* agreement with Grim, which gives D his life back pending I survive past midnight.

Something doesn't quite add up though. Why did Trick lose his freedom from The Touch? "So what'd you do?"

He scuffs his boot against the pavement; not intending to answer me.

I scowl and shrug at Damien who says, "I can't tell you either. No one knows, but we all have ideas."

"What's yours?" Trick and I ask in unison.

Damien hesitates, surprised by our single voice. "I'm guessing you finally got what you had coming."

"Fer?" Trick adjusts his position, placing his elbows on his knees, mirroring Damien.

"Fer," Damien mocks, "getting caught in The Blacklands while Grim was there, which is rare to begin with."

"The Blacklands? Is that what I think it is?"

"Depends," Trick mumbles. "What do ya think it is?"

"Hell."

Both of them laugh. I'm glad I can relieve the tension, but I'm not sure what to make of this boisterous charade. I also don't see the humor in it. I cross my arms and wait for them to stop clutching their stomachs.

"Come, my sweet Anna." Damien tries to keep a straight face while patting the step. "Don't look so upset. We can't really tell you anyway."

"Why not? I know everything else."

"Not even half of it," Trick says, pulling out his cigarettes.

I glare at Trick. "I thought you quit."

"I did!" He looks at the pack and then crushes it in his hand. "Tell her," he says to Damien.

Damien looks annoyed with Trick and seems to be weighing in his head if he wants to tell me or not. He looks at his feet before he stands because I haven't moved to sit beside him. "He's telling you the truth."

I nod but it feels wrong to stare into D's eyes as I accept the truth from him. When I look to the side, Trick isn't even looking at me. He's staring at his hand that holds a crushed pack of cigarettes. Is he regretting his decision?

Damien continues his explanation of The Blacklands as if my concern isn't worth his time. "There are many different interpretations of Heaven and Hell. The Blacklands are... not Hell. Maybe worse than Hell, maybe not." He leans toward me. "Although in there, some pray to be in Hell."

"Then what were you doing there?"

Trick's head snaps up to meet my gaze. "I dinnae—"

"Come, Anna." Damien heads inside the house and as I cross the threshold, I feel a burst of cold on my face.

Everything is dark and before me stands Damien with a black and gold scythe skewered through his stomach. Reaching out to me, his fingers covered in warm blood, he grazes my throat. From behind him, I see Trick and Nastusia surrounded by those dark shadows that chanted to me in the hotel and in my living room. The shadows come forward to overtake me. I turn to run, but fall down the stairs.

"Anna! Anna!"

I open my eyes and Damien is holding me in his arms. I'm wrapped in a blanket and his skin is carefully covered. Apparently, it's not late enough for him to touch me.

"What happened?" I look around to see my mother standing over Damien. Trick leaning against the wall so as not to come in contact with my mom, but he looks as if he's been shunned.

"You fainted, Anna. Are you all right?"

"This can't be," I whisper to myself.

My eyes meet Trick's and I'm bombarded by images that make no sense to me—images that come from another time altogether. Is this his fault? He was standing *with* Nastusia, wasn't he? It was his scythe skewered through Damien. Was he attacking her and missed? Did Damien get in the way? I try to recall the look on their faces, the stance they had, anything. But the vision is fading fast.

"Who are you?" I ask Trick. "Why are you here?"

"To punish me," Damien mumbles and I know he'd elaborate if it wasn't for my mother standing over him.

"Damien, I saw..." Now I don't know what I saw. It's in my head but I can't put any of the images into words.

I stare at Trick and he fidgets. He's tense and uncomfortable.

"She needs to lie down," Damien tells my mother.

"She should eat something," my mother adds, sounding carefree and completely unlike herself.

"Tea. It'll calm her." He scoops me up in his carefully covered arms and my mother disappears into the kitchen.

I blink and Trick is gone along with the images I can't recall.

"Tell me everything, Anna," Damien whispers in my ear and all I really want is for him to hold me. To keep me safe. But it's him that needs to be kept safe. It's him that will die on Saturday. I bring nothing but pain and sorrow to everyone. Everyone dies around me. Some doctor I would've made.

I tell Damien what I can remember about the vision and he looks concerned.

"Perhaps you should get Life Reaper to rescind his favor on Saturday."

"No."

"But—" I start.

"I'm not worried about me. I'm concerned about why you're having these visions."

"What do you mean?"

There's a knock on the door and my mother comes in with a cup of tea and toast.

"Here, Anna. How are you feeling?"

"Fine," I say without any emotion. "I'm not sick, Mother."

"I know." She glances toward Damien as if they know something I don't.

"She'll be fine." He reassures my mother with a smile and gentle nod. Keeping his arms crossed, he turns his shoulder to her as she approaches him.

"Do you think Saturday is still a good idea? If she's not..." she lowers her voice, "better, then perhaps going to Atlanta is—"

"Mother!" I can't believe she's doing this. It's only Thursday evening. Most people are just sitting down to dinner and she's acting like I'm traveling to Europe for the week. "I'm fine and one night for dinner isn't going to kill me." At least dinner won't be the cause, anyway.

"Well, if you're sure. Mrs. Durmot called and said everything will be ready tomorrow evening. Cameron said he'd take you to pick it up around five." My mother gives a sidelong glance at Damien and turns to leave the room.

Damien takes my tea and puts it on my desk saying, "Don't bother with this. It's not brewed correctly."

"I forgot. I wanted to ask you about dinner. This morning my father asked me about you and dinner..." I hesitate in order to remember the exact wording. "He said, 'If your boyfriend is paying for dinner, I'll order the most expensive dish.' Or something like that."

"Oh? Did he?" Damien is repressing a smile. I can see it in his dark, mysterious eyes.

"Then today my mother said he was just giving me a hard time and our *family* dinner is tomorrow."

He stares at me as if I already know the answer, but the only problem is that he doesn't know the question.

"I wanted to surprise you, but I suppose that's been ruined."

I scowl. I'm trying to figure out how to ask this without sounding like a complete idiot.

"Surprise? I don't understand. At dinner tomorrow I would think I'd have figured it out."

"Things never go as planned with you. I know—I have six hundred years of experience."

"Well, dinner plans aside. I'd like to clarify something else entirely."

"All right." Damien makes himself comfortable at my desk and I square myself toward him on the bed, pushing my cold unappetizing toast aside.

"I didn't bring up my father's point of speech as an introduction to my mother ruining your surprise."

Damien smiles. "No?"

He's making me drag this out. I can tell.

"No." I try not to smile back, but I can't win against that perfect, masculine face—definitely not the face of Death.

He leans toward me, but doesn't make any contact. I can feel his cold radiating on my face and time couldn't move any slower until we're relieved of this agonizing, touchless torture.

My lips part and I'm beginning to forget what it is we're talking about.

"Then tell me, Anna. Why did you bring it up?"

He knows. And he's enjoying this too much.

"Are you..." I try to clear my head, but when I open my eyes I stare into the crystal darkness of his and my breath catches in my throat. "Are you my boyfriend?" I rush out the last word. One I've never used aloud and begin to feel a mixture of emotions: fear, excitement, dread, embarrassment, and uncertainty.

I'm anxious to know what the title of this relationship is. Girl and Death? Deathlovers? Death with benefits? These thoughts are agony.

"Interesting word: Boyfriend." I don't want to look at him while he forces me to wait out his answer. "Society is bizarre. One word can mean so many different things and yet everyone knows which you mean based on the context."

"Damien," I breathe a ragged breath, "stop."

"Anna. Look at me, please." I slowly turn to face him. "You know exactly how I feel. Whatever title anyone wants to use is fine with me."

"I'm not..."

But I can't finish my sentence, let alone my thought because my father is standing in my doorway, gasping for air, drenched in a foul smelling liquid. Gasoline?

And he looks angry—sorry, *livid*.

ONE DAY
BEFORE

I'm frozen in place. My chest burns and is tight with every inhalation. The smell of gas is so overwhelming that my eyes and nose are stinging and my head is throbbing.

"Get out," my father orders.

"No," Damien says. "I'm not leaving you alone with her."

"I wasn't talking to you."

My father squares his shoulders to Damien and puffs out his chest. He must think he's got some kind of power over a Deathdrifter—one that hasn't lost his abilities yet.

"Stay right there, Anna. Don't listen to him."

I want to say something but the words seem to be lodged in my throat.

"I'm not going to stand by while you scratch your itch with *my* daughter!"

"Dad!" I can't believe I just heard that.

He takes one step toward Damien. I reach out for my father's arm and yell, "Don't touch him!"

I know it sounds like I'm trying to protect him, but even though my father has been abusive and neglectful; he's still my only father.

"He can touch me if he wants, Anna," Damien says, his arms locked across his chest.

"No," I whisper. Just because I don't have the once-upon-a-time-fairy-tale relationship with my parents doesn't mean I want them dead.

"Nothing will happen if he touches me." Damien tries to sound reassuring. I'm not buying it.

"Oh, something will happen all right." My father pushes up his shirt sleeves.

"No. Please, don't fight," I beg.

"He's not your father, Anna. Your father has been stuck inside that shell of a monster for sixteen years—longer if you count the curse reincarnations. I can stop him, but I can't kill him. Nastusia has made sure of that."

My father reaches out for Damien, but I extend my arm and latch onto his elbow. He shifts his weight and with all his force pushes me to the floor.

I must have hit my head on the corner of the TV stand because a warm tickling sensation runs down the side of my face.

"Anna!"

"I'm fine," I mutter, wiping away the blood.

I pull myself onto my knees and try to stand. Pain hammers away at my skull and I lose balance before I'm even up off my knees.

I hear a loud smack and look up. My father spits blood on my carpet. Good. Nastusia can clean that up too.

"Touch me again, boy, and I'll have your head on a stake in my front lawn."

"Touch *her* again and you can bet on losing more than *your* head, Demon," Damien growls between clenched teeth.

"Demon?" I'm not finding Damien's pet name comforting. And I certainly hope it's only a pet name.

"Been to The Blacklands lately, boy?" My father's eyes turn a searing red. His skin looks like it's literally coiling off the bone. I crawl around the side of my bed, away from them, and on second look, it's not his skin that's moving but black lines that are forming on his arms and reaching up his neck.

"Not since Grim... not for about six hundred years." Damien scowls.

"Perhaps you should pay us another visit." My father grabs Damien's wrist and they disappear.

I'm alone.

I've stared at the clock ever since they left.

Half past two.

In the morning, no less.

It's Friday. Tomorrow's my birthday, excuse me, my deathday, and I have no idea where Damien or my father is. I'm assuming they're in The Blacklands, based on their conversation, but how am I going to find them?

Trick hasn't been back since I collapsed from my vision and Nastusia hasn't shown herself either. Not like she'd tell me where they are, anyway. I just hope she hasn't killed them.

Is that possible?

Can you even kill a Deathdrifter? It never occurred to me to ask. My vision showed me that Damien will die but that's because Life Reaper will grant him his life back tomorrow.

Can he be tortured? I suppose anything is possible in The Blacklands.

So how do I get there?

Unanswered questions jumble through my brain and sleep is beyond happening now.

I wish I could talk to Grim. He should know about this. Hope swells inside me all of a sudden.

Grim.

He must know. He's got to be searching for Damien. He'd never let anything happen to *his* Doom Reaper, right?

My stomach growls and I realize that toast, as picked at as it was, isn't tiding me over.

Creeping down the stairs so I don't disturb my mother, I see a shadow quickly pass by the living room window.

"Hello?" I whisper. "Trick?"

"Mornin' darlin'."

Startled, I slip down two steps before righting myself. "Morgan?"

"Bit of a mess you're in here, isn't it?"

"What do you want?" Morgan isn't exactly my idea of a welcome guest. He's creepier than the other Reapers. To me, anyway.

"Don't be rude, darlin'. I'm here to help."

"What?" Sitting down is the only way to relieve the shock of hearing Blood Reaper offer his help.

"I said—"

"I heard you! I want to know *what* you mean."

"We don't have much time. Catch."

A small red ball flies straight at my face. I shut my eyes as I catch it. Opening my eyes, the room is pitch black. I can't even see my hand in front of my face.

"Morgan? I can't see."

I hear him mumble a strange word and the ball in my hand glows red. The blackness is thick and the red light tints my hands and clothes. And his face.

"Where are we?"

A wry smile hints across Blood Reapers lips. "The waiting room."

THE
BLACKLANDS

Sitting on the floor, or what feels like the floor since I can't see or feel anything but darkness, I spin the red ball of light in front of me. It looks suspended, but doesn't exactly float, either.

Strange.

"How long do we wait?" I ask.

"Until we're allowed in, darlin'."

"So, five minutes... five years?"

"Give or take."

"You're awfully cheery for a Reaper who's obsessed with..."

"Death?" he raises his eyebrows, fighting a laugh, which only makes Morgan look creepier.

"Murder," I half mumble, half chide.

"Oh. Yeah. Interesting, isn't it? Do you know all the possible ways to kill someone?"

He's goading me.

"No. And I don't want to know. I've experienced enough death already and I don't want to talk about it." For all I know, Doom is already dead. Again. And my father could be a demon forever—and might as well be dead too, I suppose.

"Okay, darlin'. We won't."

"Stop with the pet name already. I'm Anna."

"I thought you liked hearing your name coming from one particular heart-stopping voice?"

Now he's mocking me.

My jaw drops. "Who told you that?" It was only a passing thought. Brief. And a comparison to how I've heard it coming from my father's angry tone.

"Is Jo more acceptable?" He laughs at my sudden discomfort. "All right, *Anna*. It's time." He shifts his weight and I now realize that this whole time, he'd been leaning on... nothing?

"I changed my mind," I say in a gruff tone. "Don't call me anything."

"Come on... *darlin'*."

I don't find Morgan amusing at all.

I can't tell how long we've been walking in total darkness. It could have been five minutes or five... years?

Morgan slows and after another ten paces, or so, he stops. I slam right into his back. Luckily, he doesn't feel the need to catch me from falling on my ass.

"Little warning next time," I deadpan, getting back on my feet.

"Shh."

Normally, I would say something after being shushed; but in this case, I figure it's better to just keep quiet.

"Welcome home," a deep malicious voice booms throughout. It rattles my chest as if I were hollow.

"I don't actually miss this place," Morgan says over his shoulder.

"This was your home?"

"Is there a better candidate to fill a Blood Reaper's shoes than a murderer? Grim came here to collect me."

"Let me guess, almost eight hundred years ago?"

"Could be. Or maybe it's twelve hundred. Your guess is as good as mine."

Without diminishing, the blackness becomes brighter and we're surrounded by cliffs, ravines, stalactites, and stalagmites. The ground is gritty as if there is a light dusting of black sand. It glitters even though there isn't a light source. The walls seem to stretch out, further and further, with every step I take. The air is thick, choking me if I breathe too deeply. It doesn't help that everything is tinged in red. Or is it blood?

It's not hot but I'm sweating as if it is. My heart beats so hard I'm sure I'd faint if it weren't for the slight cool that radiates off Morgan's body. There's a sound of rushing water and the smell of gasoline is stronger here than when my father stood in my room. I hear some people like this smell, but it just makes me sick.

"He's over there. Quick." Morgan's gait increases.

"How do you know?" I pick up my pace and feel even more lightheaded than before.

"We always know where our brothers are." He sounds confused, but not because of my question. He must see something that I can't.

"What's that sound?"

"Screaming souls," he says. "Haunters."

I recall Trick telling me about the souls that the Chests won't keep—the lost, forgotten ones.

Peering around Morgan I can see my father sitting on a rock carved to look like an officious chair. He has Damien's scythe resting on his shoulder; the blade swaying behind his head.

"What took you so long? Nastusia's been waiting," my father, the demon, says condescendingly.

"Tomorrow. I have until midnight tomorrow!" I shout.

Morgan's hand glows and his black and red scythe blazes into existence. He twists the end into the dirt and the gleam from the blade dances on my father's face. There's still no light source to cause the reflection, but my father squints from the blinding light.

"Release Doom. The last thing you want is a war with Grim," Morgan says.

Nastusia appears from the mouth of a dark crevice behind a stalagmite and stands next to my father. She runs her long red nails through his hair. "That old man's insignificant runts will never come close to my power."

She doesn't look like the cleaning lady that my mother and I have come to hate. Nastusia's skin looks to be a deeper bronze, her jet black hair is in ringlets on her head and framing her face. Bright red eyes glow in the darkness and her teeth... no, fangs, shine.

My father stands up and Nastusia takes the seat he just vacated. The black layers of her dress drape around her legs, revealing her stiletto heals and curvy legs.

"Soon I'll be Queen of The Blacklands and your father will be King," she says to me.

Normally, people beam with excitement while announcing their success—especially evil villains, but not Nastusia. She pronounces her takeover as if she's been the queen forever and has already tired of it. Almost like she's finished her To-Do list and figures she might as well start from the top and redo the whole list.

"Child, you have fought my pull for too long. It used to be so simple to persuade you to take your own life. Now, you think you're strong; you think you have help, but I'll make you a deal—since you're so open to making them with Grim. Give yourself to me as a sacrifice to my divine power and I'll release your... boyfriend."

Divine?

I shake my head. The word 'no' just won't pass my lips.

"Anna." My name on sweet lips carries over the deep ravine on my right. "Sweet Anna, don't give in. I can't watch you die. Not again. Please?" Damien sounds pained—almost on the verge of giving up.

From where I'm standing, I can barely make Damien out in the darkness. He doesn't move. I believe he's slumped over, back against a rock or something big. It's like he's locked in a stasis. I'm not even sure he can lift his head, but he must hear us, otherwise how would he know I'm here?

This is wrong.

"Morgan?" I whisper.

"Huh?"

"If I distract her, can you free Damien?"

"Hmm." He takes forever to consider.

"Just answer the question."

"Yes."

Walking up to my father, all I can do is hope.

"Father?"

Red eyes peer down at me. A sinister smile of fangs greet me.

"Dad, I'm sorry."

Brown specks break through the red of his eyes. For a second he's my dad before Nastusia came into our lives. "For what, honey?"

The red returns and I stomp on his foot. As he bends over I force all my weight into him and we both barrel into the ravine.

I guess I didn't plan this through to the end. For all I know, we could very well be in the middle of the earth and lava could be flowing at the bottom. Although based on the smell, I bet it's gasoline.

I hear Damien shout my name as we plummet. And as I had hoped, we didn't hit lava, or rock, or gasoline, or anything. Nastusia won't let anything happen to my father—to her king. In turn, I hope he won't let anything happen to me.

Clinging to my father, Nastusia floats mere inches away from our hovering bodies. "Did you really think I would let you die today?"

239

"Of course not. I never agreed to be your sacrifice."
I smile. Damn, I'm bold.

"Why are you so happy?"

"You'll see."

And as if on cue, Damien Flashes above us, collects me in his gentle embrace, and then I'm surrounded in blackness again.

"Don't ever do that again," Damien grumbles. Setting me down on nothing, he leans down to kiss me, but I recoil—afraid to die from his touch. He let's out a deep sigh, "I owe you more than life itself, Anna."

"And what do you owe me, Doom?" Blood Reaper asks, leaning against the blackness, tossing his red ball of light high into the air.

SNIP AND TEAR

The blackness fades and it's as if I never left the living room. The sun glares in through the windows. The clock chimes four times and I realize I'm going to be late picking up my dress.

"Stay here." I eye Damien.

"He can't. He has to report the trip to Grim."

"Trip? What trip? You make it sound like he went on vacation. *We,*" I point, indicating Morgan and myself, "went without authorization. *He* was taken!"

Damien scratches his cheek. "Not really my idea of a holiday."

I'm glad he's so amused by all this.

"Doesn't matter, darlin'. We still went. Grim won't be happy even if it was unintended."

"Fine, but I want him back here before I get back."

"Any other demands?"

I think Morgan is being rhetorical but I do have one thing to add. "Tell Grim I want more time."

"More time?" Morgan asks, his eyebrows drawn together.

"Touch," Damien says and turns Morgan from the room to leave.

"I'll take care of it, darlin'."

I cross my arms and watch the purple smoke replace them.

Heading upstairs, I hear my mother yell from her bedroom for my father.

"He's not home," I yell back, then grumble, "like always."

"Damn him." My mother mumbles more obscenities and then emerges from the bedroom, bourbon in hand.

"I'm heading out to pick up the dress. What time is dinner?"

"Eight. What do you want?" she asks as if she'll only consider my suggestion and not really intend to make it.

"Whatever. Damien should be here soon. Ask him what he wants." She'll make anything his heart desires.

I can't hear her retort since I'm hurrying to shower and change. I smell like gasoline and slipping into the hot water makes me groan because I don't have the time to adjust the temperature before scalding myself.

Quickly, I wrap a towel around me. Leaving my dirty clothes and toiletries in the bathroom, I'm slapped by the cold of my room.

"Back so soon?" I ask as I pull open my closet door and grab a sweatshirt.

"Aye, tis true, then?"

The voice startles me. I wasn't expecting Trick to be in my room even though my mother told me he'd be going with me to pick up the dress. I guess I expected him to stand me up.

"We didn't have a choice." I feel defensive. What's Trick so upset about anyway?

He makes a sound as if he's clearing his throat. "Tis assumed that I was there and disciplined fer it. Ya three go and get praised fer... fer I donnae know what."

242

I sigh. This is a lost cause. "Are you coming or not? I'm already late."

"Aye." He reaches out, wraps his arm around me and before I can say one word we're standing on the steps of Mrs. Durmot's house.

Damien had just told me, not even twelve hours ago, not to touch Trick and here I am alive and well. If it wasn't for that fainting vision I had of Trick's scythe through Damien while standing next to Nastusia, I might be more inclined to call Trick a liar and beat him into a pulp. Although, this new bit of information could pay off later.

"You can touch me?" I'm shocked.

He nods as if I asked him a stupid question. "Can ya keep a secret?'

"Sure."

"Good, because Doom donnae know."

Mrs. Durmot opens the door before I can ask Trick anything else.

"Uh," I'm caught off guard, "good evening, Mrs. Durmot. How are you?"

"Good. Good. Come in. Come in." She sounds tired and older than the wisps of gray hair sneaking out from her tight bun indicate.

The room is darker than yesterday. It looks as if she lost a needle and tore the house apart to find it. Talk about a haystack. I wonder if she works under these conditions all the time or if she took on too much with this dress.

"I hope you didn't work all night." I smile, trying to show my appreciation for all her hard work.

Seeing how she glances at Trick, she interprets my smile all wrong. He better keep his mouth shut.

"Behind the privacy screen, dear-y. I need to make sure it fits properly."

Hanging on the back of the screen; the purple satin shimmers even in the dim light of the room. Every time

I look at this dress I fall in love with it all over again. I can't wait to see Damien's reaction when I wear it.

"The way you watch that screen, young man, one would think you could see right through it," Mrs. Durmot says to Trick.

I wonder the same thing considering the time he supposedly watched me change my clothes.

"I cannae," Trick states.

"I know that," Mrs. Durmot says and her feet shuffle to another spot in the room.

Trick whispers, "Anna, hurry up. I'm serious, I cannae see anything other than yer shadow. I donnae make the same mistake twice."

I frown. Why would he say that if he's not watching me? With my back to the screen and facing the wall, I slip off my sweatshirt and quickly slide the smooth material over my head.

The dress drapes in all the right places. For a woman of Mrs. Durmot's age, I'm surprised that she would cut this dress so low. When she said alterations, I didn't know she meant remake the entire thing. Instead of straight, the dress flares out. The bodice is a design based on a corset which laces up the front. The neckline is square with small cuffed sleeves. My waist looks so tiny that my hips look huge. Mrs. Durmot also added black velvet. I feel like I just stepped back in time. Taking a deep breath, I step out from behind the privacy screen.

Trick swallows, staring at me.

I blush.

"Beautiful," Mrs. Durmot says. "I do fabulous work."

"Aye, ya do," Trick mumbles and I don't think he's blinked yet.

"Pick up your chin, boy." Mrs. Durmot wrinkles up her face. "I'll be right back." She scuttles from the room.

Trick finally takes his eyes off me for half-a-second to see Mrs. Durmot disappear down the hall.

"Sweet Jesus, yer gorgeous, Jo."

"Thanks." I avert eye contact.

"Doom donnae deserve ya." His voice is raw and he takes slow steps toward me.

Awkwardly, I step back, but the screen stops me. "And you do?" I squint at him.

The satin of this dress is so thin it feels like I'm wearing nothing at all. Trick's hands rest on my hips. The coolness of his body causes me to shiver and as if my shiver is caused by desire and not the cold, he inclines his body closer to mine.

"Trick, don't," I whisper.

He's not listening. Staring at my lips, he runs his thumb over my cheek, his fingertips resting on the vertebra of my neck.

"Last time was fer him. This one's fer me." His lips touch mine and I freeze. I should be pushing him away; yelling at him.

But...

He's so strong and yet gentle. And surprisingly not too cold. Before I know it, I'm kissing him back. His hands slowly trace down my sides—thumbs caressing every rib, palms curving around my waist and hip bones. The shivers down my spine increase and not because he's cold. I place my hands on his neck, holding his jaw. He presses against me and his hands and lips become more urgent—reminding me that I'm not kissing Damien.

I start to get lost in him, but then I see a new face. The face I see isn't the one of the girl I've seen before when Trick's touched me. It's a face in a mirror on a wall. It's Trick's face—no, Cameron's. He looks lost. And surprisingly adorable. His hair is still slightly in his eyes, but it's a deep, reddish-brown—like cinnamon. His eyes are like green grass. Under his dinner jacket is a plaid sash with a gold pin that I can't make out in the reflection. My head vibrates with words I don't understand, but they're sincere.

Mrs. Durmot suddenly interrupts us. "I know she's stunning, young man, but you can wait until tomorrow for your date."

"He's not—" I stop. In this case I think I'd appear like a harlot to Mrs. Durmot if I told her he's not my date—not my boyfriend.

"Sorry, Ma'am." Trick releases me and I pretend to fix my dress as Mrs. Durmot steps in front of me.

"Close your eyes," she commands.

I obey and hear a snip and tear. My legs feel cold and I look down and gasp.

"Why did you do that?" I'm heart broken. Mrs. Durmot has just turned my long, flowing, satin dress into garbage.

"This is much better. I'll just add velvet in front so I can bustle the excess." Excess? "Oh, and I have the perfect necklace." She hurries away.

We're alone.

Again.

"Donnae look so upset. I think she's right."

"Trick, can I..." I reach up and brush his hair aside so it lies across his forehead instead of in his eyes. "Did we... did I know you in a past life?"

"No." He pulls himself away.

"You're sure?"

"I donnae know."

"Yes, you do. Please, tell me. I have to know."

His lip curls up in one corner. My heart thumps as he steps even closer to me this time.

"No, Trick. Stay there," I force out, pointing at his chest as if I can control his movement.

"Ya donnae sound sure of yerself."

"Yeah, well, sorry. I shouldn't have—"

"Anna?" he interrupts me.

"What, Trick?" I stare him in the eyes and try to be as cold and unemotional as possible.

"Call me Cameron."

"No."

"Ya know," he takes one of my hands and presses it firmly against his cheek, "I'd never hurt ya, Jo. Ever. But ya need to understand—"

"Okay, here it is." Mrs. Durmot has perfect timing.

Trick looks frustrated and uneasy. He paces behind Mrs. Durmot and looks as if he's late for something.

Mrs. Durmot shoves into my hands a pearl necklace with the most beautiful and biggest amethyst cut into a starburst I've ever seen.

"My husband gave that to me a very long time ago. Here, you have it."

"Mrs. Durmot, no. I can't."

"Shush. Here. Here." She pushes the jewel into my hand. Now take that off so I can run it quickly through my sewing machine."

CONFLICTED

Slipping back behind the privacy screen, I change as fast as possible. After I bring out the dress, Mrs. Durmot leaves the room to make more adjustments. Trick and I sit in silence. I feel awkward, and Trick's face is a mix of indecision and... nervousness? I don't think I've ever seen him like this.

"So, um, will you tell me about us? The us you remember."

"What do ya want to know?"

"Do you remember the first time we met?"

"Aye. We were in town. I was waiting fer me father."

Trick tells me about how embarrassed he felt being caught by a friend of mine as he stared at me. "I recall ya sayin' that just because people say me grandfather killed fer a living dinnae mean I'd inherit the business." I smile, thinking about how humorous it is that that's exactly what he does now—sort of.

Apparently someone dared me to go talk to him; seeing as how I was so open to him being a respectable person. He claimed that he was shy in life and didn't talk much because people rarely understood his heavily accented English. I had apparently invited him to my birthday party, saying that he could bring a sibling, friend... fiancée. I swallow harder than I expect hearing him tell me this story. But apparently he only smiled and nodded at my invite, something he became accustomed to since no one ever understood him.

"I guess I was nicer in that life," I say, apologetically.

He smirks. "If I wanted a nice lass, Jo, I wouldn't be here."

I place my chin in my hand and prop my elbow on the chair's arm. "Is that your only memory of me?"

"Gads, no."

"Which one do you remember most often?"

He turns his head. "I cannae tell ya." Cameron's embarrassed? Unbelievable.

"Oh, come on. You can't say that and expect me to let it go. Tell me, please?" I fake a pout.

"No."

I slide to the edge of my seat, placing my finger on his knee and run it up and down, trying to entice him. He stares at my hand. "Cam, please? I really want to know."

His eyes meet mine through his shaggy, unkempt hair. "Ya called me Cam..."

I nod once and smile a tiny bit.

He leans toward me. "Take me hand."

My nose feels stuffy with dust. A bitter wind tickles my toes, peeking out from under an old, wool blanket. I am short of breath. My heart is thundering like a raging storm and a nameless heat flutters at the base of my stomach. My legs are feeble. My whole body is crying to stay put and never move again despite the heavy weight pressing down on me. It is smooth and warm. I cannot cease skimming my fingers over the taut planes of my broad-shouldered love.

Nothing else in this world matters.

Suddenly a loud bang resounds from the room below and I start. A heavy accent shouts in a language I do not know.

Light breaks into the room and I open my eyes to see Cameron looking in the direction of what I long to be a threshold with a door. He replies in the same language and then peers down at me; wrapped in his arms. Adjusting his weight over me, he succeeds minutely at alleviating my discomfort.

With a kiss upon my nose, and a single stroke to remove the hair from my face, he appears to be pondering intently.

"Am I being dismissed?" I ask him.

He nods slowly before pushing his face into my neck.

"You must get off me, love."

He shakes his head slowly, causing his lips to graze my collarbone. I can feel his smile. He has no intent on releasing me—not that I mind. "Will," *he hesitates and I strain to comprehend his attempt at English,* "ya—"

"Return?" *I interrupt then curse myself for not being more patient with him.* "I cannot, but after the morrow. I promise."

Cameron nods once then sits up, his expression a little poignant, before rolling over to dig through a bag lying beside the mattress. I sit up to gather my dress from the floor. After sticking my arms through the sleeves and retying the corset, I flatten my hair with my hands. I smile, not a single regret washes over me for what I have committed despite my upbringing. Cameron presses against my back and reaches around me, holding his hand out. The light catches a speck of glass atop a gold band. I gasp and cover my mouth with both hands.

Cameron repeats himself with less hesitancy. "Will ya?"

"Oh, Cam" *I right myself.* "You know they do not approve of you."

251

My heart fills with regret as his arms fall away from me. He turns the small ring between his fingers, nodding slowly. I am a dreadful person. Why do I care what anyone deems appropriate?

"I am sorry."

He lies down as if attempting to sleep.

"Now, now. I hate to see you so wretched." I kneel on the uneven floor to meet his eye level. "I love you, Cam. Do not lose hope. I will persuade them."

He leans in to whisper something I do not understand. When he says, "Gu brath" my heart skips.

I lace my hands into his hair as he leans over the edge of the bed to press his lips to mine. I know I will not make it home anytime soon.

When I open my eyes I'm back in Mrs. Durmot's living room. Trick is looking at me as if he's expecting me to yell at him.

"That's the one you recall the most? Why did it seem like it was my memory and not yours?" He looks confused, as if he doesn't understand what I mean. "Never mind."

His eyes search my face. "We'd been sneaking around behind yer parents' back fer a month, but that was the first time we... slept together."

My breath catches and my heart leaps. "I couldn't see you the next day because it was my birthday, wasn't it?"

"Aye." He looks down, closing his eyes as if the last thing he wants is to think of my death.

"Does Damien know?" I wince, wishing I hadn't said that.

He shrugs. "I donnae know. Tis likely."

I'm not sure Damien really knows how close Cameron and I were. Damien may have disapproved of Cameron like my parents did or he could have "dropped in" on me at any time.

"You were learning English. What language did you speak before?"

"Gaelic."

"You don't anymore?"

"Tis ya who donnae. I worked hard to get rid of me accent but I cannae. Me father was furious, but I dinnae care. I wanted ya. I still do."

I'm conflicted. Am I in love with Damien or with Cameron? I want to tell Cam I want him too. I want to say that I feel the way I did two hundred years ago when I was in that bed with him. But when I open my mouth I don't get the chance.

HORRID
MEMORIES

"Here you go." Mrs. Durmot gives me a big white box almost an hour after she cut the front of it open. "Enjoy your dinner." She smiles.

"Thank you." I hand her a check, which I think is a little on the steep side after she just shredded my dress in half.

Once the front door is closed behind us, Trick wraps his arms around my waist from behind me.

"Anna," he says.

I freeze in place. Trick makes me nervous when he holds me. But not scared. I close my eyes, knowing I should pull away.

I can feel the hesitation in his body. The vision I saw of us together makes me long for a past I can't remember. "What are you doing to me?" I ask, unable to breathe.

"Donnae die fer me and donnae live fer him."

"That doesn't leave me with a lot of options."

"Do what ya need to but do it fer yerself. No one else."

"I thought you wanted—"

"I was ready to let ya go once, now that yer 'ere, I donnae know if I can again. I donnae think I can carry ya off."

"Cam..."

In the blink of an eye I'm back in my bedroom.

I try to take one step forward but Trick doesn't release me. He buries his nose into my hair and a guttural desire escapes him. Closing my eyes, I know I shouldn't be enjoying this.

"I thought you couldn't touch anyone?" Damien asks, standing up from the chair at my desk. "Come, my sweet. As you've asked, The Touch has been relieved early."

"Doom," Trick says as if all the air is being pulled from his lungs. I guess I'm not the only one surprised to see him.

"You bloody lied to me, you dim bastard. Why?"

"I... I wasn't going to hurt her." He sounds upset. Heartbroken. And because of my indecision, I feel guilty.

"Fan-bloody-tastic. I am now reassured." He throws his hand in the air and paces in the small area before my desk. "If anything ever happens to her, I'm holding you one-hundred-percent liable." Venom laced with every word.

"Is that so? And am I responsible fer the next skelpin' her father gives her?"

"You certainly are!"

"Am I responsible if ya kill her..."

Damien grunts. He's not answering that, apparently.

There's a silence in the room that even death can't describe. I shiver. Trick loosens his grip, but keeps me wrapped in his protective arms.

"Am no' lying to her and trying to confuse her," Trick says through clenched teeth. "Ya donnae deserve her. And I'm sure ya haven't told her about yer early days as a Carrier."

"That was a long time ago. And no longer represents who I am. I paid for my mistakes."

"Then tell her the truth. See if she still wants ya afterward."

"Truth?" I ask.

Damien glares at Trick. "Why are you doing this?"

"She deserves to know."

"Fine, I'll tell her. Let her go."

"Tell her how ya got yer name, Doom. I hope, fer yer sake, she donnae come runnin' to me fer safety."

"That's exactly what you hope," Damien growls. "Now let her go. She's afraid."

"Actually, I'm just confused," I mumble.

"Tis not me fault, Anna." Trick looks at Damien. "Tell her what ya did to me!"

"I said you have to let her go first."

Trick reluctantly lets me go. I stand equal distance between them. Damien reaches for me but I brush him away. I can't choose sides.

"Ya ought to come with me, Anna. Doom's temper can be fatal. As I said, he donnae deserve yer forgiveness or yer love."

"Someone just tell me what's going on already," I say, annoyed.

"I took him," Damien mumbles.

"Okay, isn't that your job?" I'm still confused.

"He wasn't on my List."

I look over at Trick, who's slouched against the wall and appears lost and defenseless.

"Oh, Damien. Why?"

Poor Cameron. And that poor girl... poor... me.

"It wasn't my fault either. *He* touched *me*. I didn't know he was there."

"Gads, just tell her what ya stole from me." Trick sounds tired. Depressed.

"I can't steal what you didn't own!" Damien leans toward Trick and glares as if taunting him.

257

"But I might've had a chance!" Trick pushes himself up from his slouched position. "I can still try!"

"Please don't fight," I beg, quietly.

"And now you're dead. Deal with it!"

I stare at Damien, shocked that he'd say something so rude. Glancing at Trick, he begs me with his eyes for something but I don't know what.

Damien puts his hands on my waist and I startle. "Clear off, Trick. Now. And if anything happens to Anna, I'm coming for you first. That's a promise."

"Dinner!" My mother's voice calls from downstairs, curbing the arrogant testosterone clashing in the room.

Trick glances at me again, his dark eyes lingering on Damien's hands. He still looks pained before he disappears as Damien turns me to wrap me in his arms.

"Should I be concerned?" I look up to meet Damien's gaze but he hasn't taken his eyes off the spot Trick once stood in.

"Probably."

"Then you better tell me about your past so I can dismiss all the crazy ideas I have brewing in my head."

"Later. Your mum called."

"She can wait."

He scowls and releases a full breath. Was that for show? He doesn't need to do that.

"My first two hundred or so years of being a Deathdrifter were... rough for me."

"I'm sure they were very difficult."

"You don't understand."

"No, I don't. Go on."

"The living take years to grieve before moving on. Deathdrifters take centuries." Is he trying to insinuate that Trick is still grieving? That eventually he'll get over me? "I thought... I thought that Deathdrifters were unnecessary. I started as a helper to Grim. He lost the first Blood Reaper to The Blacklands for disorderly behavior. Morgan can be... difficult, but he's nothing like that

Reaper was. Grim chose Morgan and even he's been locked away in The Blacklands numerous times for... reconditioning."

"Worse than you?"

"Me? I've never done what any Blood Reaper has done. They're murderers, Anna. In life and in death."

"Were you ever reconditioned?"

"Yes."

"Tell me." I place my hands on his chest and watch him stare past me into nothing.

"I'm getting there. Not long after Morgan started; my son appeared on his List. I had been given part of the List to help minimize the work load and help Grim. I couldn't take my son's soul. War is murder, Anna, and I couldn't handle it—it drove me crazy. Instead of doing my job properly, I got there early and took healthy, Unlisted souls of those that might attack him in the war. Grim had a bigger mess to clean up than if he'd just done the List himself. I spent almost two hundred years in The Blacklands working off those mistakes."

That means his chest is filling incorrectly. He'd created some of the Haunters in The Blacklands. And his Key may never lock the Chest. "Sounds like you've paid your debt." I sigh. "I forgive you."

"Two hundred years is four times the penalty, Anna."

"Why did you deserve longer?"

"Because I took another Unlisted soul after I vowed not to."

"Who?"

"My wife's."

"Oh." I scowl, feeling like he'll never tell me why Cameron is so mad at him. "Then why is Cam upset with you?"

He curls his lip at my use of a nickname for Trick. "I was doing my job. I didn't know he was there. He just... touched me. Now he's got some grudge against me for it."

I scowl. Is that what Damien really thinks or does he assume I haven't put it together yet? "How'd Cameron become a Carrier?"

Damien winces. "I wish you wouldn't use that term." He sighs. "Some agreement he made with Grim. I don't know, but Grim got his Trick Reaper out of the deal."

I frown. "Can you kill a Deathdrifter?"

"A scythe can kill anything, Anna."

Of course it can. And one particular one will cut through Damien.

He lays his head on top of mine as if to console his own horrid memories. "Come, my sweet. Your mum's waiting."

FAMILY
MOMENT

We sit down at the table as my mother sets the food around us as if we're having a Thanksgiving feast. Turkey with stuffing adorns the center of the table. Candied yams, corn, mashed-potatoes, gravy, fruit trays, nuts, and apple and pumpkin pies crowd every inch of space.

"Did you tell her this was what you wanted?" I ask Damien.

"Not exactly."

He slips his hand into mine and pulls it onto his lap.

"Then why are we having Thanksgiving in April?"

"I asked her to duplicate your favourite holiday."

"Oh." I was right. Whatever Damien desires, my mother will give him.

I think about all the past holidays we've had as a family, but I can't figure out why my mother chose Thanksgiving.

"You're not happy?" Damien looks hurt.

"No. I mean, yes, I'm happy." I sigh. "Damien, I don't care what I eat. I just want a real family moment."

"Then I'm happy you're happy." He squeezes my hand.

My thoughts travel back to what took place between Trick and Damien upstairs. How Damien "stole" Cameron's life. I see Trick's forlorn face flash before my eyes.

"What's wrong, my sweet?"

I shake my head just as my mother joins us and places the cranberry sauce on the table.

"You really went all out, Mom."

Tightness coils my waist as if Trick's arms won't let me go again. I look down but all I see is Damien's hand in mine. Why can't I get Trick out of my head? Is he haunting me?

"Nonsense." My head snaps up at my mother's voice. "Damien reminded me that you've missed the way family holidays used to be and you've always seemed so happy at Thanksgiving time."

She eyes Damien like a god for the idea. She actually looks better than usual tonight. Her hair is up, she looks awake and vibrant. Beautiful. Not to mention sober.

A loud bang echoes through the hallway and into the dinning room. It's my father's den door. He made it back here after all.

When he enters the dining room I search for those black tattoo marks. He's clean. And doesn't smell like gasoline, either.

My father picks up the carving knife and without a word carves into the bird. I feel uneasy watching him do it. Damien grips my hand to remind me he won't let anything bad happen. This time.

"Damien, tell me. What are you majoring in at school?" My mother makes goo-goo eyes at him. It makes me want to puke.

"I don't— "

"He's majoring in forensics," I interrupt.

"Really? Interested in the dead, are we?" my mother jokes.

"I suppose you could say that." He smiles at me, takes the plate of potatoes I pass him and puts a small amount on his plate before passing it to my mother.

"You should eat more." She scans his face, broad shoulders and long arms. "Not that you're lacking... substance. I just mean that a strong man, such as yourself, should eat more. I would think—"

"Gloria, stop babbling," my father reprimands.

"There's so much here, Mrs. Fairchild, I want to make sure I taste it all." Damien rubs his thumb over the back of my hand.

My father eyes us as if he despises the way Damien holds my hand under the table.

I jump at the sudden knock on the front door. Everyone looks at each other, but no one moves to answer it.

"I'll get it." I stand in order to get away from my father's piercing gaze.

Quickly, I reach the door and find Morgan standing there looking as if hell just froze over. That might actually be a good thing now that I think about it.

"Where's Doom?"

"In there." I point to the dinning room table.

"Doom!" He pushes past me even though I didn't invite him in.

"Hello!" my mother beams. I don't think she's seen more than two good-looking men in one room in her whole life. If Trick were here, I might be able to say three. I don't think she counts my father anymore. Poor guy.

"Uh, sorry to interrupt your... supper. Do...uh, *Damien*, we need you."

"Not tonight." Damien turns away from him.

"This isn't a request. It's an order."

"Oh? Are you in the army?" My mother's eyes light up.

Morgan looks from me to my mother, probably wondering how we're even related. "No, Ma'am. I just came to... ah, hell. I don't need this shit," he grabs Damien's arm, "come on!"

Damien stands, pulls his arm away and faces Blood Reaper, his eyes narrow with scorn. "I can't leave right now."

"Why not? What do you expect me to tell *him*?"

"Life will explain it."

"Yeah, but Trick—"

"I don't care what that bloody moron is doing."

My pulse quickens. "What's wrong with Cam?"

Morgan grumbles something under his breath then says, "How much time?"

The confusion on my mother's face is indescribable. I'm the only one who remotely knows what they're discussing and I still don't know what the issue is.

Damien shrugs.

"It won't take long. Promise."

"No!" I shout. Morgan is not one I'd accept a promise from and I don't think Damien knows how he changes my mother's mood. He's also all I have to restrain my father from hurting me or my mother. "D?"

"Darlin', it's important," Morgan insists.

"I can't help," Damien admits, but doesn't sound like he's saying no either.

"Just talk to him."

"What's wrong? Can I help?" my mother asks.

Nosey lady.

Damien sighs, "Okay. I'll talk to him, but that's it." Morgan reaches out to put a hand on Damien, but he pushes it away. "Wait."

Taking me in his arms, he kisses me as if he'll never see me again.

I hope to Death that's not the case.

GONE
ROUGE

Dinner went as I always expected it to: Quiet and full of angry hostility. My mother turned back into her self-loathing personality and refilled her wine glass several times. I ate as quickly as I could, skipped dessert and came straight up to my room.

If I have to wait all night, Grim will never hear the end of my wrath. In only the past half-hour I've hung up my dress in the closet, flipped through the eight channels I get in my room, changed into pajama pants and tried to read the book I was given for homework. Yeah, that isn't going to happen.

Now, all I can do is pace a hole in my rug at the end of my bed and think about how everything has gone wrong.

Trick loves me, which I believe is honest now that I've pieced the visions together with the information Trick told me about us. I realize how it's Damien's fault for Trick feeling betrayed right now. Damien probably doesn't care if Trick loved me in another life. What bothers me is the fact that D lied to me. He said he brought on Trick's infatuation. In reality, it was always there. Damien just didn't think before asking Trick for help. Maybe D thought I'd never remember *my* Cam.

Damien, though, took me to Atlanta so my father wouldn't hurt me and yet Trick saved me from the real threat at that hotel. Trick's there for me in times of distress. He took me to pick up the dress from Mrs. Durmot, and hid my car from my mother. Oh, and I can't forget the whole mall-murder-suicide thing.

But Damien's Chest won't lock because of what he did for his son. If I don't live so that he lives—he'll become a Haunter when Grim takes his soul. I'll never get those screams I heard in The Blacklands out of my mind. I can't let that happen to Damien.

Then there's that time Trick watched me change my clothes. But was that really so wrong? He's been watching out for me. If he hadn't been there those times at the hotel, in the car, on the front steps, and at the pool where he stopped Damien from touching me accidentally, I'd be dead. Gads, if Trick wasn't around would Damien have known it was dawn?

Gads? Now I'm using his words too.

And I thought Damien's accent was nice. Just thinking about Trick's gets under my skin and gives me goose bumps.

Trying to find reasons to forget Trick is getting harder by the second.

And that kiss.

Both of them.

At first they're complete shocks. I'm full of nervous anticipation, but he kisses me with such absolute loyalty and longing—almost as if he's never loved another and has been waiting for me for... centuries. How could any girl resist that?

Damien, on the other hand, is gentle and moves as if he'll break me. He makes me feel safe and secure. My stomach flutters when he's near, but Trick's desire is so... so...

Raw.

Provoking.

Intoxicating.

"Stop thinking about him that way, Anna," I tell myself. My heart is racing and I'm beginning to worry more and more about my indecision.

My door knob twists slowly and I hope its Damien so he'll distract me.

It's not.

My father stands in the door way, arms crossed, and stares at me.

I roll my eyes. "What?"

"You won't win."

"I can try," I say.

He advances toward me and grips my bicep in his rough hand.

"Where is he?" my father's demon asks.

"I don't know," I grumble.

"When is he coming back?"

I try to wiggle myself from his grasp but he only holds me tighter.

"Soon."

"Then I guess I'll have to be quick." He slams his forehead into mine. My vision goes hazy as the room spins before he drops me to the floor.

"Tell the Reaper that tomorrow night he belongs to me." He rams his foot into my stomach.

Gasping for air, another spike of pain radiates through my body. Footsteps leave my room as I drift off into a dark, concussed sleep.

"Anna, wake up."

I hear the lull of a heavenly voice. My angel of death wakes me from the deep recesses of a hellish sleep.

"D?"

"Anna." I'm lifted into a tighter embrace. "I never should have left you. I'm sorry."

"It's okay."

"No. It's not. I've promised to protect you and every time I fail."

"What's going on with Trick?" As much as I hate changing the subject, I don't want Damien feeling bad about my aches and pains.

"Grim suspected him of working for Nastusia. He wouldn't listen or answer any questions and now we can't find him. He's gone rogue."

"He'll turn up."

He'll show up to carry me off.

"That's what I'm afraid of. I fear he's been relieved of The Touch by Nastusia and he's doing his best to ensure your death."

I live, I get Doom.

I die, I get Trick.

What a difficult decision life or death is.

But it doesn't matter what *I* want. A sickness swirls through my stomach causing tightness in my chest and a terrible taste in my mouth. I actually don't know who I want.

"Hold me, D. Promise me everything will work out."

He hesitates before tucking my hair behind my ear. Pulling me close he says, "I promise."

Taking his face between my hands, I close my eyes and let my lips linger over his. "Make me believe it," I whisper, begging.

"I promise you, my sweet Anna."

"No. Show me."

Trick's face... no, Cameron's face flashes before my eyes.

Damien's lips urgently take mine and he tastes so sweet and yet so cold. There's a faint smell of gasoline and I know he had to travel to The Blacklands to search for Trick. My stomach turns at the thought of something happening to Cameron.

My Cameron...

Damien gently sets me on my bed, pulls his shirt off over his head and leans over me to take my face in his hands. I involuntarily quiver every time I see his long, perfectly sculpted body. He kisses my neck and slips a hand under my shirt. My back arches so that my body is closer to his. He lifts me up so he can pull my shirt over my head. His cool lips trace the curve of my neck and shoulder, move down my chest to my stomach and stop on the curve of my hip bone.

"I need you, Anna," he says in a ragged breath. "I'm can't exist without you."

I take his face in my hands and pull him up to look at me. "Don't be silly, Mr. Doyle. I'm not going anywhere."

"I'm serious. A scythe can kill anything. Even Grim."

"Shh, can we talk about this later?"

I pull him over and his lips meet mine, but this time I'm the one to trace the length of his body. Every curve of his flesh flexes with my warm touch.

I can feel how desperate he is. I know I'm like fire against his skin and as I kiss his hard body, my hands reach up to feel his chest and arms.

He groans with pleasure and pulls me up to him. Pressing my body to his, he flips me over onto my back and pulls off my pants in one fell swoop.

"I thought you said this could never happen?"

Pulling off his own jeans he smiles and says, "I'm a bloody fool for sayin' that."

I'm in agreement until...

A deep, Scottish accent repeats over and over in my head, "Happy birthday, Jo."

"Wait," I say, pressing my palms firmly against Damien's chest. "I can't."

Sunlight seeps through my windows causing me to see red behind my eyelids. I feel tired and excited at the same time. A heavy weight snakes tighter around my waist.

Cameron...

"You're awake."

No, that's Damien's accent.

Rolling over, I try not to look disappointed. "Good morning."

"Morning," he says, moving the hair out of my eyes. This is first time he's been able to stay past dawn and I should be happier.

"You slept?"

"For the first time in over eight hundred years." He runs his thumb over my lips before he kisses me.

"And did you sleep well?" I ask.

"Not really. No." I worry that his lack of sleep is due to me putting my clothes back on last night. "I felt tired, which worried me because I never am. I feared you'd disappear if I closed my eyes. And when I finally did fall asleep, I'd wake in fits wondering where I was and if you were all right."

"I'm sorry." For more than his poor night.

"Not your fault, my sweet."

"I know," I lie. "I just wanted to express that I understood the feeling."

"Being alive is certainly more difficult."

"Oh, that's right!" I nestle in closer to him. Since dawn he's been alive. Breathing, heart-hammering alive.

And he's warm. I run my lips over his neck, letting my nose trace under his jaw line.

He flinches. "Is this what you've been dealing with the whole time?"

"Dealing with?" I whisper against his neck.

"The cold. *My* cold. Before your touch was like fire, but your nose is so cold. I imagine I felt like this to you, but much worse."

I stare at him. His eyes aren't dark at all, anymore. They sparkle like a beautiful, crystal lake. His black hair is now sandy brown. I place my ear to his chest to hear the beat of his heart. His breathing is no longer a habit, but it sounds labored. When he takes a deep breath, he rises up from the bed to cough.

"Are you okay," I ask.

"Yeah." He coughs again.

I notice that his eyes have crows feet and their sunken into his head slightly. His hands are rough and look as if they've seen may days of hard work.

He looks much older than twenty-three.

Damien stands up to walk around my room and pound on his chest with his fist.

"I don't get it. Why are you sick?"

"I died of pneumonia, Anna. I probably still have it."

"We should take you to a doctor." I stand up and grab my jeans.

"And tell them what? I may be alive but I don't actually exist. Damien Doyle died, Anna."

I frown because realization sets in. How will we make it through this relationship if he's alive?

"Grim! Can't he help?"

Damien shakes his head. Either he won't ask or doesn't think Grim will bother with him now. "I'm going to lie down for a bit."

VAIN AND POMPOUS

There are so many things I want to do with Damien. Unfortunately, we only have today. Soon, we'll be doing what neither of us is looking forward to. Fighting for my life.

This afternoon is a different issue all together. Getting Damien out of bed and into the kitchen was a success all in itself. Damien's cold, grumpy, and still wheezing with every breath. He says his nap helped but I'm skeptical. It's been too long since he's enjoyed the simple things, so today, I'm making sure he feels the sun's rays and knows life outside of a bed—whether he wants to or not.

"Ready?"

"Sure." He shrugs. "Where to?"

"The park. We're going to have lunch. Well, I am. For you, it's breakfast."

He smiles, slowly gets to his feet and opens the kitchen door for me. Once outside, he takes the cooler from me and the blanket. I thank him even though I don't think he should have to bear the load. I'm still not used to his *living* appearance and feel like I can't stop staring at him as we walk to the park.

"Why did your hair, skin, and eye color change?" I ask.

"What do you mean? This is how I look."

"No. When you were dead your hair was black and so were your eyes; like Cameron's and Morgan's are. Even your skin was pale. Paler than mine." I hold out my arm to display my north-eastern skin tone.

He extends his arm next to mine and chuckles slightly, causing himself another coughing fit.

"You're different." I survey him from head to toe.

"Sorry to disappoint you."

Now I feel sick. Guilty. "No. It's not disappointment. It's just... strange. I wasn't expecting this. And it's not that you're scary or unfamiliar. It's..."

"Different?"

"Yes."

"Unfamiliar?"

"Yes. No! Oh, damn it. I'm just confused."

"About?"

"Well, you've made some big changes. For Cameron, it's only hair and eye color."

"What?" He coughs again.

"His living body is the same. Your body is... smaller now. You look older than you are. Maybe it's because you're sick."

"He lets you call him Cameron?"

"Yeah, I guess. He asked me to."

Damien's eyebrows meet in the middle. "How do you know—" he coughs so hard he grabs his chest, "what he looks like alive?"

Looking at me out of the corner of his eye, I feel as if I'm six again and my grandma just caught me in the cookie jar before dinner.

He's mad. Is he jealous?

"It doesn't matter," I say and step closer to him. "Let's slow down so you can catch your breath."

"Tell me, Anna. How do you know?"

"I just saw it, okay? I don't know how. Please, calm down. You can't breathe if you're worked up."

"Worked up?"

Bad choice of words.

"You want me to tell you why Trick is good-looking and why I'm shite? That's what you want? He's what you want now? I gave up immortality for you! Are looks all you care about, *Miss*. Anna?" he sneers.

I'm shocked. My mouth opens, but I don't know what to say. He bends over with another coughing fit and I place my hand on his back.

"No, D. I'm sorry. Please. I'm sorry."

He wheezes as he tries to catch his breath. At least his coughing is intermittent now. At this rate, Damien may die before I get to midnight. Perhaps this was a mistake. Did Grim know this would happen when I made the deal with him?

I bite my lip and decide to try another tactic.

"You're breathtaking—"

"You're a liar." He glares.

"No… you're sexy and perfect, D. I'm a rag doll in comparison."

"Sexy?" He sounds as if he's never heard this word before. Or perhaps he's never heard it said about him. Then again, he only talks to male Deathdrifters and I doubt they're calling each other sexy. Or cute for that matter.

"Yes."

A small smile peeks through and then fades too quickly. "Who're you comparing me to?"

"Every man in the world!" I nudge him and he coughs with this mouth closed.

We reach the park and instead of stopping at the first table as I have, Damien continues toward the huge, weeping willow tree by the stream. I catch up to him as quickly as I can. But his face is cold—like stone, unemotional.

"What?"

"Your comparison is between me and the living only?"

"Yeah." I shake my head at my idiocy. "I mean, no." I cross my arms and stare at the grass—anything other than his crystal eyes trying to catch me in a lie. "I mean everything living and dead, D."

"Good, because I'm beginning to wonder if I should rethink what transpired last night."

I blush and drop my arms to my sides in surrender. "I'm just getting used to this. It's only been one week."

One week?

Realization hits me again. I smile at the thought that I've been meeting Doom Reaper every hundred years. Every time we've lost each other it tears at his heart. All I can do is hope it doesn't happen a sixth and final time.

Out of embarrassment, I smile and move my hair out of my eyes to run my fingers through the strands behind my ear. Then something clicks.

"You're the breathtaking one," Damien says. In his hands is an old camera I used to play with as a little girl.

"Where'd you get that?"

"Your closet."

I frown. I've never liked having my picture taken. "The film is probably shot anyway." I reassure myself.

"One way to find out." He snaps the button again.

"Stop that!" I try to grab the camera, but even alive and sick he's too quick for me.

He pulls me into his arms and kisses my hair. Heat simmers through my body instead of cold and I love it. When it comes to Damien, I'll take any temperature I can get.

"You want to eat or not?" I ask.

"Sure, but I don't have much of an appetite," he says, looking at me as if I'm what he's starving for instead of food.

Good. Another living experience down... millions more to go.

Damien actually eats rather quickly and finishes everything that I can't or don't want. We lay on the blanket, watching families play in the park and the clouds change shape. I enjoy every second.

"We should be off. We have to be in Atlanta for dinner shortly."

"Let's not go. I'd rather stay here. Like this. Forever."

"But it's your birthday." His arms tighten around me.

"Deathday," I mutter.

He coughs. "What?"

"Nothing."

"What about the dress? You seemed happy about it after you came back from the tailor."

"Happy? No. She cut it in half and Cam..." I shouldn't explain how Trick made me feel.

"I was talking about the day you came home with your mum." He knows my mind has switched to Trick. Does he know that I'm confused and I might love them both?

"Oh!" That's good, because I don't want to discuss Trick's arms around me or that kiss.

Damien let's out a wheeze that I think is supposed to be a sigh. "Anna, I'm sorry I got so angry before. You're just curious and you have every right to be." He covers his mouth and coughs again. "When Trick died," he stops to wipe his hand on the blanket where he thinks I can't see, "it was a mistake. He was young and still wants the past he lost. He's vain and pompous and wouldn't bother to look any different even though he can."

I nod. I know Damien is trying to make Cameron look bad. Although it seems to me that Cam isn't the vain one if he isn't bothering—unlike another Death-drifter I know.

"So we'll go? I'd really like to see that dress." He coughs once, extremely hard into his hand again.

"Yeah. Okay." I say with as much excitement as I can muster.

He stares at his hand as I stand up. "What is it?"

Turning his hand toward me I see that it's covered in blood. I look at the blanket where he wiped his hand before and there's more there as well.

A NEW VISION

We made it home rather quickly. The clouds turned gray and I was apprehensive of rain. I didn't want anything to ruin our plans for the evening.

Damien promised me he'd get help. I had to fight with him about it but eventually he went out—hopefully to a doctor. I got ready, knowing Damien will return before dinner and started on my hair. I don't know where he can go for quick care and based on how he looks and the blood, I'm betting he'll be sent to the hospital. Well, if I'm going to die, I'll die in a great dress, then.

Mrs. Durmot was right. The cut of the dress looks fantastic. The low cut, square contour of the bodice hikes up my small breasts and probably adds two imaginary cup sizes—if that's even possible.

The gather of the fabric at the small of my back makes the skirt fall straight, decreasing my hip size. The feel of satin and velvet is so smooth I can't help but rub my hands over my stomach repeatedly.

I pull my short hair up with a few clips and let it spike out the back.

I apply my small make-up arsenal and even use the unopened perfume that my roommate gave me last year. I hear my mother talking to someone downstairs. I'm assuming Damien is back so I start to rush.

The light flickers to a dull, candle-like ambience and I see a face in the mirror behind me. A hand rests on the small of my back and slowly moves up to my neck. His other arm snakes around my waist and as I close my eyes I let my head fall back on his shoulder. I can feel the caress of soft lips below my ear.

When I turn my head and let my lips meet his, it's as if I'm transported to another time. He feels so warm, so comfortable and makes me crave him as if he's a drug and I'm an addict. He turns me so I'm backed up against a wall and his hands begin to urgently untie the corset lacing at the front of my dress.

I slip my hands into his belt and pull him as close as possible. In a heated fury, my hands are in his hair, our lips begging for the others' as if we'll never need air again. He gives up on the lacing of my dress and starts hiking up my skirt; lips now pressed to the hollow of my neck. One of my legs wraps around his waist. He grabs my knees and lifts me up. When I start to unbutton his shirt, I'm blocked by a plaid sash tied across his chest. His hands are cold against my thighs so I give up on his shirt and start unbuckling his pants.

As soon as he slips his fingers under the elastic of my underwear a heat explodes inside me and I can't resist him.

"I've missed you, Cam," I breathe.

He stills himself.

"They said you've gone rouge. Where have you been?"

I don't want him to stop kissing me but he moves his lips from my neck to my ear and says, "Trying to fix me mistakes."

"And have you?"

I slide my hand down the front of his pants and he closes his eyes, releasing a long kept breath.

"I love you, Anna. I always have."

"Then what are you waiting for?"

"This is wrong." He unwraps my legs from around his waist and rests his hands on my hips. I don't take my arms away from his neck. "I've prayed every day fer a chance to go back and follow ya into that library."

"What are you talking about?" I kiss his bottom lip.

"The night we died," he says against mine.

I almost stop breathing entirely.

"It was yer birthday. I dinnae know a lot of English. But ever since I first saw ya, I knew ya were all I wanted."

"I thought we were only together a month before—"

"Aye. I never had it in me to approach ya sooner."

"Wait." I put the pieces together to be sure. "You were the one standing behind Doom when I hung myself?"

He nods. "I thought if the bastirt dinnae touch ya, ya'd live."

He knows that's not how the curse works now, but he didn't then, so I don't address it with him. "You touched Damien because of me." Had that aspect really gone straight over my head? God, I'm stupid.

"Aye. Figured he'd sneak around the truth somehow."

"Why did you touch him? I was dead. I hung myself."

"Aye, but I thought I could save ya."

"Luckily Grim made you a Carrier, huh?"

"I donnae know. Grim offered me a deal. He says Fate is a bitch."

"Fate?"

"She controls everything."

"Can I meet her? Maybe if I—"

"No one talks to Fate. She's not nice nor fair. And I donnae think she'd care anyway."

281

I look down at his chest. Even in death, he's found a way back to me. "Cameron?"

"Aye?" He gives me that crooked smile I can't get out of my head.

"What do we do now?"

He thinks. Then shrugs. "We'll see."

"Do you know what's going to happen tonight?"

"No more than ya do, Jo. But no matter what happens, ya stay away from me."

"Why?"

"Gu brath, Anna. Gu brath."

"What does that mean?" The lights return to normal and I'm standing in the bathroom just as I was before. My hair doesn't have a strand out of place, considering, and my dress isn't wrinkled or untied.

"What does that mean?"

Did any of that really happen?

It certainly felt real.

And wonderful.

Damn him.

After double checking myself in the mirror, I run downstairs. High heels aren't normally my choice for foot fashion so when I get to the last three steps my toes miss the landing.

So much for a pain free night.

Strong hands gently catch me before I hit the floor. "Careful, my sweet. A trip to the hospital isn't on my agenda tonight."

Looking up into his eyes, they're dark again. His hair is black and his skin is pale. So that's how he cured himself. I'm actually relieved.

I don't linger on that fact for long because he's wearing a tux and a vest that matches my dress. I feel like I'm in high school and going to prom... again. Although this time I'm not alone.

I stand and gawk at him. "You look amazing."

"Thank you. I'd say the same for you but that would be an understatement," he says.

Mr. Smooth.

I straighten my dress and my mother pleads for a picture. "No, Mother. We're already late."

"Real quick. The longer you complain the later you'll be."

"Not if we leave right now." I start for the door, but Damien grabs my hand and pulls me toward him.

He wraps his arms around me and I can feel his cold body against my back and I start to wish he were still alive. But only a tiny bit.

I look at my mother, feign a happy smile and pull Damien toward the door.

"Have fun, kids." My mother heads up the stairs, back to her room and her bottle.

"Ready?" he asks.

"Which is the surprise, death or the tux?"

"We decided before I left that I had to get better or our relationship was pointless, Anna. Besides, I have to be at my best to protect you."

I scowl and he smiles. We said a lot of things when we walked home from the park. At the time, I didn't see a point in him coming back to life just to die again so quickly.

"We'll see who protects who."

Stepping outside and standing on the porch, I wait for him to close the door. He looks confused as he stares off beyond me. When I turn toward the street, I'm surprised that nothing looks as it should.

"What's that?" I point directly across the street.

"Looks like a house."

Thanks, Captain Obvious. "Why wasn't it there earlier today?"

"Because it appears we won't be going to Atlanta."

Just as my heart falls into my stomach the shadows of the house created by the setting sun move and lift themselves from the ground. They're the same figures from the hotel, but there are thousands of them.

A flash of light catches my attention and Damien holds his scythe at an angle in front of me.

"Ready?" I deadpan, rhetorically.

"Go back inside, Anna," he says, through clenched teeth.

"What?" I can't believe this is going to happen— now, of all times. We definitely should have stayed on the blanket in the park.

"I said inside. Now!" He swipes at the first shadow and it fades into the evening air.

I back up to the door and fumble behind me for the knob. This is my house. Isn't it? How can I not find the knob? Glancing down I see that there isn't one. This can't be.

"Damien! I can't open the door." I turn around to look at him, but across the street, it's as if I'm looking into a giant mirror. Damien's reflected image strikes at shadows, and I see myself pressed against the front door.

Damien abruptly turns, shouts for me to move, which scares the living hell out me, and kicks the door. It snaps open.

"Oh, well, sure. Why didn't I think of that?"

"Anna?" I turn to him and he looks more concerned than I've ever seen him before. "Don't listen to his lies. I'll be there soon. I promise."

I kiss him quickly and kick off my shoes before I head to the stairs. On the fourth step, it's as if I hit a wall. Glass? I'm not sure, but it's solid. My hand runs over a flat surface. It's like being in a cartoon. It looks like I can walk up the stairs, but there are no stairs.

Cold air rushes over me and I fall down the few steps to the floor. It feels like something has sucked all the air out of my lungs. I gasp for breath, but feel like I'm drowning. Darkness takes over and I realize this is a new vision.

In my father's den, books are thrown all over the floor. The liquor cabinet is tossed aside and a thin, gray vapor clouds the room. As it dissipates, I see Grim is sitting in my father's client chair. Damien is crouching in the far corner with his head in his hands. And at the entryway, Cameron is leaning over me, pulling a bottle of liquor from my dead hand. Nastusia stands with her body pressed against my father's side, happier than ever. Then Grim walks up behind them.

No. Please. Not Grim.

Picking myself up off the floor my breathing starts to return to normal. I have no idea how long I've been out. I look down the hall. My father is standing at the end of the hallway near the kitchen. Trick, to my surprise, is standing at the entrance to the dining room. He told me in the bathroom to stay away from him. After all his effort to prove himself to me and now that I care, now that I trust him—he says stay away. As I turn to head into the living room, I glance over my shoulder at Trick. What if the bathroom incident didn't really happen? Trick smiles out of the corner of his mouth and nods.

Fine. Living room it is!

I'm not sure what I can do in here, but it's getting colder by the second. I pick up two blankets and wrap them both around my shoulders. When I turn around, Trick is standing in front of me.

"What do you want?"

"You." He sounds possessed. Nothing like the Trick I'm used to hearing. His voice is monotone and almost echoes in his chest as he speaks.

"Come with me. I know you want to."

Even his accent is gone. This isn't Trick. This isn't my Cameron.

"No thanks. I'd rather live... with Damien." I step back, but a gust of air throws me up against the bookcase. The shelves dig into my back.

285

Good. He's pissed.

"Soul collecting can be... alluring," he breathes against my exposed skin.

The blankets have dropped to the floor and I feel exposed and vulnerable. I shut my eyes as Trick slides the cool bar of his scythe along the inside of my leg—inching my dress up.

"You're mine, Anna. And you know it," Trick whispers in my ear as he leans into me. His weight is causing the shelving to dig deeper into my back.

I grunt and I blink away tears. "Cameron, stop. Please. You're hurting me."

"Anna?" His eyes change ever so slightly. His accent back. "Sweet Jesus, I told ya to stay away, Jo." His hand slips into mine and he presses something hard into my palm.

"Stop!" Damien looks exhausted standing at the edge of the living room. "Don't touch her, Trick!"

His eyes fade back to the sinister color they had before. "I won't kill her... yet." His nose traces my cheek ever so slightly. "I just want a taste of her—of your *sweet* Anna."

I want to cry, scream, and pound him until he returns to his senses... to *my* Cameron. What if I've lost him to Nastusia, just like my dad? I can hardly move. Even my eyes won't scan around the room. Stupid Sorceress.

"Let me go!" I yell.

"I'll keep her quiet." My father steps up next to Trick and places his hand around my neck.

"No marks, Demon. Remember, I'm the one that carries her off."

THE ELEVENTH HOUR

Suicide.

That's why she has Trick under her control. If he collects me this time, I'm his. Has Trick made a deal with Nastusia? She wants a suicide and what Reaper fits the job better than him? Although I'm not entirely convinced that Trick is helping Nastusia. He could even be fooling all of us. And if he's really gone rouge, why wouldn't he be doing all this for himself?

My father pulls me away from the bookcase and in my peripheral vision I catch Trick punch Damien. It suddenly occurs to me that I don't really know Trick. Not any better than I know Damien. And there are some serious loyalty issues going on.

"So you want a dead boyfriend, huh?" my father asks me.

"He's better than most of the living," I mumble. Actually, all the living I know.

Suddenly, I'm dragged across the floor and scream out from the burn of the carpet on my legs. I see Trick look over and Damien uses the distraction to his advantage, knocking Trick on the floor. With Trick on his back, Damien starts toward me.

I miss the moment to crawl away when my father releases me as Damien slams into him. Books fall off the shelf behind me; some landing around me and others hitting me in the head. A vase my mother got as an anniversary gift shatters on the floor. Half crawling, half on my feet, I make it across the hall into the dinning room and head for the kitchen door. I step through the entryway to the kitchen and find myself in front of my father's den door—not where I should be.

Over my shoulder, I see Damien is still restraining my father and Trick has made his way toward them. I turn down the hall to the back door which leads out to the pool. Opening the door, I find I'm entering my house and standing in the foyer—again, my father's den door beckoning me. This is insane. I take one step further into the hall and the door to my father's den slowly opens.

I always thought survival was easy, but to survive... I have to face death.

Now or never.

The grandfather clock reads ten minutes to midnight and I have no idea how time flew so quickly. Then again, I have no concept of time for any of the visions that took place.

I look once more at *my* guys in the living room. This is it: The eleventh hour. Sighing, I step into my father's den.

Nastusia and Grim are sitting in the room just as the vision had shown me. They look like long lost friends catching up on old times.

"Grim?"

"Anna, come in." Grim waves a blurry arm in the air, inviting me to sit in an empty chair.

"Thanks. I think I'll stand."

"Suit yourself." He pauses and I wish I could see a face under that hood. Then again, maybe I don't want to. "Things have gotten out of hand." He gestures toward the living room. "Nastusia and I have reached a conclusion."

"Oh? And what does Damien say about this?"

Don't listen to his lies.

"Doom has no say."

Nastusia smiles and I know this benefits her above all of us.

"So, what, I die? Get stuck with Trick forever? Nastusia gets my father and my mother goes to a mental hospital. Or worse. And Damien... what happens to him?"

Grim shrugs, nonchalantly.

Kill himself is what he means.

"No. I don't care what you two have decided for me. I'll make my own choices."

"Anna, this could be the end if you make the right decision."

"Damien has done nothing but try to keep me alive. That's more than I can say for you!"

"It's not Doom's or my job to keep anyone alive. I'm the Grim Reaper. We are Death!" His voice booms throughout the room.

I feel angry, distraught, confused, and just plain unsure. Without thinking words start coming out of my mouth. "A dirty name. A dirty face. A curse to relive this place. Die for his shame. Die for the key. Die to become free."

"You remember it." I think Grim is smiling. At least it sounds as if he is. His blurry form even appears proud.

"And now I understand it."

"She's lying!" Nastusia stands up, anger dripping from her like lava.

Grim doesn't move.

"Do something, Charles!" she yells.

"I can't. She's decided."

Nastusia glides over to me and grabs my throat so fast I can't react. She looks around the room and her eyes light up as she sees something that will aid her in my suicide.

"Ever die from alcohol poisoning?" she asks.

She knows how I've died. She's the one who murders me every time and yet, I am proclaimed as suicidal.

"You tell me," I chide.

She yanks out the cork on a bottle of vodka with her teeth and proceeds to pour it down my throat. I try not to swallow but I cough and choke as she squeezes my throat tighter. I can't move away from her and before I know it, the bottle is gone.

Grim hasn't moved and I begin to wonder if he can. I see a slight movement from his right arm. Why is he tapping his hand on the chair's arm rest? Perhaps he's waiting for me to die. Counting the seconds?

Suddenly, a bright flash ignites in the corner of the room and Damien is hunched over, coughing, gripping his chest, and gasping for air. His hair is brown, and his eyes are blue and full of anguish. There is also no scythe in his hand, which can only mean one thing: It's past midnight.

"Stripped of your worth, I see," Nastusia says, sounding proud.

"Let her go!" He coughs and I wish I could do something. Anything for him.

I'm dropped to the floor and she turns her back, finished with me. When my hands break my fall on the floor I feel something hard in my fist.

I can't see. Colors and shapes mix together. All I want to do is sleep. And puke. I can feel my body but it's more like I'm not really alive anymore.

Pain spikes through my hand with a bracing cold. I'm surprised I can even feel it. I look at my hand, blinking several times. The gray and black mix, separate and combine. Then I remember. Cameron slipped it in my hand and I haven't let go of it.

Donnae go anywhere without it.

My pewter reaper!

"Anna!" Damien yells.

"Yup, yup." I try to stand. "Uh, nope. Very dizzy. Prab... prabably drunk."

But I remember. Damien's voice echoes in my head that a scythe can kill anything. Doom Reaper doesn't exist as a Deathdrifter anymore but...

I pull on Nastusia's arm and she spins around to face me. Pure anger in her eyes causes me to flinch.

"Wha—"

Silenced, she never finishes her question. Blood stains the carpet of my father's den and I know Ms. Cune will not be cleaning it up. My proclaimed protector has slit her throat. She gurgles and tires to talk. Her hand covers the laceration as blood coats her chest.

Grim gets up and touches her bare shoulder. Immediately, Nastusia falls to the floor. A single purple light rises from her body and Grim's scythe directs it toward him.

"Took you long enough to remember that was in your hand," Grim states.

Damien is next to me and his arms are around me faster than I can comprehend what just happened.

"Why didn't we do this sooner?" I look at Grim and Damien and they seem to be overly quiet and concerned. "Actually, tell me later. I need to throw up."

TWO HEARTS

My birthday is now over. Nastusia failed and I can't believe how different the atmosphere in my home is already. This morning I've already had my mother greet me in the kitchen with a warm smile. The smell of alcohol no longer envelopes her, but the cigarettes must be a difficult habit to kick because she's still taking long drags off the slender white stick of lung cancer.

I've already witnessed my father come in the kitchen and kiss her good morning. It's almost like they have no idea what the last seventeen years have been like. My mother couldn't have forgiven him. Do they even know we were cursed?

"Why do you look so glum, missy?" my mother asks me. I shrug in response while I pour my orange juice into a glass. A hangover is something I don't care to explain right now. "You're going to miss him, aren't you?"

My throat swells up and I swallow hard to fight the tears. "Yup." I don't want to explain the complications of the past week, so I use the least possible words to answer her.

Last night, after I killed Nastusia, I never saw Cam, er, Trick again. I've been wondering—praying—that he'll make an appearance just to say goodbye or something.

"Shouldn't he be here by now? When are you planning to head back to school?"

"I don't know." I don't bother to answer her first question. I'd hate to say Damien's been with me all night to ensure my survival but left this morning at my command to get treated for pneumonia. She just wouldn't understand.

"Oh, I bet that's him now!" My mother smiles from ear to ear when the door bell rings. She likes staring at Damien. That's all she did up until he left Friday night. And the way she runs to the door it's as if Damien only comes to see her.

"Good morning, handsome!" I hear her exclaim from the foyer. She doesn't seem to notice the difference in his appearance from the dead to the living.

"Mrs. Fairchild, how're you this fine morning?" Good lord, he's laying it on thick today.

"I'm in the kitchen!" I yell, so he'll know to break free from her childish giggling. I finish my orange juice in one last large gulp and put the glass in the sink. Following close behind him is my mother with a star-struck look in her eyes.

"How long will you be in the states after Anna heads back to school?" She might as well be throwing me out the door now.

"I don't know," he turns to look at me, "Miss Anna, when are you leaving?" He grins at me because we both know my mother eats up this kind of talk from him.

"The sooner the better," I mumble.

"What's the matter? Jealous?" he whispers in my ear.

"No," I spit out. Staring into those unfamiliar blue eyes, I know he has something he's holding back from me. Actually, I think he's holding back for my mother's sake. There's something his lips are restraining to tell me. "What?"

"Let's go for a walk. It's quite nice out today."

"All right." I squint at him as I turn toward the door. I can only imagine what happened between him and Grim in the last hour he's been gone.

Even though we're walking side by side, he's leading me through my own neighborhood. "Are you going to tell me how it went with Grim?"

"It went... well."

"And?"

"I'm a free man again, Anna."

"Free? I didn't know you were enslaved."

"Hmm. You're right. Free isn't the right word. I'm..." He stops walking and grabs my wrist. There's no cold to his touch, no deathly pallor to his complexion. "I'm alive," he beams. "And cured."

I gulp. I asked for this and Grim came through just as he said he would. My stomach and heart flutter to a tune I can't place. I wonder what price I'll have to pay for this. Hopefully, I've already paid in full—more than once.

"So what does this mean?"

"It means, my sweet Anna, that I can live my life. That I can grow old with you. Have *everything* I've ever wanted." He's ecstatic. I've never seen or heard him this happy before. It gives him a whole new persona—one I'm not very familiar with.

Everything? What about what *I* want?

He hasn't let go of my wrist as we come to the weeping willow from yesterday. The small creek running along the edge of the park caresses and licks the rocks. There's a small wooden bridge that arcs over the creek and he stops to lean against the railing.

"I've been thinking," he states as if he's giving a speech to an auditorium full of students. Other than the birds in the neighboring willow, I don't think anyone else can hear him.

"Yeah? And what have the wheels been grinding away at in that brain of yours?"

"Death."

"But of course," I chide.

"I've seen more than you'll ever know, Anna. I've seen blokes die gruesomely. Women who wish we would come sooner than expected because they can't take the pain anymore." He stops talking as if he can't go on and when his fingers slip from my wrist to take my hand, I can feel him trembling.

"What's wrong?" I press with concern and grip his hand tighter.

"Nothing. Everything is perfect." His smile is slow to surface, but he looks genuinely sincere. "Anna, my sweet, sweet Anna, I have witnessed your deaths more than I could bear and every time I begged Grim to take me in your place. You did something for me I could never have asked for by linking your fate to mine. I don't deserve you," my eyes veer to the stream at his words, "your generosity, or your love, but I wouldn't trade it away for anything. I shouldn't be asking you for a single thing and if you deny me this, I don't know what I'll do."

"What on earth are you talking about, Doom?" He's become so serious I'm afraid of what might come out of his mouth next.

He doesn't find my use of his Death name funny like I had intended. Instead, he drops my hand and grabs me by my arms to pull me closer. His free hand holds my face and I'm still surprised by his warmth after all these days of feeling his cold. Running his thumb over my lip he says, "I love you, Anna, and I would ask for nothing more than for you to be my wife."

"*What?*"

"Marry me, Anna," he whispers in my ear.

I'm stunned. Speechless. My mind is screaming, yes, yes! But out of my stupid mouth comes, "Didn't the men in the thirteenth century propose down on one knee or is that just romantic propaganda?"

His eyebrows rise in amusement and then he says, "I didn't take you for a traditionalist."

"Well, what about school? I'm heading back today. Where will you go?"

"With you, if you'll have me."

"This is... this is..." I can't find the right words. The only ones that enter my thoughts are the ones that have told him I don't want this—the conversation in the car on the way to Atlanta when he saved me from my father's fury. Then the conversation in the hotel after I woke from being knocked unconscious by Nastusia comes rumbling back into my brain. All those conversations about love, marriage, and family and he still wants me. Everything the curse has taught me about those three things, Damien has done nothing but teach me the true meaning of them.

And Cameron.

I look down at our hands pressed between our chests. I can feel our two hearts beating as one. He's waited so long for me. It would be selfish to pray, dream, or wish that Cameron will come back for me. He didn't even say goodbye. But I'm alive. Damien is alive. He removes his hand from my cheek to gently push the hair that has fallen forward with the tilt of my head. I can't deny him this.

After kissing my forehead, he rests his chin on top of my head and with a forlorn sigh says, "I know how you feel about it. And you don't have to know what you want right now."

"No," I stop him, "I don't need time." I meet the look in his eyes and I didn't intend to cause this grief. "I'm sorry. Ask me again?" My eyes search his face to find even a tiny bit of relief.

"Anna," he breathes as he lowers himself to one knee and I begin to shake. My heart pounds and it feels like it could break out of my chest at any moment. "Will you do me the honor of being my wife—letting me devote the rest of my life to you?"

My jaw drops as I catch a glimpse of movement from his hands. He holds a dainty fleck of light between his fingers. It's nothing extravagant, just a small silver ring with an oval diamond—my grandmother's ring. "Oh, Damien..." My breath is caught in my chest, tears sting my eyes. "Yes. Yes, I'll marry you." He wraps his arms around me and kisses me quickly before he slips the delicate jewel on my finger.

"Where did you get this?" I ask.

"I'm a traditional man, Anna. Where do you think I got it?"

"You spoke to my parents? When?"

He smiles and kisses me to stop my questions. "I have my ways... or I *did* anyway."

A BLINDING
LIGHT

Now that we're back at the house, I realize that my mother did, in fact, know about Damien's plan. She squealed and hugged us. I was even surprised that my father shook Damien's hand. Even though Damien still looked as if he could kill my father, I think he tried his best to hide his contempt. I flinched when my father hugged me. This is definitely going to take some getting used to.

As I walk up the stairs to my room, I can't help but look at my grandmother's ring. She had told me once that there's someone out there for everyone and if it's meant to be, Fate will find a way. I've always believed that. So now that I'm engaged, shouldn't I be able to get Cameron's face out of my head?

This isn't how it's supposed to be.

I start packing my spring semester clothes for school and slip my hand in my pocket, making sure that Doom Fairchild is still there. I'll never go anywhere without him anymore. Smiling at Trick's gift that saved my life, I start at the sight of my torn, purple dress on the floor.

"What's wrong?" Damien asks. He's sprawled out on my bed watching me pack since he has no belongings.

"Just this." I hold up the dress with two fingers as if it's the most disgusting thing I've ever seen.

"Take it with you. You did look beautiful in it." He must be joking.

I toss it at my trash can, but miss. "I'm not sure I can wear it, let alone touch it again, without thinking of last night." Without thinking of Cameron.

"Okay, don't wear it. You're beautiful no matter what." He stares up at the ceiling.

"Thanks," I mumble, not believing a word out of his mouth. "Um, D?"

"Yes, my sweet?"

"Uh, what happened to... to Trick?

"Blacklands, I assume." He folds his arms under his head. "Punishment of some kind."

"You think he'll be okay?"

Damien props himself up on his elbow and stares at me. "No. He won't be okay. He's already dead and as badly as he'd now like to die so he won't be in love with you anymore, he can't. Fortunately for him, he'll only suffer for maybe sixty to seventy years—instead of six hundred, like I did."

That's because when I die, I'll be his—if he still wants an eighty or ninety-year-old. "You think he looks at it that way?" I hope he does—a little bit.

"I don't care."

I nod and look at the crumpled dress on the floor.

Out of the corner of my eye, I see he's smiling a devilish grin which has me curious. I shake my head clear and crawl from the bottom of my bed, up his legs, and straddle his waist. "You've got a secret. I know that look," I tell him.

"I just happened across something that actually belongs to me."

"What is it?"

"You want to see it?"

"Yes!" I push on his chest to get him to stop this game.

His hands reach up above his head, under the pillows. "Yes?"

"Damien!" I whine, and he laughs. He's enjoying this too much.

From under the pillow he pulls out two pictures. The first one is of me from yesterday afternoon at the park. He had taken the picture just as I had moved my hair out of my eyes. It's actually a good picture. I'm surprised the camera still works.

The other one is of the two of us. The one my mother had forced on us just before we left for Atlanta, which we never made. I'm giving my mother my notorious fake smile. Damien is behind me, his arms wrapped around me, only he's not looking at the camera. He's staring at me as if I'm the only one that exists and I can see how much he really does love me.

"I like this one," I wave the picture of both of us in the air.

"Well, they're mine. Give them back." He sits up and overpowers me quite easily.

Overpower might be a strong word. A simple kiss and I melt. He runs his hand over my cheek and kisses me tenderly. "I can't believe I've waited six hundred years for you." He kisses my neck and a shiver runs down my spine; thinking of another that knows a certain spot so well. "I'd do it all again in a heart beat if I had to."

I wince. "You won't have to. In fact, if we leave now, we can stop in Atlanta and get married before I go back to school." Did I just say that?

"You're not serious," he says, astounded.

"Yes, I am."

"Then let's go, my sweet." He stands with my legs wrapped around his waist and then gently lets my feet find the floor.

301

I can't believe I'm doing this. I throw as many things as I think I'll need or want in my bag and we head downstairs to find my parents and say goodbye.

Throwing my bag in the trunk, I wave goodbye to my parents, who stand together at the door and watch us leave as if they've been a happy couple forever. I swear I'll never get used to this. As we pull out of the driveway and head toward Atlanta, I catch Damien staring at me.

"Hey, maybe we'll be able to get dinner after all," I joke.

"You'll have to pay for it. I don't have otherworldly abilities anymore." I think he's trying to be funny.

The time it takes to get to Atlanta flies by. There isn't much Damien can tell me about his life before me or his death, but he has a lot to say about the times he's waited for me to reappear on a List.

Atlanta is busy and it probably should be because classes start again tomorrow. The roads are filled with cars and people are all over the sidewalks shopping and meeting up with friends they haven't seen in the past week.

I'm excited to have Damien hiding out in my dorm this semester and since he's so gentle on the eyes I doubt my roommate will mind.

Damien finds this concept amusing and says, "She'll mind when I start kicking her out so I can be alone with you."

He's right. He knows her well enough from all the times he's spent as what I thought was a voice in my head.

The traffic light turns green just in time so there's no reason to break. The busy intersection is full of stupid drivers using part of the gutter to make right hand turns. Up the road a little ways is a car weaving between traffic.

"That's not good," Damien says, indicating the swerving car.

"It's just some idiot who's late and didn't expect all this traffic," I reason.

The car juts out into my lane as it passes the car in front of it. Before I can react there is a blinding light coming straight at me. Damien's hand clenches around mine and before everything goes black I hear, "Damn you, Trick!"

THREE DAYS AFTER

There is a steady, high-pitched beeping resonating in my ears. I can't open my eyes. My whole body aches and I feel like a dead weight. Muffled voices in close proximity become clearer. It's Damien and my father talking to whom I believe is a doctor. A woman's whimpers are muffled into what I can only imagine is a tissue or a hand-kerchief.

"She's sustained a great deal of trauma from the accident." This voice sounds forlorn, but rehearsed. He isn't sad for me. He's sad for those who have to listen to him.

A weight slowly depresses the bed and a shaking hand takes mine as the doctor continues, "The third, fourth, and fifth ribs bilaterally are fractured and if it wasn't for the morphine she'd still be screaming from the pain."

I don't recall any of that.

"Doctor..." I hear Damien speak slowly, "Will she be all right? Will she survive?"

"We're keeping her in the ICU until she's stable, Mr. Doyle."

"You've done four surgeries and you still can't tell me if you can save her!" Then he mumbles, "If I was... If only I never..."

"I know you're upset and you have every right to be." The doctor's voice comes closer and I hear him talk lower, "I can't imagine being in your shoes and having a drunk driver hit you and your wife on your wedding night."

Wedding night? We never even made it! I was so excited that I didn't even bother to question Damien's concern over that car. A suicide attempt is what that jerk was doing.

Wait...

Trick.

Damien saw him and it was still too late to adjust for the driver coming straight at me. With everything we knew we still couldn't help the inevitable.

Damn Fate. She really is a bitch.

I hear the high pitched beeping in the background speed up and the presence of the doctor walks around the bed.

"Are you in pain, Anna?" the doctor asks.

I can only grunt an incoherent "no." How am I to communicate? I need to know if Damien is okay. Is he hurt?

Damien's hand squeezes mine lightly and I wince in pain. I hear a few quick beeps before the doctor says, "A little more morphine won't hurt her. She should sleep now, anyway."

"Doctor?" my father's voice asks. It's pained and his breathing is sporadic. "How much longer?"

"Hard to say, right now. We didn't expect her to make it through these past few days. Maybe a couple more days or perhaps five minutes."

I hear my father grunt and Damien shout, "What do you expect us to do with that bloody information? Are you saying you're giving up?"

306

The doctor's clothes swish and crinkle with his change in posture. He doesn't answer right away and I hear my mother's weeping fill the silence. "I'm sorry Mr. and Mrs. Fairchild. Time is all we have left. Mr. Doyle, if you'll come with me, we have to do a follow up x-ray on that arm."

Damien's weight lifts from the bed and slowly he releases my hand. "Don't leave me," he whispers in my ear. I feel dizzy and like I'm floating above the bed. Is this how morphine makes people feel or is it Damien?

It seemed like an eternity until my parents left the room. I don't remember a lot since the doctor left with Damien and only occasionally did I catch parts of my parents' conversations. My mind is so clouded I hardly remember them saying goodbye.

My head clears as the room gets colder. The pain that the morphine didn't touch seems to dull and that can only mean one thing.

Death.

"How are you feeling?" the old, gruff voice asks me. I can only grunt in return. "Yes, I know. I meant emotionally."

I'm on cloud nine, Grim. Never been better. I want to shout at him. A tear escapes the confines of the bandages over my eyes and I can feel the sting of salt in the wounds on my face.

"I shouldn't have asked such a stupid question. My apologies."

I want to ask him how Damien is and why this happened this way. The curse is over. I could have had the caring father I knew when I was four. Memories of the father I wished I'd get back are erasing. I could have had more time with my mother who didn't drink and smoke away her problems. I felt a real life was just beginning on my twenty-first birthday and it comes abruptly to an end three days after a curse-free life. This isn't fair. Why me?

My face is on fire, fueled by the salt of my sorrow. "You are a strong and gifted young girl. And it's about time."

I felt his hand come closer to me. The cold radiating off his body eases me—makes me happy. At least it means he's upset enough about this whole ordeal. If it didn't bother him the room wouldn't be so cold and he wouldn't be breaking his own rule about not talking to the souls.

"Grim! No!" I hear Damien as if he's at the end of a long tunnel. "I know you're here, Grim. Show yourself!"

The cold presence retreats from my body and I hear Grim sigh. "Doom, there's nothing I can do."

"No. You can't bloody have her. Take me instead."

"I'm fulfilling my part of the bargain. You know that."

There's a sudden burst of metal against dry wall. Did Damien just throw a chair or cart against the wall? "I'm not letting you touch me, Doom. It's not your time."

I hear Damien grunt from the vicinity of where the crash came from. It sounds as if he's picking himself up off the floor. By way of Grim's words, he must have tried to touch him and fell. Cursing under his breath, in the same words that I've never recognized, I feel sorry for him.

Two sets of shuffling feet enter the room and they must be nurses because one woman says, "Mr. Doyle, are you all right?"

"Fine," he grunts.

"The doctor should look at your arm. The pins shouldn't be at that angle."

Pins? He shattered his wrist in the accident.

"I'll take care of it later. I'm busy now!"

"Mr. Doyle, stop struggling. We need to get the pins reset. She'll be fine. Come with us now." The younger voice of the two nurses sounds the most concerned for him. And why wouldn't she? He's even more attractive alive than dead, which means I'll never be seen with such a gorgeous man ever again.

Their shuffling feet start to exit the room and Damien must have seen something the nurses didn't because the last thing I hear before the silence is, "Charles, I'm begging you. Let me say goodbye!"

Cold envelops my whole body. I feel pain free and weightless. Then the blackness slowly brightens to white.

THE
WHITELANDS

Grim places a black box in front of me with an intricately woven skeleton key and says, "Here's your Key."

I stare at the small silver key. It looks the same as the one that Trick had shown me. This one though has the face of a roaring lion instead of a rose.

It's the Key to the Chest—*my* Reaper Chest.

"You are my newest Deathdrifter. I've found that curses are as prevalent in today's age as it is to sue someone." I believe he's attempting to be funny because he pauses for my reaction. I'm not laughing, nor am I smiling. I'm still mad at him for not letting Damien say goodbye. "Nastusia wasn't the strongest sorceress," he continues, "more of a nuisance. I want you to collect the cursed souls. Granted you will be reincarnating the same soul multiple times but I think you understand this necessity more than any other Reaper. Inside the Chest is everything you'll need to help you fill it."

"A scythe won't fit in here," I deadpan.

He grunts in an unamused way. "No, that comes later."

"Are you training me?"

"No," he sounds reluctant to answer me. "Trick is."

"Oh," I pause, "was this part of the deal?"

"He told you about that? I'm surprised. He's actually quite reserved."

I shrug. I learned a lot about Trick Reaper during that week, but death might shed a new light into the mystery that is Cameron McKinney. "Is Damien... I mean, Doom, ever going to return? Is he on your List?"

Grim hesitates. "You don't recall our deal?"

"I've heard you've hidden it well. Should I?"

"Let me show you." A hand of bones holds out a monstrous scythe from the shadow before me. "Grab it."

Hesitantly, I grip the pole under his hand. The shadow envelopes me and in a typhoon of darkness, I'm looking at a horrid view of myself—cuts at the wrists, arms, and neck—watching a man leave me behind in the empty whiteness. I see myself look up and meet the face of a blurry, black cloaked figure. I assume this is Grim.

"What is the matter, tortured soul?"

"I don't want..." I wipe away tears and hiccup from all the sobbing.

Grim interrupts with an assumption, "*You're* afraid of dying? That's something I did not expect of you."

"No. I'm not scared for me. Damien..."

"You remember him? Interesting. I believe this is a first. Then again, it was bound to happen with one of the reincarnations."

"What do you mean?"

"I'm sending you back again."

"Again?"

"There's no Chest for a cursed soul."

"Cursed? How many times has Damien had to come for me? How many times will his heart break?"

"I've never known a soul to be as unselfish as you. I'll make you a deal."

"A deal with Death? Sounds like a bad idea."

"I'm true to my word."

"I guess I don't have anything to lose. What's the deal?" I cringe while listening to me say these words. If I knew then what I'd lose, I may not have made that deal. Then again, I remember how I felt at that moment too. At least, now, Damien will never endure another one of my deaths.

"When the curse is broken, I will grant life back to Doom."

"Doom?"

"Sorry, Damien," he sneers. It sounds as if human names disgust him.

"What do I have to do?"

"Nothing." I think I hear a slight chuckle. "Just follow your heart."

"Okay..." Sounds easy enough. "Deal."

Why didn't I ask for specifics?

The scene before me goes black and the encircling typhoon diminishes. Everything is white again. Though I'm hugging my knees, wishing I could have yelled at myself for not making any stipulations, I'm still glad the curse is over and Damien can live the life he never got to.

"I broke the curse and I still died. Why?"

"Trick made a deal too. He's smarter than I gave him credit for. Since he became one of my Reapers, controlling The Touch was all he cared to learn. That and English. He has more self-control than Doom ever had. But when Doom went to him for assistance, he knew all he had to do was aide Nastusia along the way —she just didn't know his aide was for his own benefit." Grim smiles, proud of his Trick Reaper. "For your safety he made a deal with me that you'd be with him when you died—no matter how long the wait."

"So when I originally made my deal with you, it should have been for me to die without reincarnation and spend eternity with Damien, here?"

"Not really an option."

"Too late now anyway."

313

"Doom made his own choices too."

"He must be in so much pain." My heart aches for Damien. I desperately want tell him I'm okay and that I'm happy.

"More emotional than physical."

Of course, he spent six hundred years waiting and then watched me die. He had it planned not to see the sixth death and though he didn't *see* it, I still died a sixth time. Emotionally, I can only imagine what he's going through now. "Can I talk to him?"

"You know very well that that is against the Deathdrifter policy." I should be yelling at Grim right now. I think he's rehearsed that line on all of his Carrier's and yet he breaks it himself and doesn't change the rule.

"Can you at least tell me if he's okay?"

Grim sighs so deep I already know the answer. "He could be better. He had a gift as all Deathdrifters do. His presence had the ability to nurture, heal, and pacify. Some interpret these feelings as love—especially if they already do for someone else."

I'm a little miffed. Did he know he was doing this? I could see how he changed my mother so easily, but...

"Though he no longer has you," Grim continues, "he has chosen to continue your dream of a healer."

I'm a little surprised. He's setting goals for himself, which means he must be happy to be alive, right? I smile at Grim and though I can't read his face through the black hood, he puts one hand on my shoulder. "He's dealing with this in his own way. It would only make things worse if you visit him."

I spin the ring on my finger and try not to think about how I almost married him. "Does he remember? Does he remember me? Everything from the past eight hundred and nine years?"

"Yes. I couldn't take all those memories from him." Grim sounds sad—as sad as a Reaper can sound. He must have wanted to reduce the heartache from his favorite Deathdrifter but I'm sure Damien didn't let him. "Perhaps someday, he'll be... relieved."

"He was like a son to you. You wanted him to take your place someday. Will you wait for him still?"

"No. I have a new Deathdrifter I'd like to offer the position to."

"Trick?"

"No. Not Trick. And I'd rather not say just yet."

"Oh, all right, fine." I bite my lip. I'm excited to see Cameron again but there's one thing I need to know first.

"Show me Cameron's death, Grim. Please?"

He makes a guttural sound of disappointment and then slams his scythe down in front of me.

A huge staircase appears in the distance. Slowly, the surrounding scene comes into focus and I see the beautiful girl that I've seen every time I touched Trick running up the stairs. She looks behind her as she reaches the landing and slams into a young man's chest. He gives the girl a cooked smile and she blushes, apologizing for getting in his way.

I hear Trick's voice but don't understand the words. Apparently she doesn't either because she curtseys, he kisses her hand, and then they linger—eyes locked on each other.

After she disappears behind a pair of large wooden doors, Cameron puffs his cheeks, takes one step toward the closed doors, but then turns to head down the staircase. When he reaches the front door, he lights a cigar and for reasons I don't understand, looks over his shoulder toward the balcony.

He freezes. The cigar falls from his lips and ash mixes with dirt as he screams my name. He runs—without any hesitation in the least. He runs so hard and so fast. When he reaches the balcony he extends his arms but the girl is in the arms of another man. The noose still around her neck.

Cameron doesn't say a word. He just grabs the man's hand as he touches the girl's face.

Up close I can see now. I know for sure.

That girl *is* me.

"It was a mistake," I whisper. "Why are they both punished?"

"Not punished. Both were given options. You had to choose. I benefited also."

"How?"

"I needed a Trick Reaper. Cameron and I made a deal. He had to work for Nastusia so I could end her reign in The Blacklands. If you failed, he'd have you after your sixth death."

"So he was okay with me dying."

"Not exactly. He wanted you to be happy. Even if it meant you chose Doom. He didn't have to like it, but he had to play his part with Nastusia."

"That's why he gave me Doom Fairchild."

Grim doesn't speak for some time. He lets me think. Organize my thoughts and feelings.

"What does gu barth mean?"

"It's Gaelic. It means forever."

I sigh. "Is it normal for me to love two people?"

"Open the Chest," Grim says, ignoring my question. He always sounds so annoyed when anyone talks to him about love.

I wonder if he ever... Oh, stop it, Anna.

I slide the Key into the small lock and hear the click of acceptance. Slowly, lifting the lid, the bright whiteness overtakes the darkness inside the box. On top of everything is a book. It's small, like a pocket dictionary. The cover is black with an abstract purple design. Flash smoke, perhaps? Otherwise, it has no identifiable marks—not even a title. I flip through it and there is the policy for the Deathdrifters to follow, an employee list with their job description, a map of the world, directions for understanding your watch, and blank pages for notes. This is obviously an important item for new Deathdrifters, although I've never seen Damien or Trick with one, and Trick was supposedly the newest Deathdrifter.

Setting the book aside, I pull out the folded black cloth. It's surprisingly long and I have to stand up so that it hangs straight to the ground. It's a simple cloak with no markings or visible stitching. The hood is large enough to cover my face and veil it from anyone's sight.

Looking back into the box, my jaw drops to the floor. I see the dress that I had bought from that small family owned store. Only this one hasn't been tailored by Mrs. Durmot. It's dark rich purple glistens in the whiteness—the satin reflects a light that doesn't exist in this world. I want to cry because it reminds me of Damien and how badly I had wanted him to see me wear this, touch the soft material—and feel his cold. I'd die again just to feel a cold touch from him.

"Try it on. Think of it as your work uniform. Though, you'll never actually have a need to change your clothes."

"But it's not black."

"And Deathdrifters are not women. If one policy can change, why not another?"

I squint at his comment and hold back my smile of rapture. One day, I might understand why he thinks it's irresponsible to talk to the soul you take, but until that day I'll keep my mouth shut for once. "Are you going to watch me change or can I be alone for a moment?"

"You need to Flash into it."

"I don't know how."

"You know whatever you *want* to know. Do what you *want* to do. That's all any Deathdrifter can ever be."

I sigh with confusion. This won't be easy. Closing my eyes, I picture myself in the dress—the satin hugging my body in all the right places. The soft fabric feels paper thin curving over the arch of my shoulders. The cut of the skirt brushes past my legs as I walk.

When I open my eyes I'm in the dress. It's perfect and it wasn't has hard as I thought. I spin around and watch the satin skirt expand slightly from my waist. The fabric clings to my torso and accentuates the shape of my hips, waist, and chest. I've never felt more beautiful.

I swing the black cloak around my shoulder and fasten the clasp at the neck of the hood. "This is amazing, Grim."

"Aye, ya can say that again," a young, deep voice echoes through the whiteness.

"It's time. You will be working with Trick, as I've said. He will take you to get a scythe and time piece. He'll also go over the routine with you."

I nod and slip the little black book into a pocket in the cloak, but not before placing Damien's ring inside the Chest.

I follow Trick, who had Flashed beside me without a word, through the whiteness to a little old man sitting at a desk with a metal file. The man is shaving away at a small circle with notches in it which I'm sure is a gear for a watch.

He doesn't look up at us right away and Trick takes this moment to slide his hand from my elbow to my fingers. I smile a tiny bit and, in return, I get a slight upturn to the corner of his mouth.

"Ah, good, good, you're here," the little man says after Trick clears his throat. "Come, come."

Do all old people repeat themselves?

From a small rectangle in the white wall behind him, he pulls out a black rod with purple vines woven around it. "Here, here. Take this." He shoves the rod at me. "The blade is around here somewhere." His eyes search the whiteness as if he can see something we can't.

"Oh, oh, the time piece." He opens another drawer and an amethyst hanging from a silver and pearl chain twists and glows in front of my face.

318

I take the pocket watch in my hand and pop it open. It's the same as Trick's watch that I've seen before. The overlapping circles and phases of the moon slowly change within the dial. The small numbers and symbols are the same deep purple as my dress on a snow white background.

"Now, you have what I need?"

I furrow my brow. Cameron puts his hand into the pocket of his trench coat and hands the little man Doom Fairchild.

"Let me get that blade and secure this to it. It's my best work yet, it is!" The little man runs off and I turn to raise my eyebrows at Trick.

I can tell he's been watching me this whole time and not the crazy, little old man. He surveys me up and down as if he's never seen me before and with a crooked smile he says, "Welcome to The Whitelands, Curse Reaper."

ONE
❦ YEAR ❧
LATER

ONE
& YEARS &
LATER

ALIVE

Damien is staring at himself in the mirror of the men's bathroom of my old college. His hands are clutching the side of the porcelain sink; knuckles white with tension.

Trick kisses my cheek and says, "He's all yers, Curse."

"Cameron?"

"Aye?"

"Don't go far, okay?"

He kisses me and lingers over my lips as he says, "Such big concerns fer such a wee lass."

I smile. "Thank you for this, Cameron." He returns my smile and Flashes from the bathroom.

Damien's feet and the hem of his scrups are wet from the over flowing sink. Trick showed me his List and if I wasn't already dead, I would have died again seeing: Damien Doyle, Drowned, Twelve-Ten. This is the same time I died one year ago today.

I watch as he leans his face down toward the water. "D," I whisper.

He stops. "Anna..."

His knees give and he falls to the floor, shaking and holding his head in his hands. All I want to do is hold him. Tell him life is a gift and it's too short. But he already knows that, even if he hates it.

"I'm here, Doom."

"Anna, you've come for me," he sobs.

"Trick told me. You're on his List." I'm more upset that he'd consider suicide than him actually succeeding.

"*He* brought you here?" he growls and turns his head in my general direction even though I haven't revealed myself to him. Mostly because learning the powers of Death takes a while.

"Do you remember the fourth time I died?"

"Of course," he answers, as if he's been thinking about every single one of my deaths every moment for the past year. "And whatever Trick told you—"

"Grim *showed* me. I *know* it was an accident. But you made me a promise, D. You said you'd do anything to put an end to my curse."

"Yes, but I also promised I wouldn't let you die a sixth time. I failed. Life is now a punishment. A horrible bloody punishment."

"Life was my gift to you. After my fifth death, I remembered you. Grim was amazed with me for it. I made a deal with him that when the curse was broken you would be given life. At that time, I failed to ensure that I would live with you. All the protection you gave me from Nastusia, I couldn't be more grateful for."

"But the car accident! He knew. He could have saved you, at least."

"The car accident wasn't Trick's fault. He couldn't stop that woman any more than we could have." He pulls his knees up to his chest as I continue, "Every time you had to leave me after every death, my heart broke to see the sorrow on your face. Our entire week together last year had me only thinking of you and the life you were cheated of. I want you to move on. Have everything your heart desires."

"*You* are everything my heart desires. I lost everything when I failed to keep you alive."

I take my time concentrating at this moment to become visible. Trick told me it was a risk to Flash in a public place. I'm not concerned with that right now.

Damien needs to know the truth.

"Oh, Anna..." Damien's staring at me. He's so much thinner than he used to be. His hair is longer and looks disheveled. I wonder when he last slept. Even in this state I still find him to be breathtaking. "My sweet Anna."

"I can help you forget, Damien. It's my ability to alter memories. That's why I had those visions. I can make you forget. I want you to be happy."

"Forget? I don't want to forget you. Ever."

"I hate to see you in so much pain—with so much regret."

He pulls himself up off the floor and stares at me with his lips slightly parted. "You're so beautiful. It kills me that I almost forgot."

"I'm not the same dead as I was alive. Remember?" I straighten my purple dress with hopes that he notices it and doesn't think about the argument we had in the park. I remove my black hood and my curly, dark hair cascades down over my pale shoulders.

"You're... Anna," he says with longing as he takes a step toward me. "Trick's Anna."

"Cameron's," I correct.

"Why?"

"Why the fourth me?" I sigh. No holding back now. "We've decided..." I kick my foot out. "Grim let me have my memories back. Reminding me of my feelings from when I was alive then. Before you took that noose from my neck I wanted to marry him and he me."

Damien shakes his head, not wanting to believe. "but what kind of...death can you have together? It's not life, Anna."

"I made a deal." I look at my feet, feeling ashamed.

"What? What kind of deal?"

"Grim's giving us both another chance when I fill my Chest."

"A chance at what?"

"I want kids, D. I want... him."

He shakes his head, looking like he wants to throw up. "I would've—"

"I know. Love makes people do crazy shit, right?" He nods, looking ashamed. "We want the life we never got."

"And what about me?"

"You had a wife once. You, unfortunately, died of pneumonia—robbed of a good life. But that didn't mean you had a right to me over Cameron. I chose him in life. You only led me to believe what I felt for him was really for you. Let me have a least one of my lives back."

He looks sad and I bite my bottom lip. Now I know why Grim doesn't want us talking to the souls we take. Even from this distance, I can feel how warm he is. The wonderful smell of life encompasses me. His velvety voice pumps through my veins and I feel the sensation of life back in my body.

I close my eyes and hold my breath, trying not to think about touching him. "You've taken the path of a healer," I say, changing the subject, "still trying to keep people alive, Dr. Doyle?"

He smirks and finally turns the faucet off. "Actually, I'm doing it because I want to be closer to death. Closer to you. Healing is what you were aspiring for and I just felt it's what you would want."

"I only want what makes you happy."

"Me too," he whispers and takes another step closer to me.

326

I still feel drawn to him so I take a step closer too. "You only want what makes you happy?" I tease.

"I only want you," he doesn't whisper, but his voice is light and incredibly seductive.

I stop. Fear has my stomach in knots. "You can't touch me."

"I have to. I don't care if it kills me. It's worth it."

"I think you should forget about me, D. Live your life."

"No. Not yet."

"When?"

"Just let me look at you."

"She donnae got all day."

"Trick." Damien's tone drips with contempt. "You bloody—"

Trick cuts him off. "Fer being such a lazy bastirt, at least I figured out how to control The Touch."

"When?" Damien asks.

"Before I could Flash."

Damien scowls at Trick, but his desire overrides his anger. "Show me," he demands as if he's still part of the club.

Trick walks over to a plant on the ledge of the mirror. He fingers the leaves gently and it remains green and vibrant.

"How'd you do that?" I ask, amazed.

He gives me that crooked smirk I can't get enough of. "Come 'ere, my love."

"Careful, Anna." Damien says, as if he can still protect me.

I stand next to Trick and he puts his hands on my face as if to kiss me. My stomach flutters as if it's still the first time. I start to close my eyes but Damien's shift in posture draws my attention. He looks angry. I know he's jealous of Trick and the time we can spend together.

"Touch the leaf," Trick whispers in my ear after releasing my face and slowly sliding his hand down my arm to my wrist. I hear Damien swear in that dead language of his and I notice he's staring at the ring Cameron had offered me instead of his.

Before Cameron brought me here, we discussed telling Damien the truth. I wanted to be honest with Damien, but Cameron felt that the less he knew the better. I love both of them, but it's impossible not to doubt myself. Cameron accepts that I'll always have a soft spot for Damien, but can Damien ever accept how I feel about Cameron?

"I told him," I whisper to Trick.

He kisses my neck, under my ear. "I knew ya would, Jo."

I'm hesitant as I touch the leaf. It feels so soft and it remains the same when I let go. My eyes don't leave the plant as Damien quickly scoops me up in his arms and turns me away from Trick.

"Let her go," Damien scolds Trick.

"I cannae. She'll kill ya."

Cameron has every reason to kill Damien, but he doesn't—for me.

Damien holds me tighter around my waist and kisses my forehead, eyes, nose, and cheeks. He runs his stubbly face lightly down my cheek to kiss my neck. I think he'll cover every spot on my face before he finds my lips. I feel so warm in his embrace.

I turn my gaze on Cameron. He's looking away—jaw clenched tight with anger.

"I can't let you go. I need you, Anna. I need you." He has tears lightly raining down his face. I'd cry too, if Death could.

"I'll always be here for you, Damien." I smile faintly because I know, for his sake, this is goodbye.

He knows its goodbye too when he says, "I'll never stop loving you, Anna." His lips press to mine and warmth washes over me like I've never known before.

Before it's too late, I take all six hundred years of memories. All his Deathdrifter ones and especially the ones of his wife and son.

I'm especially erasing me. He deserves to move on.

As he slips into a deep sleep, I realize how Damien felt whenever he got close to me or kissed me through out that week.

He felt alive. He felt free.

THE ✺ LAST ✺ TIME

A PERFECT
HELLO

"I can't believe we're here!" Fiona says, pure excitement running through her tiny body. I stare up at the lights, the tall buildings, the thousands of people scattered around us.

"I know." I take a breath, realizing I'm so caught up in my surroundings that I stopped breathing all together.

"Thanks to you, Anna, I'm not stuck inheriting my grandma's store." She releases a contented sigh. "Why do you think they call it Piccadilly Circus?"

I shrug. "Who cares? We're here on scholarships and my birthday is in three months, so let's just enjoy it. Okay?"

"Look!" Fiona points across the street. "Maybe I can exchange my traveler's checks there."

"Try it. I'll wait here."

She runs across the street, half skipping out of joy. I laugh at her childish way but glad that I have the best friend in the world.

Turning to look at a group of guys making a commotion down the way; one tall, attractive guy is pushed by another. He glances at me as he's separated from the group and then stares down at his feet. The one who pushed him is just as gorgeous, but a little shorter and a little leaner. He's wearing a sweatshirt, the hood up over head.

"Hey!" he shouts at me in a heavy British accent.

Great, now I'm going to be mugged. And the sun, what sun there is in London, hasn't even dropped below the horizon yet.

I look for Fiona, but she's still talking to the man at the kiosk about exchange rates. Working at her grandmother's store has made her good with money. She won't back down anytime soon.

The guy in the sweatshirt approaches me and says, "Do I know you?"

"Doubt it," I respond, dryly.

"American," he points out, rather rudely. "What's your name?"

"Anna."

"Hello, Anna. I'm Damien."

"What's up?" I incline my head.

He crosses his arms and turns his head toward the group of guys. "Anna!" he shouts. "Get over here, you dim bloke."

The guys push the shy tall one toward us. I feel sorry for him. His friends are jerks. Slowly, the dejected one comes over. He's wearing a heavy, dark jacket with a red plaid scarf. His hands are bunched into his pockets and he won't look at me, despite glaring at Damien.

"Cameron, this is Anna," Damien says, then lewdly adds, "She's American."

"Aye, so?" This guy's accent is different from Damien's, but not overly so.

"So invite her to the University gala."

"Oh, um, that's okay. Really. I have to study. My friend and I are here on a scholarship and if—"

"Oxford?" Damien interrupts.

"Yes."

334

"Then you don't need an invitation. Cameron here is an exchange student also."

"Really? From where?"

"Scotland," he mumbles, still not looking at me.

"Cool," I say, afraid to ask if he's really considered an exchange student or if Damien is still being cruel.

"Hi!" Fiona pops around the side of Cameron, saving me from the awkward silence.

Once he moves, she meets Damien's eyes and I can tell, he's all she'll talk about the rest of the semester.

"We should be going," I say, embarrassed when Cameron finally glances at me as I make for our exit.

"Aw, no," Fiona whines. "Introduce me, Anna."

"Yes, Anna, introductions are always polite," Damien says.

I roll my eyes. "Fiona, this is Damien and Cam. Guys, this is Fiona."

"How do you do?" Damien bows as if Fiona is some kind of princess. He's actually right about that on most counts.

Cameron turns to me and for the first time stares directly into my eyes—as if he can see my soul. "You called me Cam," he says.

There's a strange, comforting feeling over-whelming my body as I stare into his green eyes. My heart aches as if the last time we parted was our last time, and yet it soars as if this is a perfect hello—one for the rest of our lives.

"Sorry," I say, unsure if I am or not.

"Tis fine. I sort of like it," he whispers, hiding a smile.

I like him and for some reason feel the need to reach up and touch his plaid scarf. He stops me, taking my hand in his. His heat warms me so that I forget how cold and overcast it is. I forget that Fiona and Damien are here, watching us. I forget I'm in London or even still on earth.

But wherever I am right now, I really like it.

GLOSSARY

None of the Deathdrifters are American. They all originate before The New World was founded. It's not too difficult to figure out what they're saying, but if you'd like to know the exact meaning of their words or idioms, the following should help:

Across the pond: The other side of the Atlantic Ocean. Referring to the US or UK depending on the speaker's location.
Am'no: I'm not
Argue the toss: Refuse the decision and argue about it.
Aye: Yes, sure, yeah.
Bastirt: Bastard
Beer and skittles: Self-indulgence and pleasure.
Belt up: Shut up.
Bite your arm off: Want desperately.
Bloke(s): Man or men; informal.
Bloody: Emphasizes almost anything. Considered a swear word.
Bollocks: Bullshit
Budge up: Move over or make room.
Cannae: Cannot

Carrying coals to Newcastle: Doing something that is unnecessary.

Clear off: Get lost or leave.

Cupboard love: Showing love to gain something in return.

Dim: Stupid.

Dinnae: Did not

Dobber: Idiot

Donnae: Do not

Driech: Miserable or ugly; usually referring to weather.

'ere: Here

Fer: For

Helfy: Awesome

Holiday: Vacation or time off.

Jo: Scottish term of endearment for wife or his intended; short for Joy

Lad: Young boy

Lass: Young girl

Make a song and dance: To make an unnecessary fuss about something unimportant.

Me: My, as in ownership when used before a noun

Nip: kiss

Nod's as good as a wink: You have understood, even though it was not said directly.

Pure: Very

Prat: Mildly insulting term for someone.

Right royal: Extremely exciting, memorable and fun.

Shite: Shit

Snog: make-out, kiss

Tis: It's

Tosser: Derogatory term for jerk. Considered worse than wanker.

Ya: You

Yer: Your, You're

Yerself: Yourself

ACKNOWLEDGMENTS

There are always too many people to thank in situations like these. And I, for one, am no good at giving thanks. If you know me personally, that's no surprise. You may also know that I'm blatantly honest to a fault and I'll openly admit that when it truly matters. I am also quite forgetful, though, I could tell you many tidbits of useless information.

Now, if you are listed here, it's probably because I, either: a) see too much of you or b) you have an extremely quirky nature that I just can't resist. Either way, you're being thanked.

First of all, I have to thank an inanimate object: A radio. Music has its way of delving deep into my soul and lyrics are a great motivation for staving off writers block—which is why I haven't had that problem, yet.

Secondly, the people that have made all my dreams and "nightmares" come true are as follows:

My husband, my parents, step-parents, in-laws, aunts and uncles, brothers and sister: You have no idea how important family is to me. And you're nothing like my crazy characters.

Dad, Betty, as morbid as it may sound, you two have always indulged me in the concept of death and what could become of a person—afterlife or no afterlife. Thank you for never showing fear and instilling that strength in me as well.

Lin, thank you for all the work you do and for your genius perspectives. Perhaps, one day, all our dreams will come true... wait, is that a good idea?

Marisa, your first read-through and questions page that I assigned for "homework" was a big help. Thanks!

Working Girls or My Accomplices: Whether you're asking me about my progress, how to do something, telling me to stop "over-analyzing", or just picking a "fight" with me—you're indispensable.

Also, thanks to my fellow authors, bloggers, tweeters, facebookers, and website members. Reading what you have on your mind gives me insight for the future and something interesting to read in the world! I hope you all enjoy the stories and crazy worlds I envision for years to come.

ABOUT THE AUTHOR

J.T. is a Rochester, New York native. Her newest addition to the house is her daughter, born in 2011 and such a joy and muse to her "library of personalities." Her husband, though not involved with any of the story planning or ideas, is a wonderful addition to the continual search for unpredictable reactions and conversations—as well as cover art.

She has spent her whole life "making up" stories. Forced to stay in bed as long as possible at a very young age, she would daydream the early morning hours away. When she couldn't sleep at night, imaginary friends amused her until she could. Nowadays, "real" characters keep her up no matter what time of day it is. And an audience is always welcome to hear her develop the colorful scenes and character traits.

And as far as she is concerned about Death; it's not the process, or the unknown that's worrisome—it's all the people she loves that she hates to leave living with grief.

Love you...